SMASH IT!

FRANCINA SIMONE

SMASH IT!

inkyard PRESS

ISBN-13: 978-1-335-14650-2

Smash It!

This edition published by arrangement with Harlequin Books S.A.

For questions and comments about the quality of this book, please contact us at CustomerService@Harlequin.com.

Inkyard Press
22 Adelaide St. West, 40th Floor
Toronto, Ontario M5H 4E3, Canada
www.InkyardPress.com

Printed in U.S.A.

To the past, present, and future theater kids.
Y'all are always braver than most of us. This one is for you.

ACT ONE

ACT ONE—Scene One—
Here I Come

CAST—Center stage—spotlights

Othello:
I KNOW THEY THINK I'M DIFFERENT
I'M THE SAME AS THE REST
WAS SCARED TO LIVE AND LOVE
THEN DESDEMONA STOLE MY CHEST

Desdemona:
AND NOW I'M FALLING, BABY, I COULD DIE, I COULD
DIE
I'M FALLING, BABY, I COULD DIE
YOU'RE MY HEART SONG, BABY, I CAN'T LIE, I
CAN'T LIE
I'M FALLING WHEN I LOOK IN THE EYE…

Othello/Desdemona:
…OF THE ONE THAT I BELONG
MY LOVE, OH HERE I COME
LOVE, HERE I COME

Iago:
NOW IT'S MY TURN TO CONFESS
I WANNA RISE ABOVE THE REST

Cassio:
THE WINDS OF CHANGE ARE HERE

Bianca/Emilia:
A STORM IS BREWING NEAR

Othello/Desdemona:
OUR LOVE CAN BRAVE THE WEATHER
WE'LL NEVER SAY GOODBYE

Iago:
LEAVE IT TO ME, BROTHER
I WILL ENSURE THAT YOU ALL DIE

Chorus (Iago exit stage left):
AND I'M FALLING, BABY, I COULD DIE, I COULD DIE
I'M FALLING, BABY, I COULD DIE
YOU'RE MY HEART SONG, BABY, I CAN'T LIE, I
CAN'T LIE
I'M FALLING WHEN I CATCH YOUR EYE

CHAPTER 1

Fuck.

I'm an idiot.

It's Halloween and I'm the only one in a packed club on Teen Night *not* wearing a costume. Girls are jumping and screaming lyrics in cheap shiny wigs, and all the guys, dressed in a motley of cheap polyester, are scoping out the dance floor, their gazes hopping right over me. Even the bartender, slinging water bottles, has on pink bunny ears.

This isn't an *I'm seventeen and too cool for dress up* moment. I *like* wearing costumes. I just thought I'd look like an unintentional clown doing it. We're at a club. Who wears a Halloween costume to the club? Apparently, everyone except this freak in an Old Navy hoodie and khaki shorts. I'm wearing *khaki* shorts, like a nerdy loser.

Some girl bumps into me and does a double take at the

sight of my hoodie. It's Florida; I know October everywhere else is like that meme of the dog in a wig wearing a scarf because "it's sweater weather," but we're in Florida; the leaves don't change here. They just fall off sometime between hot-as-fuck and damn-where-that-wind-come-from? So even though this white girl has on a mesh shirt over a nude bra—I don't know what the hell she's dressed as—I can tell by her raised brows and attempt to act like she didn't see me that she doesn't know what in god's name I'm doing right now either.

Oh my god. Why am I like this?

This is what I get for not doing the *yes* thing. My mom bought this book by Shonda Rhimes, *Year of Yes*, and—I'm not going to lie—some rich black lady with a gazillion TV shows shouldn't be able to tell me, some sad black girl, how to be all, *Say yes to the dress!* But right now, I'm really wishing I had said yes when Dré asked, *Are you sure you don't want to put on something? It's a costume party at a club. Don't you have something sexy? Sexy nurse? Sexy vet? Hell, cut up your hoodie and go as a sexy hobo.*

I'm wishing I had scissors or the foresight to go as Sexy Hobo, because now, while my best friends are onstage at the hottest teen club in Orlando, singing their asses off like rock gods, I look like the freak who has no social shame.

The truth is I have too much social shame. So much shame that it seeps out of me like fresh cut garlic on the back of the tongue.

I make eye contact with Eli. He's on the keyboard, belting out lyrics and twisting in and out of a rap. His voice is the love child of Sam Smith and Adele. He's all suave and mysterious to everyone here, but I know him as the boy who shaved off half an eyebrow when we were thirteen and those Peretz Hebrew/Palestinian hairy genes started coming in. His mom and dad were on that Romeo and Juliet vibe back in the day, and even though it makes for an epic love story, with real war and faking deaths to escape their families and countries (epic as hell), their genetic combo gave Eli thick brows and hair like nobody's business.

He smiles at me with his dark brown eyes just under his fedora. Of the three of us, he's definitely the broody one, writing poems about nostalgia and love.

Dré, on the other hand—he's got on shades. Who wears sunglasses inside *at night*? Dré. When we were in middle school, Dré used to hide his Spanish and pretend his name was Andrew. I don't blame him. Our school had a lot of white kids, and they always asked dumb as hell questions. I always got, "If you can't get your hair wet, how do you wash it?" One kid asked Dré if *Puerto Rican* meant *legal Mexican* in Spanish. The kid *legitimately* didn't know. I know our education system is shit, but come the fuck on.

High school has been a game changer for all of us. Our magnet school pulls in kids from all over the county. But now there are too many kids from way too many places. Now we *have* to be different to fit in—cue Dré's flashy, Spanish-heritage-day-is-*every-day* evolution. He's a self-proclaimed Puerto Rican papi, and he kind of radiates like a sunny day on South Beach.

Then there's me. In my hoodie, khaki shorts, and Converse, stuck in the middle of a club with hundreds of kids basking in the glory that is Dré and Eli. I look like an outcast from a bad '90s movie. I'm not uncool, but I do these uncool things as if I'm addicted to self-sabotage.

Mesh Girl looks at me again; she's probably wondering why Dré keeps pointing and making steamy eyes at me while he spits some rhymes in Spanish. I know she's thinking, *How'd she get him?* Girls *have* asked me that. They see me, with my not-slim body and my brown skin, and say, *No offense, but damn, girl, how you got with Dré?*

I'm not. Never have, never will. This flashy thing that he's doing is our signal for me to check his hair. My only job is to make sure it still looks good. I nod and sway to the music, ignoring Mesh Girl's eyebrows, which are raised to the top of her blond head. Is it bad that I like the attention? I enjoy her envy, even though I'm not the girl she thinks I am.

Some girl dressed like a pumpkin shuffles past me and reaches out to touch Dré's hand. What she doesn't know is that he's transferring half a store's worth of product onto her fingers. He spends so much time on his hair, we have to speed to school—which is the last thing we should do in Dré's rusty old car, the Bat Mobile. It's already two gearshifts away from blowing up with us inside. We call it the Bat Mobile not because it's cool, but because it looks like a hundred bats dropped turds all over it and eroded the paint.

Even though it's pretty much trash on wheels, I'm so jealous. I can't even get my mom to let me practice my learners in her car. The queen of burning out engines thinks I'll mess something up. Then again, here I am on Halloween, the only girl in the club not having fun because of my shitty choices.

Mesh Girl bumps me with her shoulder. "He's hot, right?" She's talking about Eli, and I do a weird laugh thing and nod, because I'm the worst at small talk, and it's too much to yell, *Yeah, I've thought that for years. I can like the way he looks, right? That's normal, right?*

She doesn't seem to care that my laugh was borderline psychotic. "Oh my god, we should totally dance for them. Guys love that shit." Suddenly this girl that I don't know from Eve is pulling me toward the stage, and I start freaking out.

I've watched enough romance movies to have this scene planned in my head—but those are fantasies, and this is getting too real. People are staring at us as she starts twerking and swinging her arms around.

She waves at me. "Come on!"

Nope. I just smile and shrink back into the crowd. She's clearly one of those people who *really* believes in herself—like, no one has ever told her she can't do a damn thing, because, here she is, shaking her ass like she invented the booty pop.

Mesh Girl isn't looking at me anymore. She's dancing and looking at Eli, and—he's looking at *her.* I know I'm not supposed to care, because he's just my best friend and he and Dré are supposed to interact with the crowd—that's part of the gig—but he's looking at her and smiling like he's impressed. He thinks this girl's half-baked dance moves are cool. He thinks *she's* cool.

I can dance better than that. *I* could be that cool.

Except I'm not.

I'm the girl who hides in the crowd. I'm the girl who isn't even in costume. And now, the guy I maybe-sorta-like is smiling and singing to the girl who is doing the scary thing, even though she's not that good at it.

Fuck my life. My crush is about to go up in tired-ass flames like the rest of my dreams. This isn't the first time I've passed up doing what I want because I'm afraid of looking like a clown. It isn't even the tenth or the hundredth.

Hell, just this morning I walked by a flyer for the school musical auditions, and when the drama teacher offered me one, I did the weird laugh, and—let's just say she'll probably never make eye contact with me again.

All I had to do was say *yes*. All I had to do was tell myself I'd *try*.

Why am I so chickenshit?

I make my way to the bar and order a soda.

The guy at the bar eyes me as he sprays Coke into my glass. He puts the Coke down in front of me, and just when I want him to walk away and leave me in my despair, he pulls off his pink bunny ears and puts them next to my bubbly soda. "Take these. I don't want you to stand out."

I shake my head. Honestly, he's got long hair and it's kind of greasy, so there is no way I'm putting that on my head. "I'm cool. Don't need pity ears, but thanks."

He laughs, and it's low-key judgmental. "Yeah, because cool people don't wear costumes, right? You must be a blast at parties." He looks around at the club behind me. "Oh, wait."

Rude. "Look. I happen to be a very cool person, thank you very much." I shouldn't talk when I'm in my feelings, because my voice goes up an octave and I can never get my eyebrows to stay still. They're up in my hairline now, showing the whole damn world that I have no chill.

Dude puts his bunny ears back on and leans on the bar. "Yeah, it's so cool sitting by yourself at a Halloween party with no costume." He shrugs. "I'm not saying high school is going to be the best time of your life, but you should get over yourself enough to have a little fun while you can. Otherwise, you'll be a cool adult sitting alone at a bar wondering why your life sucks." He stands up, crosses his arms and looks proud of himself.

Is there a sign on my head that says, *I'm having a hard time. Please do pile on*? I take a deep breath and hate myself, because my first reaction is to smile and nod. But I stare him dead in the eye and say, "Because being a bartender at thirtysomething is so great." I feel a little badass for saying it, but also super guilty for being a bitch.

"Well, one of us is having fun." He wiggles his bunny ears. "And the other one is at a party full of kids and only has the bartender to talk to." He pulls the white towel off his shoulder and starts wiping down the bar. "Don't forget to tip." And then he's moving away and pulling out waters for a group of guys in some anime costumes.

I drop my head to the bar, which, regrettably, is sticky. That turd of a bartender doesn't know me, but he's kinda right. Some girl on YouTube—the one with the minimalist white walls that look chic instead of broke as hell—said everyone has a moment in life when there are two paths before them. The cool one where you change your pathetic ways and everything gets brighter and better. And the other one where you die sad and alone.

She obviously knows what she's talking about, because she manages to make millions of people listen to her talk about *hacking procrastination* and how to make your room over with just a succulent and a few black-and-white photos strung up on the walls.

I don't want to be sad and alone, or to freeze every time my moment comes to shine. I want to be the fierce inner beast I know I am. I want Eli to look at me like I'm the only one in the room.

Something has to change, because that bartender and the succulent girl are right. If I don't, I'm going to disappear like I was never here.

CHAPTER 2

It's almost midnight. I'm leaning against the Bat Mobile in the E.T. parking garage of Universal Studios. Nothing like closing time at the Park to send hordes of people to their cars. The exhaust from the hundreds of cars roaring to life on our floor alone is starting to give me a headache. We get free parking because I work here—not at the garage; at a gift shop at the front of the theme park. I can't complain. I get AC, three free tickets every quarter and flexible hours. But when I say I'd rather *not* spend my free time near the place I work, I mean it.

The Grove is smack-dab in the middle of Universal's City-Walk; it's the only teen club that pays for gigs. But it is Halloween at Universal—Halloween Horror Night—and *everyone* is just now leaving. People are screaming and laughing, and cars are packed in an obscene line, trying to get out. It's a mess.

And just my luck, Dré is busy taking a selfie with some chick who has rotting flesh plastered on her face while Eli and I pack the car. Dré jogs over, his long legs and arms swinging with ease like he's running off a football field for a drink of water. I can't stand him sometimes, but whenever we make eye contact, he laughs and then I smile. It's been that way for years.

We're doing it now, but then I stop, because he's shaking his head while looking at my tragic outfit.

"You look ridiculous. You know that, right?" He's got this Freddie Mercury costume on—heavy eyeliner, a yellow leather jacket with buckles, and white pants lined with a red stripe on each side. He puts his arm around me and pulls out his phone for a picture. "You could have pulled off Sexy Hobo. Woulda been bangin'." Before he snaps, he kisses my cheek, and I'm forever captured on camera rolling my eyes.

I refuse to answer him. He has this way of picking at my insecurities while making me feel special. But that's Dré. He's friendly with everyone; affection rolls off him like hair off a cat. He leaves behind his touches, but get too comfortable and he'll scratch you for no fucking reason.

Eli ducks his head around the car as Dré uploads our picture onto his Instagram. Dré has over 50,000 followers, and the number goes up faster with every gig they do. "We need to start doing original songs," Eli says, and I can hear Dré roll his eyes—not literally, he does this breathing thing that makes him sound tired, and he jerks his leg and scrunches up his shoulders. It's a whole sound, believe me. He does it

when his mom yells and anytime Eli or I say anything remotely close to *what if we try something else?*

"Chill, brah. We will, but damn, covers are hot. We give
the people what they want, and they'll make us kings."

I can't help but think Dré doesn't want to do originals because he sucks at writing songs. I'm just being honest. We're all
in band class, so music is our thing—but just because you like
playing concert music doesn't mean you can write songs. Eli
has almost 90,000 followers on Instagram, and it's because he
also posts his poetry. Sometimes it's a tad angsty, but it's good.

Personally, I don't know what I want to do—I wish I had
a *thing* like them. Something beyond showing up to class and
practicing my parts.

Eli pulls off his fedora and throws it into the back seat.
His dark brown hair is curled tightly from sweating. He's
dressed like a 1920s mobster. I don't know which one; he's
into the details of the past, but that stuff goes right over my
head. It suits him though. He has this stoic, classy vibe even
when he's just woken up and answering the door in a white
T-shirt and basketball shorts. He's what my mom calls an old
soul, and when you look into those brown eyes, you can feel
all the lives he's lived. "We're never gonna stand out copying everyone else."

Dré looks in the car window, checking his hair. His lips
pull back as he inspects his teeth. "Tell him he's impatient
and delusional, Liv."

"I'm not in it." I hate being dragged into the middle. I
move from between them and to the trunk to make my point.
It's always Dré who uses me like a shield when Eli starts making sense.

Eli checks the trunk for the third time. Everything is packed, but he never leaves anything to chance. He would still be hoarding all the poems he shared with me if I hadn't told him to post them. Ten months later, and I turned out to be the brains of the group—except when it comes to myself.

I'm looking at my Chucks when Eli pokes my side and whispers, "Sexy hobo isn't a thing. Takes balls to come as you are."

"Hey—quit whispering." Dré can't stand to be left out of anything. "Don't do that. Don't take his side." His head pops over the top of the car. "I'll leave you here and make you walk."

"We're not even talking about you." I point at the line of cars inching past us like snails, one of them leaving a trail of oil. "And if I have to hitch a ride and my mom sees me coming home with some rando who belongs on a headline, she'll fuck you up. She's still pissed about the tire marks on the grass."

Dré sucks his teeth. "She's always pissed." He waves at two girls as they shout his name from the window of a car. "Wanna picture?" He jogs over to them. Some dudes honk at him and shout song lyrics. Dré eats it up. He was born to be a star.

"You're missing it," I tease Eli.

Eli looks up from the trunk again and smiles. He's got big front teeth, and they're so straight. He never needed braces, and he's got beautiful full lips to frame them. Elijah Peretz won the genetic lottery. "Everything I need is right here." He means his keyboard. I know it looks like he means me, because he's staring at me with Eli eyes—they kind of squint when he smiles, and sometimes he dips his head like he's embarrassed and his lip catches on his teeth—but that's just Eli. He makes that face to everyone.

Regardless, I can't hold eye contact when he's like that. My god, it's like staring at the sun—I am Icarus, or some chick who will get really bad heart cataracts if I keep looking. He can't help it—it's the broody thing—but I *can* help being the idiot girl who falls in love with one of her best friends. Besides, I'm not his type. Eli's last crush was a redheaded choir chick. She used to sing jingles about the bagels the choir sold in the mornings. I still can't look at a bagel without remembering her line about spreading cream cheese with ease.

Also, contrary to me having the balls to *come as I am* to a Halloween function where everyone and their dog are in costume, I do have lines. Falling for a best friend and doing the unrequited-love thing is one of them. At least—I *had* that line. I lost track of it somewhere in between Eli's smiles.

Eli closes the trunk, and we pile into the car. He's flipping through a playlist, playing me songs he thinks I'll like. He knows I have a thing for love songs, and he finds all the best ones.

Dré is still soaking up attention from passing cars.

I honk the horn. "Hurry up, Dré." My mom can be chill about curfew, but it's late as hell and she'll beat the black off my ass if I waltz in past one in the morning. I can hear her now, *What, you think I raised a ho?* As if staying out late is synonymous with sleeping around. And I know girls who *do* sleep around. If anything, they're something to look up to. They've got this air of independence; like they own something I don't have but really need. Or maybe it just seems like that because I've been a major horn-dog ever since I watched

Titanic and saw Leonardo DiCaprio draw Kate Winslet like one of his French girls.

Anyway, I'm not wrong. We pull into our neighborhood where the houses are all two stories and, as my sister always says, *look way too damn much alike.* I like the tall arched entryways, the alternating white and beach-sand colored painted houses, and our bright orange Spanish villa roof.

What I don't like is that the entryway light is on. By the time I get inside, it's five minutes after one and my mom is standing in the kitchen with a glass of wine and a face full of attitude. On our white marble counter is another glass with pink lipstick stains and I know Dré's mom, Gloria, was here, too. They watch the new *Housewives of Atlanta* episodes together but that had to have been hours ago. Why my mom is still drinking wine at one in the morning is something I'm not allowed to ask—not while she's being all quiet and looking me up and down.

"What time is it?"

Damn, Ma…like you're not standing next to the oven clock.
"One."

She sips her wine and then crosses her hands over her body, the wine swirling as she rhythmically circles the glass. "What day is it?" I love my mom, but she's so annoying. She doesn't just get to the point. She drags it out like I'm a dog and she's rubbing my nose in shit.

"Halloween."

"You smart now?" Her eyes cut at me.

I know not to push her, but I have my limits, too. I'm not a bad kid. I don't drink—I think alcohol is nasty. Like, who chooses to drink that burn-your-throat-flavor when you could drink a smoothie? I'd rather die fat than from liver problems. I also don't do drugs—just not my thing. I'm not having sex—not that I don't want to, it's just no one has asked me out, and I know I'm in the new age where women are taking their power, but have you met my mother? I don't have power of my own to take.

"Wednesday," I correct. I'm not even going to try to explain myself. That just makes her twist my words. I'm literally five minutes late. I didn't kill Jesus.

Still, I keep my face blank, because one twitch and this bitch will go apeshit. She's got a job at a fancy event management company downtown planning weddings—the kind of place with big windows, shiny marble floors, and granite reception desks. It pays well; we have a four-bedroom house, and I've never had to worry about food in the fridge or asking for new stuff, but it's long hours and she's always bringing work home.

That, plus the fact that she doesn't turn off the boss bitch attitude, means she's always in a bad mood and she'll take away all my privileges until she remembers I'm actually a good kid. I ain't got time for all that, so… I keep my mouth shut.

She looks me up and down again and scrunches up her face. "Did you wear that?" She says it like I'm actually in some version of the sexy hobo Dré suggested I wear. She's staring at me like she can't compute.

I swear to god if my mother roasts me for being lame on Halloween, I will burn this house down.

Her gaze is stuck on my shorts. "First of all—" oh my god, she *is* doing this "—you're wearing a hoodie *and* shorts. Either it's hot or it's cold. Pick one. Second—" she waves the hand holding the wineglass at my shorts "—you have way too much booty, and there are nasty men out there who will look at your ass and they don't care that you're only seventeen."

I groan. This is worse than a roast. My mother is tall and has a willowy figure, and she's always telling me I'm too curvy and too fat for anything *except* clothes thirty-year-old women working at *less* fancy management companies wear.

These shorts are midthigh. My ass isn't hanging out. These aren't *shake'em* shorts, and I sure as hell ain't getting any play in these.

I let my face slip a little, and my mother is all over it.

"No. You think you know it all until shit happens and mama's not there to save your ass. You have too much body. You can't walk around like your little white friends. You're a black girl, sweetie. People look at you different."

I can't stop myself. "Oh. My. God. Really?" I look at my skin. "When did it happen?" My mom thinks that, because I'm not all Black Panther, I don't know I'm black. She's always sent me to schools with a lot of white kids, so, yes, some of my friends are white. I don't get why that confuses her. And as usual, she conveniently forgets my two best friends are both brown. Every time. I can't win with her. If I'm not surrounded by black kids all the time, I'm wrong.

"Fix your attitude. It's about how you present yourself in public."

I really look at my outfit, because, other than it being Halloween and me being the only idiot not in costume, I don't understand what she's talking about. I have an ass—nothing short of a tent will cover that up. I have breasts, but you can't even see them under my hoodie. I don't even look my age—

especially with my hair pulled up in a bun of thick curls. I look like a kid.

I'm about to burst; I can't stand to have her pick me apart. For some reason, it hurts more when she does it than when I think other people are doing it. Nothing is good enough. In her eyes, I am flawed.

She looks at the clock and sighs. "Anyway, I'll let it slide this time. Let it happen again and it'll be the last time." She takes another sip of wine before pouring the rest down the sink. I can't leave the kitchen soon enough, but she calls me back before I reach the stairway leading to my room.

I don't trust myself to speak, because I'm still so pissed, I can't even look at her.

"You don't understand it now, but I love you. You and your sister are my everything, but this world will take you and break you." She's wiping the counter and fishing for eye contact. It's just me and her. My sister's been doing her own thing for five years now. So, my mom is *extra* focused on me, like I'm her last egg and she doesn't want me to hatch. I don't have the stamina or the patience for it anymore. "Go get some sleep," she says.

She's like the Lifetime movie where it turns out the monster is the lady keeping you locked in the house by telling you the world will kill you if you leave her. Honestly, I can't take her crazy.

In my room, I kick off my shoes, scuffing up my purple rag rug. Twinks, my cat, is curled up on my bed and barely cracks an eye to look at me. Just under my *Aida* poster, a bag of her favorite treats are on my nightstand with teeth marks all over the packaging. I grab the bag and toss a few treats to her as I eye the poster.

Aida was my first live musical. I can still remember sitting in the Dr. Phillips Center, sinking into the chair as the lights dimmed. My skin chilled during the "Dance of the Robe" and I've gone every time they tour in town since—except this year. We get notifications of the shows in the mail and my mom accidently threw it out. By the time I thought to look it up online, the tickets were already sold out.

It's fine. Just another reason why my life sucks.

I put the bag of cat treats back on my nightstand next to that Shonda Rhimes book, *Year of Yes*.

I pick it up.

Shonda Rhimes started out as this weird kid talking to soup cans in her pantry, and now she owns TV. As much as I rag on her rich black lady problems, I want to be like her. I want to be the confident woman she is. She wouldn't let the shit my mom says bother her—she wouldn't be so concerned with what others think that she'd end up the only person not dressed up at a party. She would dance at the party to get the guy she likes to notice her.

I lie back on my bed, feeling too dirty to touch the sheets, but I run my hands over my worn, soft comforter. It's my favorite shade of blue; the same blue they used for the school musical audition flyers.

I can't believe I'm about to let another audition pass by. I've *loved* musicals ever since I was ten and I saw the *Phantom of the Opera* movie. Every day for a year, I performed a one-woman act as both Phantom and Christine in front of my cat and anyone I could corner—including the checkout lady at Target. I was a kid with *gumption*.

Then I got a body. Boobs, butt and birthing hips, as my mother calls them. People started staring at me for all the wrong reasons, and then I stopped calling attention to myself altogether. I wanted to be invisible, and now look at me—I don't even have the balls to dress up for Halloween. *Halloween*, the one day you can actually look ridiculous and no one cares. And I know Eli doesn't care about the flashy stuff, but he *looked* at Mesh Girl the way I want him to look at me. I'm not saying a *supportive* friend isn't a great thing to have, but I want a *has-the-hots-for-me* boyfriend, too.

I want to be seen.

I stare up at my ceiling fan going round and round, and I hear the bartender's unsolicited advice… *You should get over yourself enough to have a little fun while you can. Otherwise, you'll be a cool adult sitting alone at a bar wondering why your life sucks.*

He's so right. I want to try out for the school musical—it would be epic: the songs, the late-night rehearsals, getting onstage, and getting a standing ovation. The thing is, how do I become the person who auditions for the school musical?

Fuck it. I'm not going to let some guy at a bar get me in my feelings. Instead, I'm just going to do it. I'm going to go to school tomorrow and put my name on the sign-up sheet and do the damn thing.

CHAPTER 3

I wake up to Twinks pawing at my face. She does this every morning and it wouldn't be so bad, but she's missing a few teeth so she drools while she does it. "Oh my god. Get off me." I would push her off, but she's got a bum hip and I'm not a monster.

So here I am, 6:30 in the morning on three and a half hours of sleep, trapped in my bed with stank cat drool on my face. She's not fat, but she's super heavy and she's squishing my boobs into my neck. "Get off, Twinks." I can't ever die like this. The headline on that—"Florida Girl Smothered by Gigantic Twinkie-colored Cat"—that's not a way any seventeen-year-old girl wants to go out.

My phone buzzes, and she plops off with some prodding. I reach for my phone and pull my blanket back over my head. I know who it is before I answer. "I'm awake," I say.

Eli sounds groggy. "I'm not ready to wake up yet. Is it sunny? Is it beautiful?" He's so goddamn weird. I love it though. He's been my wake-up call since sometime over the summer, and we never stopped. I have no idea why we keep doing this or how we even started. We don't talk about it— he just calls, and I answer. He sounds different on the phone, his voice low and thoughtful.

"Open your eyes and look out the window." His house is next to mine. His bedroom window is literally *across* from mine. It's how I met him and Dré when I moved to the neighborhood. Dré was at Eli's house, and they were watching me with binoculars while I unpacked. It was weird, but back then I was more interested in making friends than talking about why peeping into my window like we were on some made-for-Disney kids movie was extremely creepy and problematic.

We've been the three of us ever since.

Eli breathes and says my name. I'm used to it now, so I don't hold my breath and wait for some declaration of love like I did over the summer. The thought makes my face burn. I know I'm not the usual type of girl Eli goes for, but I'm pretty sure we've got *something* going on between us. Maybe—I think.

"Eli?"

I imagine him under his covers the same way I'm under mine. His are gray and just as soft, and they smell like his deodorant and cologne. I know this, but I also know what Dré's sheets and bed smell like, so I mark this as *not stalker-ish* in my book.

"I need you—to do this for me." He says that every time,

and the pause between *I need you* and *to do this for me* is getting longer and longer. I'm making it up in my head, and I really need a shrink or to stop watching so many romance movies with my mom.

"*Liv...*" He's doing that dramatic *I'm dying* voice and it's a crime. A crime against hearts; he doesn't even know he's committing it. What does this thing we're doing even mean? It's so secret and between just *us* that it makes me feel things I shouldn't feel—and asking outright could potentially destroy a solid friendship, not to mention our group dynamic. I cannot be *that* girl. Unless he wants us to be *those* people, then I'm totally down.

But I can't read him. Once I posted an anonymous question on his Ask Me Anything with my burner Instagram. I asked who he had a crush on—I mean, I knew he wasn't going to just name his secret crush for the entire internet to see, but I figured he'd put something a lot less cryptic than The girl of my dreams is still just in my dreams. Apparently, his dream girl doesn't exist yet.

I make a fuss about getting out of bed and being exhausted, and I pull back my curtains. He's staring at me through his window. This, too, is rehearsed and expected. I know it started out as a way to get me out of bed, but that was months ago when I was pulling early-morning summer shifts at the Park. He was my alarm clock, forcing me out of bed so I could prove to my mom I'm not a spoiled princess who can't work for her own dime.

Now...he's a boy staring at me in my good pajamas, because I know that, every morning, he's going to see me.

What does he see? Why does he keep looking?

I lean on my window. "What do you know. It's another sunny day in the Sunshine State. It's probably already eighty degrees and climbing." I cross my arms over my stomach. It's my problem area, and this tank top is cropped a little high and the neckline a little low. Maybe I shouldn't have worn this one to bed.

"Liv. Is it beautiful?" He's getting weirder these days, and sometimes it makes me want to be weird, too. Even if he doesn't *like* like me, is it a crime for me to enjoy this feeling?

"Elijah Peretz," I say like his dad does when he's about to say something worth thinking about. "It's beautiful."

He looks up, surveying the sky, and nods. "It is. See you in thirty." He hangs up. I really hate it when he hangs up without saying bye—but maybe he does it because all we are is one long, ongoing conversation not really going anywhere.

I'm in Biology II when the reality of three hours of sleep starts to hit me. Dré, Eli, and I were running late again with no time to stop for coffee, and to be honest that shit never works on me anyway. I'm pretending not to slump over my desk when I hear my name.

Everyone is staring at me.

"Ms. James?"

Ugh. I hate it when the teachers use that name. My dad gave me nothing but big eyes and hips. I use my mom's name for almost everything. Johnson. The old man didn't stick around long enough for me to remember what he looks like, so why should I have to suffer the *Do you know Lebron James?* questions. Okay, I got asked that only once, but Sperm Donor is the worst man in the world for leaving my mom with a freshly baked baby and a lifetime of childcare bills and worries to suffer alone.

I look up at Mrs. Darcy, who told us on the first day that she's tired of the Jane Austen jokes. She's got wild frizzy hair and it's red—box-color red—around her pink face. She's always wearing bright-colored shirts that make her face look extra flushed, but she's a nice lady, so I try really hard not to judge her and wonder, why *these* choices?

"You're with Ms. Baker." Mrs. Darcy looks down at her clipboard, and I have no idea what's happening. She goes on to the next student, calling out partners.

I don't know who Baker is. I don't really know anyone in this class. I picked Biology II because I got good grades in Biology I, and I heard the physics teacher sucks on epic proportions. I can't afford to bring home bad grades, and rumor has it Mrs. Darcy is hard but fair, so—Bio II it was. I glance around. Everyone else is slowly getting up and breaking into pairs, and I still can't find this Baker girl.

Someone taps my shoulder. I turn around, and Dreads is behind me. That's what I call her in my head. She's a skinny mixed girl with these long dreads wrapped in wires and jewels. Big, gold hoop earrings dangle from her ears and she's wearing a red plaid button-down over a rocker tee. None of what she's wearing should make sense, but she looks cool. The kind of cool that matters *after* high school. "Baker?" I ask.

"Lennox," she corrects with a nod of her head. She takes the now-empty chair next to me. "Olivia, right? You always raising your hand and shit."

I nod. I'm not embarrassed about being *that* kid. I want good grades, and I'm not afraid to do what it takes to get them—well, the legal stuff, like asking questions and doing my homework.

"That's lit. I'm not trying to be fucked up with a slacker. Good stuff." She leans back and fills me in on what we're supposed to be doing. The unit we're on is forensics, and we've been given a crime scene to solve by the end of the semester. We've got crime scene A, and she opts to be the detective, because she can "spot a lying mutha fucka from a mile away."

She pulls out her binder and opens it to a fresh piece of paper. On its other side is the audition flyer for the school musical, *Othello*. Well, damn, you put something out into the universe and it delivers—overnight, apparently. She sees me looking and puts the flyer on my desk. "You like theatre? You should try out."

I know what *Othello* is about; we read it earlier this year in English. Basically, a really psychotic dude, Iago, was pissed he got passed up for promotion, so he manipulated his boss, Othello, into believing Othello's wife, Desdemona, was sleeping with Cassio, the guy who got the promotion. And because it's Shakespeare, Desdemona gets smothered with a pillow, and just about everyone dies at the end.

Normally, I'd be all about Iago's manipulative ass, and I know last night I said I'd sign up, but I'm getting images of me singing and dancing onstage in a costume that will make me look like an Oompa Loompa.

A bunch of weird words come out of my mouth, and she's looking at me like she's spotting *a lying mutha fucka* right now and I settle on, "I do, but I'm not good enough to try out." I know I'm punking out and proving that bartender right, but—a girl is not ready. I need more than three hours sleep before I start diving into the deep end. I know change requires bold moves, but this is bright, neon-yellow-jacket bold, and it's not even ten in the morning.

"Says who?" Lennox is the kind of girl who wears red lipstick, and it doesn't look weird on her. Everything about her is bold, and she doesn't know me—the me who is pretty much pastel-on-top-of-pastel bland—so I don't expect her to understand that a chubby girl like me is hesitant about stepping onstage to do *Othello*. I mean, let's face it. I made that vow last night out of desperation. I should have promised something like *I will wear eye shadow to school and not wash it off before first period*.

Plus, my cousin is in the theatre program, and in my family we have an unspoken rule that music is my thing and theatre is hers. Our moms have this weird competition going on to determine whose child is the most talented while simultaneously trying to force a friendship between us. I have nothing against Cleo, but she's about as interesting as a brick wall. We've never really been more than cordial at family get-togethers, and when I see her at school, we sort of wave and keep it going.

I know she doesn't own the theatre department, and there's nothing to stop me, a kid on the music track, from trying out, but our moms would go into extra gear if we were both in the same production.

I open my mouth to tell Lennox this—she seems cool enough that she won't make fun of me or my family drama—

but then I remember standing in the club with my khaki shorts. I remember the look in that bunny-eared freak's eyes as he showered me with his rude AF pity.

My lameness is leaking out so much that people are starting to take notice, and I'm supposed to leave my punk bitch ways behind. If I say no...I'm just perpetrating the same nonsense. I mean, what's the worst that can happen? *Besides* invading Cleo's territory or looking like an Oompa Loompa while being smothered with a pillow?

"Fuck it," I say.

Lennox seems to get it and nods her head. "Exactly. Fuck it." She also puts the packet of papers on my desk. "I have drama next, I'll get a new audition form. The girls' section starts on page five—memorize the lines and the song. Mrs. G casts our roles based on just those two things. It's not a lot to go on, but she says she 'just knows.' That bitch is mean as fuck, but she do be knowing."

I don't know much about the theatre program, but the band room is next to the theatre and we hear Mrs. G yelling all day. I set the papers aside, internally screaming. The punk in me is cursing me out so dirty right now.

We work on our forensic project while the *Othello* packet burns through my desk. Lennox is looking at her phone; it's another one of her bold moves. She does it like it's natural and not the quickest way to get your phone snatched by some overworked, underpaid, baggy-eyed professional. Mrs. Darcy doesn't even notice.

Lennox makes a *hmph* noise and turns the phone over for me to see her Instagram. "You know Dré?" It's the picture from last night, where he's kissing my unamused face.

"Yeah. We're friends." This is going to go one of two ways—she's going to ask me to hook her up with him, or she's going to be passive-aggressive because she thinks I'm competition.

I wait for it, but instead she drops, "Yeah, I slept with him over the summer. He's all right. It was his first time, so he wasn't too sure where to put his hands, but he can lay it down."

My jaw drops. Like, I don't have it anymore. R.I.P solid foods. I look like a fish, but I can't move my mouth and be a mature adult about this.

Lennox looks up, pockets her phone, and pulls together her eyebrows. "Girl, you all right?"

I still haven't fixed my face. I'm usually good at pretending nonchalance. I once told my band teacher, *If you strip naked and jump up and down on this table, it wouldn't surprise me.* He was highly disturbed, but in my defense, he thought I'd be shocked about placing first at nationals. Psh. Nah, I ain't surprised. I know I'm an amazing flutist.

But *this*?

Dré alludes to being sexually active but the way he talks about it always makes me think he's putting on a show. Why would Lennox tell me their personal business like that?!?!

"Olivia," she says, tilting her head. "We both have sweet lady vaginas. We're in this game together. We can talk about this stuff."

No.

No.

No.

No.

No, we can't.

She raises her brows. "Dick not your thing? I get it, girl. I swing that way, too."

"I'm not gay. I just—" I get an image of them...*together*... Lord Jesus help me.

"Neither am I, sis. This shit is fluid. Some days I like it—"

I cut her off, because I don't need to know about who and how or when this girl likes to have sex. "I've known Dré for forever and—I just don't want to know about *that*."

"Oh," she says. And to my relief, she leaves it alone, like I'd just asked her not to bring up movie spoilers.

Dré's first time has been reduced to an *oh*.

The bell rings, and she pats on my audition packet. "Make sure to put your name on the sign-up sheet."

I'm nodding, because, let's be honest, I haven't recovered yet. But when I walk from Bio II all the way to the theatre and stop in front of the bulletin board, I pull out a pen from my bag. The tip of my pen touches the paper, and I freeze.

There *really* is no going back once I put my name down.

Just when I'm about to pull my pen away, a group of girls walk up behind me. "Hey, can I borrow your pen when you're done?" the closest one asks.

"Uh—yeah," I say as they stare at me expectantly. I take a deep breath, write my name, and pass the pen. I'm actually doing this.

I'm proud of myself—I mean, I kind of hate myself, too, because WTF am I doing?! But last week I couldn't even take the flyer the drama teacher was handing out. Today, not only did I take the packet from Lennox, I put my name on the list.

I'm pretty much turning my whole life around—except, in a few weeks, I have to get onstage, and I have no clue what the fuck I'm going to do.

CHAPTER 4

It's lunch. A normal lunch except—I can't look Dré in the eye. I'm sitting on the big staircase with my pizza, and he keeps leaning over and taking my fries, and I'm just thinking, *But your hands, how the hell did you not know where to put your hands?*

"Liv." Dré's got a mouth full of fries and, even though he's saying my name, he's looking at Eli on the other side of me. "Tell him he's fucking crazy." They're arguing over whether they should enter Battle of the Bands or not. Dré's on Team *We're a band*, and Eli's on Team *We're two guys who sing covers with a keyboard and a guitar*. I'm on Team *I don't give a rat's ass because all I can think about right now is Dré's junk*.

It's right there, under his too-tight jeans, and it's been inside Lennox. She said he knew how to lay it down, and now I'm freaking out all over again. Why would she tell me that?

I know we're supposed to be all open with our sexuality and fly our freak flags, but I am a prude. My sex education has been my mother randomly scaring the hell out of me with way too much personal information about her dating life.

Then there is my sister, who is gay. Amber doesn't know I know this, but I do. She's so painfully awkward about keeping everyone in the dark, and we all know but are just waiting for her to be comfortable. And no, I don't mean she's in the closet—she's *very* obvious about being gay—I think the thing is she's just as terrified as I am of being openly *romantic* around the family. I'd die before announcing I have a boyfriend. All our family would hear is, *I'm having sex,* and they'd want to meet said significant other and—it'd be a whole thing and sometimes it should just be a small quiet thing.

Anyway, we've never talked about this stuff. She's just as prudish as I am. We *do* have the same traumatizing mother. My mother is the *worst* when it comes to having private conversations on the phone. She's loud—and once I heard her loudly talk about how much she likes oral.

I nearly ended it right then and there. No one should have to live through hearing their mom's *sexy* voice.

Anyway, I am not ready for this. I want sex, but at school, sitting between Eli and Dré and thinking about Dré's stuff in Lennox's stuff—it just makes my stomach turn. How was Lennox so open? Am *I* the weird one here?

"Liv, stop staring at my junk."

I snap my head up and meet Dré's eyes. He's smirking, and I swear if I was a white girl, I'd look like a tomato right now. I mumble something about looking at ants, and he and

Eli keep arguing, accepting that they've lost me somewhere to the clouds. I am literally staring at the clouds right now. Our school is an open-to-the-elements campus. Though we are inside, we are also outside.

There's a palm tree next to our staircase, and I'm pretending to be interested in a squirrel chewing on a burrito wrapper when Dré puts his arm around me and squeezes my side. Eli's already gotten up to throw away his trash.

"You home?" Dré is touchy like this because he's Puerto Rican. That might be a gross overgeneralization of an entire group of people, but I swear he, his mom, his cousins, his aunts, and the other Puerto Rican kids at school—they are all handsy. *HOW DID HE NOT KNOW WHERE TO PUT HIS HANDS?*

I move out of his embrace and put my pizza down, then pull a notebook out of my bag. "Yeah. I'm just thinking. Behind on homework."

Dré rolls his eyes. "Homework is institutionalized racism."

"Is that why you don't do it?"

"It's for white kids who don't have to work jobs to support their families." He's back in his personal space, and I'm back in mine with my Bio II notebook on my lap. Eli is settling in again and putting earphones in. His music blares. He doesn't want to argue about the band thing anymore. Eli's way of resolving confrontation is to hide from it.

"Dré, you work because your mom wouldn't give you $500 for clothes and cologne."

He takes a bite of my pizza. We've been sharing since forever. "And because the ladies like a man with independence. I can't have my mama paying for my dates."

Or condoms. I hate Lennox right now, because I'm looking at Dré in a way I didn't before. I'm looking at his arms and thinking about them around me. I have hormones and wants and needs. And Lennox should have thought about that before planting seeds of sex with Dré in my mind. I feel both intrigued and nauseated—not to mention I'm thinking about his arms around her tiny little body and how mine is much bigger.

And then there is Eli. I can't even think about sex with Eli; it just leaves me feeling embarrassed and overexposed.

"What's that?" Dré says, reaching into my binder. Thinking about where and when he'd done *it* means I forgot to be stealthy about the *Othello* audition packet. It's in his hands before I can explain it away. "Damn, Liv. You trying out?"

Dré leans over me and flicks Eli.

Cautiously, Eli takes out one earphone and raises one of his bushy eyebrows into his thick, curling hair.

"Liv's trying out for the musical." Dré's announcing it like it's a thing.

"I didn't say that." I don't want them to know. Dré is still that cat, purring one minute, then shredding your couch the next. He's bound to say something to make me feel stupid about it, and I don't want Eli to know because—I just don't.

Eli takes out the other earphone. The look on his face is... almost offensive. "Wha—?" He laughs. "Why?"

I roll my eyes. *This* is why I don't do things. "Because I *want* to," I say.

Eli holds up his hands. "I didn't mean anything—I was just surprised, that's all. It's not…really something you'd do."

I want to tell him he doesn't know what I'd do, but Dré's already interjecting with *his* stupid laugh. "Liv, you refused to wear a costume on Halloween. How the hell are you going to get onstage in one?"

Eli's trying to cover up his own laughter, and I just want to die. "He has a point, Liv."

Dré slaps Eli on the shoulder. "Dude, she had dance lessons for five years and still won't dance in front of us."

Is this how they think of me? Like a joke? They think I'm just as lame as that bartender did, and worse—Eli's laughing. I expect Dré to roast me. He drags everybody for just about everything. But Eli's supposed to be in my corner. I can't stand that he sees me the same way the world sees me.

I grind my teeth. "Shut up."

Dré's nudging me. "Don't be mad. We're just shocked. It's cool though."

Eli gives me a small smile, but it doesn't erase the shame in the pit of my stomach. They think I'm incapable of doing anything remotely cool. Their first reaction was to laugh.

"It *is* cool." Eli reaches for the packet and looks it over. They're both quiet. Trading papers between each other like I'm not sitting in the middle having my personal life victimized.

"Dude, let's do it," Dré says. He looks to Eli for the final answer. Something no one knows, from the outside looking in, is that Dré's like a puppy on a leash. We do everything

Dré wants, but only because we let him drag us around. In the end, Eli pretty much steers our ship.

Eli looks to me and I shrug, pretending I don't care. I do. Them doing it, too, means *I* can't back out. It also means they'll be watching me make a fool of myself. They're the ones used to being in the light, singing and dancing like they don't care what anyone thinks, not me.

But because I care way too much what Eli thinks of me, and I *want* him to think I'm the kind of girl who gets up on the stage, I hold back all my cringing as I say, "Yeah, let's do it together."

After the lunch bell, I go to English. We have a substitute, and he puts on *Jurassic Park* for god knows what reason. I'm glad though, because I can't focus. I've got Eli's and Dré's laughter swirling in my head along with yesterday's debacle that was Halloween.

Enough is enough. I've wanted to try out for a school musical since ninth grade, and every year I've made excuses—I'd tell myself I needed more practice, more time to get a singing voice that would make it past auditions, or another year to lose fifteen pounds so that I could fit in whatever costume they gave me.

I'm not wasting another moment standing on the sidelines.

I'm not just going to try out. I'm going to say yes to everything that scares me. I'm not gonna let anyone—most of all, myself—punk me anymore.

On the TV, the T. rex tears up the porta potty, and the girl next to me screams. Everyone's laughing. I have goose bumps on my arms, and my stomach is on fire. I feel so alive. I feel like this is it. This is my moment. My fork in the road.

I fish a notebook out of my book bag and make a list:

1. BE BOLD—DO THE THINGS THAT SCARE ME.
2. LEARN TO TAKE A COMPLIMENT.
3. STAND OUT INSTEAD OF BACK.

I can't think of anything else, but it's a big piece of paper and I can always add things as I go. I had an English teacher who always told us to write it down if we meant it, and *title* it if we planned to do it. I write out, *The Year of...*

I meant to write *The Year of Yes* but—ew. That sounds too much like I'm having a midlife crisis.

The Year of Balls to the Wall! I'm gagging, that's so stupid.

The Year of Free the Tits—that's not even remotely close to what I'm trying to do.

YOLO—No. It wasn't cool when Drake did it; it's not cool now.

Maybe this is a sign. I'm not supposed to be wild and free— maybe this neurotic, cares-too-much-what-other-people-think person *is* me.

"Fuck it," I breathe.

It hits me. *Fuck It*. This is a *Fuck It* list. This is the year of giving no fucks. I finish the title and close my notebook as the boy next to me yells about how white people always make the dumbest decisions when it comes to survival. Now the white kids are throwing out that the black guy died first, and the black kid whose name I can never remember is freestyling a comeback and telling people to check out his SoundCloud.

Honor's English—you'd never guess it though.

The sub waves his hand at us, but doesn't bother to look up from his phone. "Thank you for the hot take, but settle down, everyone."

I run my hand over my notebook. *The Year of Fuck It*.

I spend the rest of the school day doing all my schoolwork *and* homework. Between finding time to practice my parts for band class and my part-time job at the Park, I don't have time for homework. I have no idea how I'm going to fit musical auditions in.

Universal Studios is literally across the street from my school, which leaves no time during the commute for homework. Technically we're on the back side of the Park and there's so much foliage that I only notice the Park every now and again when one of the roller coasters shoots a bunch of screamers across the sky. I'm not mad about it today, because being busy distracts me from thinking about my new Fuck It list and Lennox and Dré's sex scandal, until I'm standing in line for my work uniform and the guy in front of me starts talking about going down on his girlfriend.

He's telling the guy in front of him how he likes it; they're literally debating cunnilingus in public like they're debating the virtues of being a vegan. The guy who's totally into his girlfriend's taco looks back at me. "Ah, shit. Sorry, shorty. I didn't know you were there." He elbows the other guy and they change the subject.

I don't know if I'm more offended that they were talking

about it in the first place or that they stopped *after* seeing me. Am I not worth talking about sex in front of? Do guys only see me like that? A shorty? It hits me, and I wish I'd never thought it—Dré had sex with a girl like Lennox. I know it's not rational, obviously she's active and open about it, but I can't help but think I'm not the kind of girl he'd be into. Not that I want him to be—but I don't seem to be the kind of girl *any* guy is into.

When I've changed into my stiff blue polo and long khaki pants that belong on a flat-assed geriatric man, I head to my gift shop. I don't work at Hogsmeade or anywhere cool like Ollivander's Wand Shop; I sell Scooby-Doo plush toys and light-up swords at the store in front of the exit. Which means I just walk around the store fixing everything people keep knocking over and listening to the same thematic music on loop. And every now and again, if I'm lucky, I work in the candy shop, where it's super cold and management doesn't bother me.

Today, despite the turn of events at school, I *am* lucky. I'm in the candy shop with Al, an old Italian dude from the Sunny Oaks retirement community. He's working split shifts for *something to do* besides waiting to die. I like the way he yells at the customers in his thick New York accent when they spill candy on the floor or how he laughs even louder when pretty old ladies stop by. He's all right.

"How's it going, Livia?" He always drops the O. He's cleaning the window to the candy apple display and stops to smile at an old lady walking by in a dress.

I can't tell him I'm depressed because my best friend whom I don't want to have sex with didn't have sex with me. First of all, Al's an old guy, and I'm not going there with him. Second, I'd sound like a lunatic. "It's all right, Al."

He puts the cleaner down and shakes his head. "That's no good. You're young. It should be great."

"Spoken like an old man who's forgotten a few things about what it's like to be young." He hates it when I call him an old man, so I do it every chance I get. Everyone else tiptoes around Al, because he's the kind of guy that takes up space. He looks like he's in charge, and people act like he is—everyone except me. Maybe that's why he doesn't call me a pissant kid. He calls me Livia without the *O*.

"You're a pretty girl. What do you have to be sad about? There's no war. You work at a candy store. You've got those rock star friends." Al knows everything about my life, except the sex stuff; he's an old guy and I don't need him all up in my vagina's nonexistent business. But he knows about my mom and how annoying she is, he knows about Eli and Dré, and yes, even that I had the briefest of crushes on Eli over the summer (that I admit turned into a full-blown crush).

"Al, we're at war with like two countries, not to mention all the underground government crap." We talk about everything. Even politics. He'd be a raging anarchist if he weren't so Catholic. He says God and the Mother keep him democratic.

"Okay, but *you're* not there. They've got drones blowing up stuff now—oh, that's too depressing. It's a Thursday, Livia, let's not talk depressing stuff till Tuesday." Tuesdays are reserved for topics like death and family members who suck.

"I didn't bring up the war, Al." I sigh. "I'm kinda freaking out over something stupid I've decided to do. A musical." So far, the first thing on my list—be bold—is starting to feel like a dream so vague that it's unattainable. "I have no idea what I'm doing." Man, Dré and Eli were right. This is so out of my lane.

Al frowns but nods his head. It means he's surprised but interested.

I explain to him the Shonda Rhimes book (which he's read and says is A plus—he's a *Grey's Anatomy* fan and enjoyed the references) and my Year of Fuck It. When our assistant manager comes in, we break and pretend we're restocking the fudge. The assistant manager hates Al with a passion, because Al always shits on his made-up rules about organizing the stockroom.

"I don't care for the title but I like your concept. You know, saying *yes* to opportunities makes room for new ones." He scratches his short-manicured beard. "Everyone thinks you have to always be *doing* things. Always creating opportunities for yourself. That's not how life works, kid."

He picks up the glass cleaner and the paper towels. "By simply being open to new experiences, you create opportunity for more. What is it they say? *If you're always looking longingly out the window, you'll never see the open door next to you.* Make sure to see your doors, Livia."

I nod, because, jokes aside, the old man knows his stuff—but it's me, and I can't let a joke go. "You been reading *The Alchemist* again?" He gave me a copy over the summer, and—well, I didn't get it. It's about a boy looking for treasure and traveling through Spain and North Africa. Honestly, not enough dragons or sexy elves. Al said I'd get it one day, but he's got more faith in people than we probably deserve.

"You being a smart ass again?"

I smile. "*Well*, when presented an *opportunity*—" I stop talking when he squirts glass cleaner at me.

"Listen. Your cousin doesn't have a monopoly on the theatre. You should do this musical thing," he says while I start boxing up a slice of cheesecake for a lady decked out in Harry Potter gear. Al doesn't get the wizard stuff, so he always stares and points like he's at the zoo: *My god, she's got a broomstick between her legs. This is not appropriate for children.*

"I don't have a choice anymore—Eli and Dré are going to try out, too. There's no way they'd let me back out." I leave out the part where they basically dragged me for stepping out of my comfort zone. Al's the only person in my life who thinks I've got *moxie*, as he puts it. I can't ruin that.

Al scowls. "I don't like that Eli kid. He doesn't know his own heart. You're a woman now, Livia. You need a man who knows his own heart. You hear me?" He thinks Eli's a punk kid for leading me on, but Al's old-school and thinks boys always have to take the first step.

"Jesus, Al." I sneak a gummy worm from the candy wall. Al's a romantic. He's always complaining about how we're all too loose and disconnected from each other. He thinks people are like swans and mate for life—he was a self-proclaimed swan until Veta, bless her soul, left him three years ago to be with *the* Father.

For all Al's flirting, he talks about Veta like he's going home to see her every night, and I'm one of those emotional people who gets teary thinking about him sitting home alone reading memoirs and watching *Grey's Anatomy*.

"Don't be blasphemous." After a while, he nods his head. "I think this musical stuff will be good for you. And if you

need help, ask some of those theatre kids. But don't do it because of the boys. Do it for you."

Al goes back to lady watching and throwing compliments
at grandmas leaving the Park. The problem with the old man
is he's right about a lot of things—for example, the forty-year-
old lady zooming by on the broomstick *really* needs a longer
skirt. But he's also wrong—how the hell am I going to ask
the competition for help? They don't even know me.

I set aside a candy apple to take home, and after we've
packed up I decide—maybe there is a loophole. Maybe I *can*
ask someone for some help.

Eli.

CHAPTER 5

I'm home, and after a long shower and washing my hair, I want to sleep. Problem with being a black girl is I have to sit with conditioner in my hair for at least an hour before I can even think about going to bed. I've spent way too much time on YouTube learning how to grow my hair past my shoulder blades to mess up now.

As I secure the plastic shower cap over my curls, lathered in conditioner, I go back to my room and pull out the *Othello* packet. I can't believe I'm doing this. It's a rap musical. I hadn't noticed that before. I don't rap—I mean, I can keep rhythm, but I sound stupid as fuck and look possessed doing it. I always get way too into it and shake my head around like I'm Nicki Minaj on too many Red Bulls. It gets a laugh out of my cousins, but I'm not ready for the entire high school to see that—even Dré and Eli haven't seen my way-too-animated rap game.

I go to my window and peek through the blinds to see if Eli's up. His blinds are open and his lights are on. I don't get why he does that. I have this irrational fear of leaving the blinds open when the lights are on. Actually, I get it from my mom. Whenever we drive home late, she always points at the houses with the blinds open and says, *That's why white people are always getting robbed. They never close the blinds, and then they wonder why Johnny the Criminal is up in there murdering them the next day.*

I don't even reach my phone before it's buzzing.

"Stop spying on me," Eli says. I can hear him getting up as his bed squeaks.

"You need to close your blinds." I've told him this a thousand times.

"The only one looking in my window is you." He's laughing. "What's up?"

"What makes you think something's up?" I love that he knows me better than I know me. This has to mean he feels like I do. How else can two people be so connected? We spend most of our time talking around everything that matters and diving deep into things that don't. And yet, he *knows* me.

I can never answer the question *Tell us about yourself.* I don't know who I am like that. I look around my room at the white walls with a couple mismatched Harry Potter posters I got from the Park. I've got a few pictures of the boys pinned to the wall, too, but honestly, this room could belong to anybody. Well—my dresser is purple and matches my rag rug, and the decorative pillows that have now fallen on my floor are lime green, so it takes a special kind of anybody to exist in all these colors, but anybody nonetheless.

So. Who am I? I don't know. Who do I want to be? No clue. A better version of myself…but who is that?

Yet with Eli, I know I am a thousand things all at once, and sometimes there aren't words for that. He makes me feel at home with myself.

Oh my god. Al's right, I'm a sucker for this kid.

"Liv." Why does he say my name like that? Like he's saying *love*. *Liv. Love. Liv. Love. I love Liv.*

"What do you really think about this musical stuff?" Most people ask someone what they think because they want their opinion. I ask Eli because he's got freaky psychic powers. He *knows* things. Not about trivial stuff, like answers to a test or if I'm in love with him…I think.

He knows things like whether it will rain if we go to the beach, even if it's been sunny for days. Or like when Dré's abuelo died. Or like that time at band camp when he knew I'd get hurt if I went to McDonald's with the flute section. He didn't know what was going to happen, but he told me not to get into the car. They crashed, and luckily everyone was safe because they were all wearing seat belts. But there were six of us and five seats and, if I'd gone, I wouldn't have had a seat belt.

He *knows* things.

"I think you should try out. You can sing. You can dance. You're funny."

Tell me more, sir.

"I think you'll regret it if you don't."

Twinks jumps on my bed and drools on my papers as if to say, *Dooooooo it*. I move the papers and run my fingers over her massive body.

"Is that Twinks?"

Did I mention she purrs like a busted lawn mower? Eli and I talk, and as I procrastinate popping my question, our conversation drifts from the musical to him not wanting to do the Battle of the Bands without an *actual* band. I listen, even though I know he doesn't want my opinion. He knows I'll default to *talk to Dré about it*, because last time I got between them, it turned into World War III, and I honestly don't know how Switzerland does it.

We're still on the phone after I wash the conditioner out of my hair, and he says my name again in that way that makes my whole body warm and my stomach flutter.

"Eli." I never know what else to say. Except I know I'm supposed to boss up and make a move. "Help me with auditions?"

There's a pause, and I'm pretty sure he's thinking of how to politely tell me I'm barking up the wrong tree. "I'll help you with the singing part of the auditions if you help me with my dancing."

Sweet Jesus. Truth be told, I *am* good at dancing. I danced for five years before high school, but I quit. Things stop being fun when everyone's goal is to become a professional jazz dancer or to get into some fancy dance academy—not to mention when you overhear your teacher tell your mom your body is getting too curvy.

Whatever. I don't need lessons to love dancing. I just like that feeling that comes with making the lyrics mean something with my body. But I don't do it in public, not since I got ass and breast. Now, when I move my body, everything moves. I feel like a walking porn show. I don't want him thinking I look like a thirst trap every time I shake my hips.

"You've never seen me dance. How do you know I can teach you?" I'm still salty as hell about them laughing at me today. They brought up me being too much of a punk to dance in front of them and that hurt—even if it's true.

I know Eli's picking up on all my petty because he starts talking fast. "Liv, I didn't mean to hurt your feelings. I was just surprised. That's all."

Mmm-hmm. "I never said you hurt my feelings." I don't know why I lie about things like this. I know pride is, like, the leading cause of self-sabotage, but it's all I've got these days.

"I just want you to know that I believe in you. Hundred percent."

Wow. If my heart wasn't doing somersaults before, it is now. I mean, yeah, they roasted me, but what they said was true, and the whole point of change is—to change. So of course they were shocked.

Also, Eli believes in me. I try to get my shit together and stop swooning long enough to say, "What if I'm bad? Will you laugh at me?" What I'm really asking is, *What if I look like a big-boobed sex show—will you scratch your eyes out and pretend you never knew me?* And what I want to hear is more of this *I believe in you* heart-melting stuff.

"Yes."

I choke.

He said it so fast, at first, I thought he said no—the default answer to a question like that. "But," he adds, "I'd still love you. Hot mess and all."

He does that. Says the *L* word without actually saying it—and I always ignore it. There is no way to confirm whether he means it in that friend way or more-than-friend way—but I try to get that confirmation anyway, because my heart is beating in my damn throat.

"You love everyone." I wait on edge for the words I want to hear. *No, just you.*

But he sighs and says, "I'm a lover, what can I say."

I'm glad my blinds are closed and he can't see me slump onto my bed like the sad, parched girl I am.

Yeah. Okay. Cool. Cool. It's all cool. I can't tell if this thing we have is exhilarating or really putting a beating on my self-esteem.

"It's a deal, right?" he says, and I hear him clicking off his lamp. Normally I'd say no faster than my mom when I ask to borrow her nice purse, because I don't want Eli to hear me rap like I've been possessed by the devil, or see me shake my big ass like I'm putting out a mating call. But my Fuck It list is on my mirror where I put it when I got home, and even Twinks is looking at me with her squinty eyes like she's saying, *Don't be a punk bitch.*

So I say *fuck it.*

"What?"

"I mean, yeah. Let's do it."

I'm on my way to band class when I bump into Cleo. She's outside the theatre pinning up musical flyers.

She raises her eyebrows at me and does that weird smile where she bunches her lips together. Welp, this is going to be awkward as hell.

"Hey, little cuz," she says. She's tall and willowy like my

mom—and everyone else in our family—and her hair is as straight as her spine. She's got it in a ponytail, and it swings as she reaches up to tape a flyer to the brick wall. We're only two months apart, but she always has this air of the *older cousin*, which is ridiculous, but whatever.

I'm doing the usual wave when she hands me a flyer.

"We're doing a rap musical this year, hang this up by the band room for me?" She does this small laugh that means she's about to say something she thinks is clever but I don't get, because we don't frequent the same universe. "As if band kids will put down their instruments long enough to try their hand at lyrical Shakespeare." She laughs at her own joke.

As usual, I don't get how that was supposed to be funny, but okay. At best, it was sorta rude.

There are two types of magnet kids—the ones who go really hard for their department, like Cleo, and the ones like me, who really don't care about who is in which department. I don't think music defines me. It's just a thing I do—something my mom picked, actually. While I was in middle school, she thought all girls who played the flute were pretty. And now I play the flute and take music theory.

I nod at a passing oboe player who's looking at the flyers and squealing about the new production. "Actually," I say to Cleo as she grabs the rest of the flyers to plaster the school, "I'm trying out."

I'd have to tell her eventually so I just put a small smile on my face so she knows I'm not trying to be combative. It's weird, this relationship—we aren't friends, we're not really family—I mean we *are*, but we don't act like it.

We have other cousins, who I *love*. We have a blast when

they come up for holidays, so I don't know why Cleo and I are like this. I've always blamed our moms, who have this sibling rivalry thing going, but one day, it just seemed like Cleo and I went from being uninterested in each other to eyeing one another like we're on *Survivor* and one of us is about to be cast off the island.

Cleo, still processing, tilts her head. "You're trying out?" She's squinting her eyes like it's a joke, but just when I think she's about to get all Aunt Rachel on me and make some smart-ass comment about how it's *so unlike me*, she nods. "That's ballsy."

I don't know how to take that, so I just wiggle my hips. "Yeah, I've got plenty." I don't know why I said that, and she's shaking her head like, *Girl, stop.* And I do. "Well, it always looks like a lot of fun, so—" Talking with her is so awkward. Once, we went to the mall with my mom and spent the whole trip not talking. We just sat on a bench between stores on our phones while my mom shopped.

We both like musicals. You'd think that'd be something to bond over, but she *hates* the ones I like. WHO HATES *RENT*?! Cleo, that's who. I'd say she's a horrible human being, but she's my cousin, so...

Cleo's adjusting her book bag. "They're totally fun—but *super* hard. I mean, auditions are a beast to get through, and even if you get a small role, it's *so* much work."

I nod. "Yeah, but worth it, right?" Is she trying to talk me out of it?

A few other kids from band walk around us, and this one boy who plays the trombone spins between us, nearly knocking the pile of papers out of Cleo's arms.

"Of course, I just mean you already have a lot going on,

and Mrs. G is a harsh judge. But if you're serious about it, I can totally help you with lines." She's smiling like normal now—which is still a tight-lipped half smile, but with Cleo and me, that's about as warm as it gets.

"Sure," I say. I don't know if I really want to take her up on it, because deep down the ugly part of me thinks she might try to sabotage me. I know that's super paranoid and borderline self-obsessed, but Cleo's still holding her face in the exact same position—stiff and forced.

She's not a bad person, and I know I'm being extra. Not to mention she is a theatre kid, and like Al said, she could give me legit tips—so I try the fuck-it thing to get out of my head—but before I can ask her when she's free, the bell's ringing and she's taking those long-legged strides away from me toward the theatre.

Eli is leaning on one of the brick columns in front of the band room, watching me with a smirk on his face.

"Don't," I say as his smile widens and his bottom lip catches on his teeth. He knows about the weird thing between Cleo and me. A few years ago, my mom hosted a Fourth of July party in our backyard, and Eli and Dré stopped over. Cleo was there, and our moms kept asking us to perform things. *Cleo*, Aunt Rachel would say, *do your skit from recitals.* Then my mom would shout, *Liv, go get your flute.*

Needless to say, I went inside to grab my flute and never resurfaced. We all ended up playing Xbox at Eli's, and Cleo was clearly the odd one out.

Eli laughs. "You two are so awkward. It hurts just watching."

"I'm not awkward. She's the weird one. I just told her I'm

trying out, and she pretty much told me I'm too busy and not good enough."

Eli opens the door to the band room, and we're blasted with a wave of noise—a flat trumpet and high-pitched flute shrill at the top of the sound cloud. "Don't listen to her. She's just trying to whittle down the competition." He winks at me, and I walk with him to his French horn locker, since I've already got my flute with me. His fingers roll through the combination—I know it like I know everything else about him.

I have to raise my voice over the random notes and timpani bangs. Everyone is warming up like a responsible ensemble after yesterday's practice, where Mr. Kaminski yelled at us for being total garbage on every song we rehearsed. I was well rehearsed, of course, but that's because I know what I'm doing. The flute comes easy to me—boring but easy—unlike theatre. "To be honest, I'm having second thoughts. All the drama kids are going to be trying out for these parts. She has a point. I've never done this before."

Eli pulls out his mouthpiece and buzzes on it. I wish I could say it wasn't sexy. But everything he does just looks *right*. I'm making myself sick. I *am* sick.

I spot Mr. Kaminski popping his head out of the office, surveying us like he's readying for battle, and I drop my book bag next to Eli's locker to start unpacking my flute. "I'm just saying, this is starting to look like a crazy idea. I mean—where will I find the time?"

Eli pulls the mouthpiece from his lips and shrugs. He holds his locker door open for me to put my case in—it's things like this that make me feel like, if he gets a girlfriend, it will ruin our entire friendship. I share his space—his room is across from mine. I can't look up one day and be the girl who has to stop sharing Eli's space because his girlfriend has taken up residence.

He's already off grabbing a music stand, and I pull my sheet music from my bag and take my seat—second chair to the world's most neurotic flute player, Zora Jackson. She's always marking up my music when I don't take down every note that is rather *obvious* to me. I just let her do it—better to go with the flow sometimes and not make waves, as they say.

Except trying out for this musical *is* making waves.

Someone taps my shoulder, and I look back—but no one is there, and I immediately know it was Dré. He does that all the time, and I can't believe I looked. He's walking with his trumpet to his seat and pretending he didn't just pull a *made you look.*

He's carefree, relaxing in his chair while everyone else is trying to look productive so as not to catch Mr. Kaminski's wrath. Dré's like that. He'll find a way to make the musical work in his schedule; he doesn't care about auditions, because he doesn't really care about anything. He's just *good* at things.

The horns are settling in, and Eli's still buzzing on his mouthpiece when he catches my gaze. He raises his eyebrows and winks before going back to his music.

I want an ounce of their confidence. If I'm honest, Cleo has me feeling a little overwhelmed with all the shit that can go wrong—that I'm up against kids who do this every day and might as well be professionals in comparison to me. Al told me to get help. Eli is great but he's never done musical theatre before either, and the obvious person to give it to me just sashayed her tiny little ass away from me, taking my hope with her.

Zora is in her seat next to me, pulling out her flute and music. She looks a little ruffled as she grabs her pencil and starts rattling off a bunch of words that should make sense, but because it's Zora, they don't. I have no clue what she's talking about, and her music is all marked up; it looks borderline serial-killer-esque.

Zora is a star pupil as far as Mr. Kaminski is concerned. She does all the extracurriculars and goes out for leadership roles during marching band season. Hell, she's got her eye on drum major next year, and I think she'd literally kill for the position. No doubt Zora's going to play in the pit for the musical. She did the last two years. That's what I'm supposed to be doing—but I just don't care about band like she does. I don't want to be in the pit.

I want to be onstage.

Even if Cleo, no doubt, believes I don't belong there.

Zora leans into my stand with her pencil at the ready, and I stop her just before she puts some of her crazy on my copy. "No, thank you," I say, blocking her twitchy little fingers.

Wide-eyed, she looks at me and then around the room like she's taking in the world for the first time and then goes back to chattering a mile a minute about crescendos and key changes.

Maybe making waves is better than getting swept away.

Mr. Kaminski leaves the podium, and I pull out my phone and type a quick message to Eli.

Practice. My house tomorrow?

I watch as he pulls out his phone and shoves it back into his pocket.

We lock eyes, and he smiles. "Definitely," he says, just as everyone stops their honks and shrills. Everyone's looking at him. I am, too. But he's only looking at me.

CHAPTER 6

Eli and I are standing in the middle of my garage. It's Saturday, and my mom gets off in the late afternoon on Saturdays, so we only have three hours before she pulls in and makes fun of us, calling us *cute* for *putting on a show*, or some such mom nonsense.

He pulls off his shirt, leaving just a sleeveless black tee that's tight on his chest. It's not even hot in here, but I'm pretending not to care about all the eye candy because old me wouldn't have cared—wait. Maybe old me would have roasted him for showing off his chest. Where is *that* girl?

He's smirking now. "Checking out my pecs?"

"I was wondering what ate the rest of your shirt." I roll my eyes and pretend to check if we have everything we need: water, Bluetooth speaker, phone—yup.

He smiles wide, and the bottom of his lip gets caught on

his tooth. I know that it's always done that, but I didn't find it sexy before. Now I think about it whenever we talk. I double-check the water bottles and phone again. Fantasizing about us alone and flirting until one of us jumps the other is a lot easier than living it. What kind of weirdo tries to stage a romantic scene?

"You don't have to lie." He's next to me, and I look over because I can't tell if he's joking or not. He's got that smirk on his face again, which means it could go either way.

I throw a towel at him and put on music so I don't have to respond. "We'll dance first so I still have time to duck out of all this singing business."

"Aye aye, Captain. Just show me how to bust a move." He can say stupid stuff and still be cool. When I do it, I sound like that one old-ass teacher who creeps on teens. There's one at every school. They still think we ride skateboards and say things like, *Rad, man!*

I move to the middle of the garage and close my eyes, because I can't do this with him staring at me. It's a lot, knowing that I'm the only thing in the room he has to look at. I even put on my tightest bra and undershorts under my shorts to keep things from jiggling because the last thing I want is my boobs flipping and flopping around like fucking balloons.

I find the beat and let my body step into it. When I dance, I feel like I *am* the beat. I twerk and grind in my room when no one is looking, I do it in the club when I think it's too packed for people to see me, and most of all I do it with guys I know I'll never see again. I've always been able to slide into a song like it's telling my story.

I open my eyes, and I don't know what I expected, but

Eli's small smile is enough to make me feel…like this isn't weird. It's fun. The music's loud, and I scream over it, "Just go with it."

He nods and starts moving along with me. We're not close, like in those weird dance movies where people all of a sudden practically start having sex on the dance floor. We're just two people in the same space, dancing. And then we're jumping and pounding our feet against the pavement.

He takes it to a whole other place and hoots into the music. He starts singing, and his moves—they're so bad it actually looks good. He's hopping on one foot doing some rendition of the chicken dance, and I can't stop laughing. Eli never dances onstage. He's got three moves that keep him in the same spot, and now I know why. But the more he weaves back and forth, like he's Stevie Wonder in the middle of a riff, the more I actually wish he would.

He grabs my hands and twirls me around him. We are Beauty and the Beast, and for the first time *I* feel like Beauty, but Beast Boy is nothing to snub my nose at.

The beat is thumping, and Eli shouts the lyrics even louder. Even when he's not trying, his voice is smooth and full. He lets go of me and claps to the song. "Sing," he yells.

I open my mouth, but the words stick in my throat. I am a walking hesitation. Why is it so hard for me to just *do*?

He dances around me, clapping and jutting his head back and forth.

I'm laughing so hard, and for a minute I'm back in middle school when we used to make these dumb home videos of ourselves singing and doing skits. I don't know what happened to that girl. She wasn't afraid of anything.

I sing.

"Louder," he shouts.

I'm screaming the lyrics, and I know I sound ridiculous, but it's too much fun when we're both yelling and dancing like nothing matters. We're in this moment, not a second before or after. Just now.

He mouths words at me, and I can't hear anything between my screaming and the music.

"What?" I yell.

He moves closer, jumping with me. His lips nearly touch my cheek as he says, "You're amazing."

We spent an hour dancing and laughing around the garage. It's November and some of the leaves are falling off the trees, but it's still 70 degrees outside, and in this closed garage, I'm sweating bullets.

We're lying down with our backs on the cool cement when Eli says, "I can't remember the last time we laughed like this." We laugh all the time, but I know he means the last time we did really stupid shit and laughed so hard we cried. The kind of laughing that sounds like we have really bad asthma.

My head is next to his, my shoulder touching his shoulder, and even though we spent the last hour transported to our middle school days, I'm very aware that we're back in the present. Me in this body I didn't ask for, and him to a chiseled jaw that makes me swoon.

His hair is curled around his face from all the sweating, and I hope I don't look half as crazy as I feel. My curls are slicked back in a bun, but I can feel some pulled loose on the back of my neck. "I don't know," I say. Then it hits me. *"Eighth grade."*

His eyes go wide, and we're laughing again.

The summer before eighth grade, I found my sister's old camera and we reenacted all eight Harry Potter movies. I can hardly talk. "When Dré came out of the bathroom with his mom's wig…" I can't even finish.

"Oh my god." Eli snorts, and tears collect in the corners of his eyes. "He thought he looked so good. *Behold the Mighty Draco, bitches*. Oh my god." He sits up. "We have to find that. He had on eyeliner and everything."

I remember it like it was just this morning. We were doing the emo version, and we thought we were geniuses. The editing on it was absolute trash, but it was *us*.

Eli wipes his eyes, still chuckling. For once, I'm not envious of his thick lashes. I want them in a different way. The way you want to see something on a person who belongs to you.

With the music on low and us in a bubble of silence, I realize we're staring at each other. A smile plays at the corner of his mouth, and I want to know all the secrets that make up Elijah Peretz. I thought I knew them, but now I know I don't.

He doesn't look away, but he doesn't lean in and kiss me either. He says, "Ready to sing for real this time?"

I pull away from his gaze and stare at the ceiling. I'm the biggest sucker in the candy shop. I breathe out the nerves that were collecting in my stomach.

"Liv." He's saying it like he does when we're on the phone, and I know I can't be making up this whole thing between us. "Liv…" He's singing my name now. He stands up with his water and holds out his other hand for me. I let him pull me up as he drinks half the bottle. He gives me the rest and I finish it.

We share like this all the time…but it feels different right now. I'm waiting for something, but nothing comes next. He just walks over to the table with my phone and puts on his own playlist. He knows my music, because my music is *his* music. We share everything except for the truth about what is happening right now.

He starts to sing with the track and raises his brows at me. His voice is liquid gold. It's deep, and it does its own thing. His voice is my body with music. It doesn't hesitate or need an invitation to be. It just *is*. "Sing with me."

I look up at the ceiling again, mumbling out the words, because I'm not the kind of person who can look longingly into someone's eyes and sing. I die when they do it to me. I squirm like a slug dying as someone sprinkles table salt on my little slug body.

His fingers tickle my neck, and I push his hands away, kind of hoping he'll push mine back and lock them together, but he just laughs and says, "Look at me."

"That's super intimidating and awkward. I'm not fearless like you," I say, but I scrunch up my face so he knows I'm being funny instead of honest. I can tell him the truth if I cover it up in a joke. Maybe that's my problem.

"I'm not fearless. Everyone's scared. We're all scared to fail or scared to admit we're in love. We're all stupid and smart all at the same time. We're all good at something someone thinks is stupid. Being brave enough to do it anyway is the difference."

Did he just say we're in love? I can't tell if he's being abstract or if he's saying he loves me and he's scared. This is going to haunt me until eternity, because I'm too chicken-shit to get clarification.

"All right." He moves next to me; we're shoulder to shoulder facing opposite directions. "Now I can't see you." He sings again and nudges me.

I'm still stuck on the love thing. I used to be able to figure him out. I knew when he was sad, angry, bits of both. I knew it all, and Eli used to be the kid of *very* few words. Now, he talks so much, and I can't figure out what he's saying.

I let the lyrics fall out of my mouth, and he doesn't laugh at my shaky voice. I'm terrified right now, but fuck it. That's what this year is supposed to be about. Fuck the terror. I take a deep breath and keep going. Song after song, he makes me sing louder and louder until I'm shouting and we're laughing all over again. At this rate, we'll never be ready for auditions, but I want to keep going like this forever.

Maybe this is the way it is with us. We'll dance around it until we fall into each other. Maybe we're making that secret contract right now. To do this thing naturally.

I don't get Eli anymore, not like I used to, but I'm stupid in love with him. And I'm pretty sure he's in love with me, too.

CHAPTER 7

Eli and I don't talk about our secret dance parties or how my rap game is kinda scary. (Luckily, as we go through the audition pieces, I realize that most of the female parts are sung anyway.) We've been practicing most nights when no one is around, so I'm bummed when Dré announces he's booked them another gig at the Grove. It pays double this time, because their Halloween gig sold to maximum capacity.

I'm happy for them—I am—but I'm also positive that Eli and I are one practice away from throwing our panting bodies into each other and sucking face. Actually, that's a lie—I just keep hoping it'll happen, like the sad sack I am. Al would be so disappointed in me, but I haven't the guts to tell him I'm back on the Elijah Peretz train and still apparently going nowhere.

I was *sure* Eli was sending me vibes, but now I'm back to

not having a single clue. When we get close and I look into his eyes, he does...nothing. I give him *the* eyes. The ones where I look longingly at him for a second too long after a flirty joke. I find the cheesiest excuses to touch him. To brush our hands against each other—and yet he's giving me nothing back.

But at the same time—when I least expect it, he'll drop a line like, *How you single dancing like that?* Who says that without a follow-up? I thought we were doing the *when the mood strikes, it will happen* thing. But it doesn't get more romantic than singing love songs together in my bedroom—unless he's just not into me.

I just want to cry into a bowl full of mini Reese's Cups.

I'm sitting in Bio II across from Lennox with our DNA results from the fake crime scene, when I realize the only person I have to talk to about my non-love life is a seventy-year-old man who thinks Twitter is the work of the devil.

Lennox is staring at me, probably because it's the fifth time I've sighed and I haven't added anything useful to the conversation in ten minutes. "O, what is up with you, girl? I can't have you fucking with my grades." She calls me O now. No one calls me Olivia except my grandmother. And when she says it, it's like she believes I'll be a debutante with white gloves and a black boyfriend named Cliff.

"I'm fine." I'm so not fine. I'm far from it. Not to mention my jeans keep falling off my butt and I don't have a belt, because I hate the extra bulk buckles add around my waist. All the black girls at my school have pants that fit but I swear they all have those tiny bellies that stay flat when they sit down.

Lennox puts down her pen and leans forward, surveying my face. "You in love?"

This girl is like the psychic version of Bob Marley. I don't even know how to answer her. "No." I don't want her telling me about who else she's slept with. There are over three thousand kids at our school, but if she says Eli, I'll fucking lose it. So I change the subject. "I'm nervous about auditions." It's true, I am. They're at the end of next week, and I am low-key freaking out. Every time I think about getting onstage and singing or delivering my lines, I get that deep dread in my stomach.

"Don't even sweat it." Lennox has gold wire wrapped around her dreads today, and it accents her light brown eyes. Those eyes are already intense as is with the color, but she's also an eye-contact person. Normal people blink away every three seconds. Lennox is a slow blinker, and her gaze never leaves mine. "My first time auditioning I was scared, too, but everyone is supportive. We're all there for the same reason, so it's like being in front of friends."

I want to tell her that, until recently, my friends couldn't say they'd ever seen me do anything—but she tilts her head like she's got an idea.

"You know what. Come to our audition party."

I blink. I'm at a magnet school, and I've seen those PBS specials about performing arts schools and kids doing all that off-Broadway kinda shit. My school isn't really like that— we're just normal—but I won't lie, the theatre kids, they're like a cult. They break out in song in the mornings, by the lockers, in the pizza line. They move in groups, and unless you're one of them, you don't know what they're up to or when they're going to flash mob you. So, while I'm surprised they have parties for occasions like *auditions*, I'm not surprised at the same time.

"When is it?" I don't even know why I'm asking, because I know I'm going to settle on *I'm sorry I can't make it*, no matter what she says.

"Tonight." Lennox is all chill about asking me *the day of.*

"Girl—that's real short notice." I don't even have to come up with a clever excuse. I get ready for a resounding no, but the annoying voice in my head saying *fuck it* is getting louder. So far, this fuck-it thing has not come easy. Every choice is forced and uncomfortable. It's not like I live a wild and crazy life. I go to school, do homework, practice my flute, and do chores. I started this list thinking I was making some huge change in my life, and so far it's been a week of—nothing life changing.

Al said change isn't about creating opportunities, it's about taking advantage of the ones present, but does going to a party with strangers count? I'm not scared. I'm just not interested. I don't do parties without Dré and Eli, because they're my people. *They're* the reason I *go* to the party. I don't even know anyone in the theatre program besides Cleo—oh god, what if Cleo is at the party and we get our awkward-stank all over the place?

These are starting to feel like excuses, and I groan. "Fine."

Lennox raises an eyebrow. "Damn, I take it back if you're gonna act like that."

I hold up my hands and laugh. She looks really insulted, and I can't help but laugh harder—no, really, when people get mad, my first reaction is to laugh. It's so messed up, and my mom has slapped me upside the head more times than I can count because of it. "I'm not saying that to you. I'm say-ing it to me."'

She doesn't look convinced.

"I'm doing this Year of Fuck It thing and—" I can tell I'm losing her, so I explain it to her the same way I explained it to Al, and she, like Al, is into *Grey's Anatomy*. It's like the show to bridge all generations. Obviously, if Shonda Rhimes can do that, she's got to be onto something about this *Year of Yes* thing.

"I get it. Is that why you're doing the musical?"

I nod, and just when I think she's about to say something slick, she smiles. "That's boss. Shit, I want to do it, too—well, I would if I didn't already say yes to everything that scares me. But I dig it."

Lennox picks up her pen, and we get back to work try-ing to match blood samples. Before we leave class, she offers to be my ride and puts my address in her phone. Again, she just whips it out and no one even bats an eye. I swear, once I just checked the time and had admin all over me like drug dogs on a bag of cocaine. I don't know how she does it—but I dig it, too.

She puts her phone away with this look on her face that I can only describe as devious. "Bring that fuck-it attitude with you—you're gonna need it." She leaves me standing in front of the lockers, trying to figure out what the hell I've gotten myself into.

Eli and Dré's gig is tonight, and I feel bad for canceling on them, but I don't know why. It's not like I do anything for them; they have all the moral support they need when they're onstage, with a fan base that spans a few schools. They don't need me. But I'm looking at Dré's message in the group chat, wondering if his Cool means *Yeah, it's cool you're going to a party*, or *Yeah, whatever, we don't need you anyway, asshole.*

Eli just sent a K. Nothing else.

It shouldn't bother me, but I want them to fight for my attention a little. Maybe they've gotten so used to me being around, they don't even notice when I'm not. Or, most likely because I'm my mother's neurotic child, I'm reading way too much into two one-word messages.

I put on my best pair of jeans, the ones that ride high on my waist and make me look slimmer, and a white tank top with a billowy kimono blouse.

I stole the blouse from my mom's closet, and as she watches me put on some of her red lipstick, she nods in approval. "You look cute," she says, eyeing her sheer kimono.

I'm always stealing her clothes when I want to look nice. She's got fashion sense, but apparently not enough of it to pass down to me. She helps with mascara, and I can't help but ogle her poreless skin. She's not even wearing makeup. My mother looks like a doll. She's in her late forties, but everyone thinks she's my sister. Not in that lame flattery kind of way. In the *she tries to buy wine and they card her and eye her like it's a fake ID* kind of way.

Because she has vampire genes, I look like I'm twelve when I wear my hair in a bun or try bringing back coveralls. I'm not mad about it, but I get the *cute* comment from guys while girls like Lennox get the *hot damn!* kind of recognition.

"You really should do something with that hair." My mom thinks natural hair is nappy and unruly. She doesn't get the *embrace the curl* movement. She's all about weaves and—to my unfortunate middle school days—thick braids that don't belong on a girl with a round face. I was *that* girl. The one who looked like she didn't know hair could be pretty.

I don't know what it is with my mom. She *always* looks flawless, but she would dress me like I was Oliver Twist—like she wanted people to take pity and toss me a few coins. To be fair, I was a big kid. I was shopping in Junior Miss before I was a *miss*. I was the kid who thought everyone ate a box of cookies in one sitting.

Now, I'm not fat, but damn, I'm not snatched either. Clothes just don't fit me like they do other girls—except these jeans and this sheer, flowy blouse. Perfect outfits only happen on magical leap years, and though I'm thinking about it, I have too much shame to wear the same outfit every day just because it's banging.

My mom's talking again, and I have no idea what she's saying. Over the years I've learned to tune her out like background noise. "I'm sorry, what?"

She cuts her eyes at me. "I *said*—you should put on some of my heels. They'll give you height, trim a few pounds off your thighs."

OH MY GOD. This is why she lives on mute most of the time. "I'm good in flats." Who does she think I'm trying to impress anyway? And I'm short and have thick thighs; no amount of heel is going to change that.

She's rolling her eyes, like, *why do I even try*. And I want her to try, I do. I want to know how she can piece together an outfit from just a pair of shoes, or how she learned to ombré her lipsticks. I want to know these things, but she always comes at me with some whack-ass nonsense that just doesn't look right on me. Last year, I let her do my makeup for home-coming, and I swear she had me looking like a clown.

Twinks jumps up on the counter and puts her tail in my mouth while I tweeze a few rebellious eyebrow hairs. Twinks is probably on her last year or two, and I don't have the heart to yell at her. I try batting her tail out of the way and get a streak of drool on my arm instead.

I'm checking myself in the hallway mirror when I get sec-ond thoughts. Lennox's words haunt me like flashbacks from Halloween. *Bring that fuck-it attitude, you're going to need it.*

But there's no time to call it off, Lennox is five minutes early, and I'm honestly surprised. I don't know anyone with an ounce of melanin who is ever on time. "Damn, girl." She's checking me out, and I can't help but smile. I tried. I really did. This whole look took me three hours and four changes of clothes to get right. "Bitch, you fine as fuck. Stick to high-waisted jeans. I don't know why you don't wear them to school."

I look at the jeans—she's not wrong. My sister gave them to me last week. Amber's always giving me her castoffs when she's down for a random weekend. She lives in Atlanta doing—I actually have no idea what she does. She's always changing careers, and every time she starts explaining her job, I hear that, *whamp whamp* sound all the adults in *Charlie Brown* make. It's not that I don't care, it's that I'd rather talk about what she's going to cook. She can throw down in the kitchen, and once, I really did scream, "Hallelujah! Take me, Jesus!" after my sister made me a key lime pie.

The party isn't too far from where I live. There are four cars parked outside the house (none of them belonging to Cleo, thank god) and at the door I can't hear anything. The parties I go to are thrown by people I know and involve us sitting around talking about what we should do. I don't know whose house this is and I'm not trying to be cliché, but I halfway expected to hear loud music and see people with red Solo cups standing on the porch.

A guy opens the door, and I barely register some light thematic music in the background. He's a big, thick guy, like he could be a linebacker, and tall, with dark, straight hair pulled back in a man bun. He definitely belongs on a beach.

"Lennox," he says, holding out his hand and giving her a half hug. He's got a deep voice, and as he's telling her who's already here, I notice his accent. He's Hawaiian. I sing enough *Moana* to know it from anywhere—that, and he *looks* Hawaiian. I'm gawking, because he's hot.

And he's looking at me, too.

"Kai, this is O." Lennox doesn't even say my whole name. I want this boy to know my whole name *and* my number.

I hold out my hand, and he laughs, pulling me into a half hug. "I'm a hugger. Nice to meet you, Olivia." He knows my name, and my face gives my surprise away. "I've seen you around school. You're always hanging out with Dré and Eli."

I nod. What the fuck happened to my words? I have no game.

"Come in. We're still waiting on David before we start."

Start what? I'm trying to slow my breathing.

I get like this when I'm nervous. I smile until my jaw hurts from clenching. My shoulders get tense, and I regret every life decision leading me to the event in question.

Again, I realize I don't know anybody here except Lennox, who might not want me hanging on to her like one of those socially anxious lapdogs.

Upside—Kai's house is gorgeous. It's got Polynesian carvings on the wall and paintings of the ocean. He has a dog, a retriever who moseys over and licks my hand. Dark wood floors lead to the living room, where a bunch of kids are sitting around a big floor table. I don't know how to describe it, other than it's a table with short legs.

"Have a seat by the kotatsu." He's pointing at the table, and Lennox is already headed there. He disappears into the kitchen and so I follow Lennox to the group of kids already around the table.

Yep. I don't know any of these people, and worse, it's a small group. Nowhere to blend into the background. No way to avoid conversations I don't belong in. As soon as the inside jokes start, I'll be that weird girl everyone keeps thinking *who invited her?* about.

Lennox is pointing around the table and rattling off names: Steph, Markus, Jackie, Rodney, and Javier. Steph's a white girl with a messy bun of auburn hair, Markus a black kid who keeps looking at Jackie while she's talking to her phone—I think she's making a video. Rodney is leaning in next to Jackie, saying, "Yaass, girl!" with his blond hair slicked back, and Javier is a tall skinny dude with thick black glasses who looks up from shuffling cards to wave at me. "This is O. O, this is everybody."

They all stop, even Jackie, who is in the middle of vlogging, to say, "Hey, O!" Jackie points the camera at me and says, "Damn, check out sis, rocking the kimono. She a fine piece of chocolate."

I don't even have time to respond before the camera is pointed back at her.

Lennox grabs two pillows from a big basket near a window with a view of a lake. She puts them on the floor next to the only empty pillow. Then she puts me next to the empty pillow and winks. I'm not even going to acknowledge that she's low-key trying to hook me up with the Hawaiian Sunset coming out of the kitchen with two cans of Coke.

And then it dawns on me—she *is*. The ratchet chick in my head is laughing like Goofy, and I hope to god Kai can't see my crazy.

He sits next to me and hands me one. He smiles.

I pull out my finger guns. "Yo-la sweet Cola. Uh—I don't know why I said that—um—let's start over? Hi." What is *wrong* with me?

He laughs, and his shoulder brushes against me. "Ever play Wolf?" He's smiling at me like I'm Little Red Riding Hood and I want him to take my basket of baked goods. I don't even know what the hell that means, but I really want him to.

"Wolf?"

Javier starts dealing cards. Everyone gets one. Kai explains the rules. There are two wolves, a sheriff, a psychic, some kids, and townspeople. We have to guess who the wolves are, and everyone has to agree on naming those people. We have to catch the two wolves before they completely destroy our village or we accidentally hang everyone accused of being wolves.

What kind of party is this? I'm waiting for the kicker: *Wolf takes the town; you lose your clothes!* I can't believe these people are sitting around playing card games like middle-aged couples without kids. I'm not mad. I just thought it was going to be a night of awkwardly hanging out with kids smoking pot and drinking way too much alcohol.

We play a few times, and as I figure out the game, I get really into it. When I play games, I play to win. So, when I'm the wolf, I make it my job to infect every last player with my venom. I have people burning innocent villagers at the stake, and I feel so gloriously evil.

The third time we play, I get the wolf card again and so does Kai. He nudges me with his leg every time we get the others to go after someone else. We win that round.

The game is the icebreaker I didn't know I needed. My cheeks hurt from laughing at Jackie pleading her case like she's fresh off an episode of *Law & Order*. Everyone is way different than I imagined. I was expecting over-the-top personalities, and—well, Jackie's a little out of this world, but for the most part everyone is really chill and welcoming. I'm not the new kid in the group. I'm just a girl competitively playing a card game and laughing so hard I'm choking on my soda.

We take a break from cards and go outside to pretend we can see the meteor shower that's apparently happening tonight. I sit on a hammock, and Kai sits next to me. "You having fun?" He hands me a new Coke and I open it, swinging my legs back and forth. I'm really glad I didn't wear heels. I'd have been so overdressed.

I want to impress this guy. The way he looks at me—no one

else does. I thought Eli was giving me eyes, but Eli is more like a puppy looking fondly at his favorite toy. This guy is a tiger ready to pounce, and I'm that one deer—or whatever tigers eat—standing in the meadow screaming, *Me! Take me!*

"Yeah," I say looking up at the cloudy sky. I can't hold eye contact with him. I like that he's looking at me, but at the same time I hate the attention. It doesn't make sense, but while I want him to look, I'm terrified of what he sees. I want to say something funny to get the attention off me but, *fuck it*. How can I get up onstage and have hundreds of eyes on me if I can't stand having just two take me in?

I take a small breath. Will this discomfort ever go away? Will I wake up one day and feel like a flawless boss bitch, or will it forever be a fight?

Jackie and Rodney are walking around the backyard filming and screaming, saying they can see a gator in the water. The yard is fenced, but, according to my grandmother, gators can climb fences.

Kai leans in and taps my arm with his. "I'm glad you came." Then he leans in more, and I almost lose it because I think he might kiss me, but he just smiles. "To be honest, I didn't know if you'd be cool. Dré's kind of a dick, and I've seen you hanging with him, so I assumed you might be one, too."

I laugh, because, wow, what an accusation. But Dré *is* kind of a dick, so I get it. "Well, you know what they say about assumptions."

"Duly noted." He's still doing that Lennox thing where they stare without looking away. Three seconds is the acceptable amount of time, but nobody told *them* that. "So, I've got a full schedule with my package." He pauses when I glance down. This dude is bold and—wow.

He laughs, and it's big and earthshaking. "No. *No.* Not like that. It's the senior projects for drama. We have five skits to perform before Thanksgiving break." He relaxes again next to me. "You want to hang out sometime after that?"

My throat clinches and I try not to show all my teeth as I smile. This stupid giddy laugh erupts from my lips. I've never been asked out in my life. It's sad. I've kissed boys, but it was that *shh, don't tell anyone* kind of stuff. Mainly because I never wanted Dré and Eli to know who I liked. I always figured they'd make fun of me, which, in hindsight, is idiotic and doesn't make sense.

Regardless, *this* has never happened before—and though I'm not trying to think about my old pal Al, I want to tell him he was right. I said yes to the musical and then Lennox was right there with the audition packet. I said yes to going to this party. All these things I'd have shut down without hesitation before—and now I've just been asked on a date by a boy I never would have met otherwise.

I made this happen by just saying yes. By *choosing* to say yes to these things that have been there all along. I'm mentally adding: *4. Go on a date* to my Fuck It list, because when God hands you fresh squeezed lemonade, you drink that shit.

He takes my stunned silence as a no, and I have to correct him. "I'd love to." I sound like such a chump.

"Okay, then." He takes a sip of his Coke, and I'm pretty sure he's smiling at the same time. "You're making me nervous." He's doing that unwavering stare again, and I can't help but point out that *I* actually do the three-second thing. So if any-one should be nervous, it's me. "Nah," he says. "You're a lot."

I have no idea what he means by that, and I don't have to mention I'm sensitive about my weight, so I just sit there looking at the black lake.

"Like—I feel like I have to plan something big for you. You're funny, smart, and hot as hell. That's a lot of pressure. It's intimidating."

Kai, the Hawaiian Sunset, is getting my best *I'm totally into you but I'm not desperate* smile. I kind of can't believe this is happening. I've never met a guy who just…says what he thinks. Or maybe I have, but I've been too busy saying no to talk to them.

I can't help but compare him to Eli. Yeah, they're differ-ent people, and maybe Eli's way of being interested is quieter than Kai's—or maybe he's not interested at all. The problem is I can't say yes to a bunch of fucking maybes.

There's no question with Kai. He put it out there, and now, so can I. "I trust you'll come up with something." I don't even know who this bitch smiling and batting her eyes is, because I've never been this bold in my life.

The door is open—I just hope walking through doesn't mean leaving Eli behind.

CHAPTER 8

When I'm back in the car with Lennox headed home, she side-eyes me. She's got a playlist going, but it's low-key old-people jazz. The saxophone kind that's two steps away from being retro porno music. "So," she says as a smile creeps on her face. "You met Kai."

I don't indulge her and keep my cool. "I met Kai," I say.

She reaches over and shoves me with a laugh. I get why Dré had sex with her. She's effortlessly sexy. If I were gay, I'd want to have sex with her. I don't tell her that though, I refuse to be the straight girl all over the bi girl.

"I saw y'all on the hammock making eyes." She leans back in her seat with her hands relaxed on the wheel. "You gonna tap that?" Sex is on the brain with this one. I mean, it's always on my mind, too, but she just puts it out there.

"I don't even know him."

She makes a noise like a snort but it's softer than that. "I can look into the eyes of a person and see their soul. That's all we need to know."

"Maybe you got them witch eyes, but I don't. I look into his eyes and I just start hyperventilating."

She laughs shaking her head. "You're so stupid."

"I'm serious."

Lennox glances at me. "I mean, if you're not ready, that's cool, too. No pressure here, I was just curious."

I let down my guard a little. I mean, *fuck it*, she's open, and I need someone to talk with about this stuff, so I can be, too. "I think, after I get to know him, I could. He looks at me and I can tell he's looking *at me*." I don't have to explain to her what I mean. She nods. She gets it. "I've never had sex before though. Dudes are always worried about putting it in the wrong hole and I'm like, what if *I* put it in the wrong hole?"

We both laugh, but I do, in fact, know my ass from my vagina.

"Don't think about it so hard." Lennox turns down the jazz. "On the real, everyone is always saying how that shit's gonna hurt, or be bad, or how it needs to be special. Girl, the only thing it needs to be is good."

I look at her, because that is legit the first time anyone has said that. Granted, I don't talk to too many people about sex, so, low bar—but I feel like what she's saying is right. "How do I make sure it's good?"

"You can't. But you can pick somebody who seems like they'll take the time to make it good." She turns into my neighborhood and in a minute, we're sitting in my driveway, but I don't get out.

"Explain."

Lennox puts the car in Park like she had no intention of letting me out anyway and turns to me. "It's like this. If you want a special time, you'll end up with a dude trying to smash you like the only thing he has to go on is a shitty teen movie where they fuck on prom night. You don't want that trash."

I don't. I don't know what I *do* want, but I don't want that weird *we go to a hotel with rose petals* thing. I'd die of second-hand embarrassment.

"If you go into it just wanting to get it over with, you'll end up with a jackhammer dude." She grabs her purse. "You don't want that either." Lennox pulls a Coke out of her purse and pops the top. She offers me first sip, and I take it.

I've never had a girlfriend. I've been friends with girls but none past elementary. Growing up, Cleo and I were always pushed to be best friends, and I think by rejecting Cleo, I sort of rejected all girls. I always thought I was that girl who got along with boys better—I'm starting to think I missed out on a whole lot of cool conversations.

"You need a solid dude," she says before taking a sip. "Forget everything you've ever seen on TV. Dudes are scared shitless and can't handle all your hang-ups *and* theirs. You have to go into it your own sexual beast. You masturbate?" She just drops it like she's asking me if I sometimes cook my own freaking breakfast.

"Jesus Christ." Why is it necessary she know this? I'm doing the fish face again, because my jaw is on her dirty floor mat.

She hits my arm. "Don't be a punk. I told you we both got

girl parts. We're in this game together. You need a dildo? I can get you one if your mom is weird and checks your mail."

"Oh. My. God." I'm laughing, because she's so serious I can't believe it. "No, I don't need a fucking dildo. Do I? Look, I've done stuff, but I'm not over here sticking carrots and cucumbers up my hoo-ha."

She's cackling and I start laughing again, too. "Girl, there is nothing embarrassing about using a cucumber. I've been in some desperate situations."

"TOO MUCH INFORMATION." I want to regret my choice to have this conversation but—I don't. I don't want to know all that, but I do want to know other things. I have no clue how to go about any of this sex shit and I want to know everything.

She's cackling again as she looks over my shoulder. Dré's Bat Mobile is pulling up in front of Eli's house, and the music is blaring. They both look over, and Dré nods his head. I know he's doing it to Lennox, because Dré *does not* nod with me. He makes faces and licks windows and other weird things when it's just us three. When he's trying to be cool, he nods.

Lennox raises her can at Dré. "He's your dude."

I look back to make sure she's talking about some dude I missed in the car with Dré and Eli. Dré's staring at me, probably wondering how I know the girl he lost his virginity to, and Eli's face is lit up from the glow of his phone, probably not caring that Dré's shitting his pants wondering if I know. He's saying something to Dré—or singing, I can't tell.

Neither of them will ever guess Lennox just told me to sleep with Dré. *I* can't believe it. "I'm sorry, who?"

Lennox starts her witchy cackle again. "He's somebody you know. You're comfortable with him. He'll want to treat you right, and I've already taught him how."

I want to gag. "Um, I know Eli—and other guys, too," I add, because I don't want to give away my big-ass crush.

Lennox shakes her head. "You and Dré have chemistry. You're all over his Instagram, not to mention that cute pic with him kissing you."

I wave her off. I'm not going to explain to her that Dré is just handsy—she should know that. Jesus. "I am not taking your sloppy seconds."

"He's a *person*, O. Not a bowl of half-eaten cereal."

"He's *Dré*."

She puts up her hands. "Well, Kai is cool, too." She's got this wicked smile on her face. "When I told him I invited you to the party, his whole face lit up like it was Christmas Eve and I was ringing Santa's sleigh bells."

My eyes get big. I don't want to know the answer to this question, but I need to know. "Have you slept with him, too?"

"Watch it, Janice." She rolls her eyes. "No, and even if I had, so what? Sex is an experience, not a pink slip. And it sure as hell ain't anything to be embarrassed about."

I can tell I hit a nerve, and I swear I'm not trying to call her a ho. I'm just not used to this. I breathe out. "Sorry. I'm just a little—"

"Green. It's fine, just don't get all judgy."

That's fair. I look over again, and now Dré's face is lit up from his phone. He's talking, too—no, they're definitely singing. That's the kind of stuff I'm used to. Sharing memes in the car and talking about the funny videos people are posting—or them singing and harmonizing like it's breathing. Not cucumbers and screwing my best friend.

Lennox is smiling again, and she shrugs her shoulders. "What?"

She takes the car out of Park. "Nothing, just looking at a girl about to trade in her V-card for some D."

"Oh. My. *God*." I get out of the car with her cackle following me. "Bye," I say, bent over with my head in the window.

"Bye, sis." She pulls out of my driveway, and in a few seconds, she's gone.

I stare at Dré and Eli, and I swear I feel like everything has changed. I don't know how to be with them after being with somebody else. It feels like I just cheated on my friends. It's weird and doesn't make sense, but with Lennox, I was a girl—a full-fledged girl, flirting with a boy at a party and talking about masturbation and sex.

I don't do that with Dré and Eli.

When I get to the Bat Mobile, Dré's already getting out of the car, and he gives me a once-over. "You have fun?" He's wearing jeans and a white V-neck shirt fitted to his body. His eyes keep flashing down the street like Lennox might reappear.

"I did." I'm looking at him in this way that makes my cheeks burn, and it's all Lennox's fault.

His eyes squint ever so slightly, and I feel caught.

I look away.

He pokes my stomach. "You look cute." I smack his hand away. I hate it when he does that. I almost think he does it because he knows I hate it, and the way he said *cute*—it's like he's trying to get me to admit I tried to look nice.

Ugh. Just like that, I feel like that kid playing dress up in Mommy's closet. Chemistry is *not* what I have with him. I have pure fiery rage that's about to flick him in the middle of his forehead.

"What?" Dré says. He's bending down, trying to catch my eyes.

Eli's putting his phone in his pocket and opening the trunk.

"How was the club?" I say it to Eli, since he still hasn't said anything to me.

His head pops out from the side of the car. "Normal. Except no one was there to tell Dré his hair was okay, so he kept running his hands through it and all that shit in his hair made his hands slick."

Dré's rolling his eyes. "Dude."

"He dropped the mic on some girl's face." Eli's laughing as he shuts the trunk with his keyboard in his other hand. He walks over to me, and I swear to god, if I hadn't seen him lean in, I'd never have known it really happened.

Eli kisses my temple. Just under the hairline—quick, like he's kissing a kid sister—except I'm not his sister and even Dré raises an eyebrow.

Eli looks down at me. "You do look nice."

What the fuck just happened.

Dré's face is back to normal as he gets back into his car and leans out the window. "Anyway, all I know is you ruined my night. Thanks for not being there for me." He winks. Then he pulls out of the driveway and shouts, "You're dead to me!" as he drives away.

Eli's still looking at me, and when I meet his eyes, he's back to normal Eli. Except we're standing outside in the middle of the night, staring at each other. We're both doing the Lennox thing—and neither of us is doing anything about it. I can't help but think about Kai, who was so direct. He said I was *hot*. He asked for my number, and he asked me on a freaking date.

The guy I've known for years—the guy I talk to every *day*—is just staring at me, and even though he kissed me, I still don't know what it means. It had to mean something—but we're alone with no one else around, and he still won't say anything.

I want to provoke him into it, tell him about Kai so he knows the clock is ticking—but that's petty, and I don't want to strong-arm him into asking me out. I want him to do it of his own accord.

Eli scratches the back of his head. "Tonight was crazy. The crowd was way into it, and some girl even gave me her number." He's biting the bottom of his lip, like I'm supposed to be impressed.

Is he serious right now? This might be a tad irrational, but I want to take Eli's phone and chuck it into the nearest lake. I'm grinding my teeth, and I have to force myself to relax. I don't want him to know how much that bothered me. "Wild, I just got asked out by a guy at that party."

Eli's eyebrows shoot up to the top of his head, and he shoves his free hand in his pocket. "Wow."

I want to say I'm not offended by the sheer shock on his face, but I am. "Why is it so shocking someone would ask me out?" Why is *he* shocked that someone could find me attractive and datable?

He lets out a small laugh and shakes his head. "Don't go crazy on me. I only said wow."

This. This is why I can never figure out if he actually likes me or if I've just deluded myself into thinking something is going on between us.

He sighs. "Liv, chill, I meant it as a good thing. Anyways it's late. Go to bed before midnight for once in your life."

And he's off—walking to his house. After all the practices where we've spent time dancing and laughing and singing stupid love songs, I thought we were *seconds* from taking the plunge. But then he kissed me on the temple...and told me he got a girl's number.

What. The. Actual. Fuck.

I'm inside, slamming my keys on the counter, and my mom asks about the party. She's on the couch working on her laptop and I expect her to half listen to me but I've got her full undivided attention. Great.

"It was okay." I'm trying not to sound like someone peed in my apple juice, but Eli's driving me up the wall.

"O-kay," she says all slow, pulling off her glasses. "Were Dré and Eli there?"

I don't know why she's fishing for information. She saw me take off with Lennox. "No. They had a gig."

"Hmph." She leans back onto the couch pillows. "You three are usually joined at the hip."

I plop down in the armchair and wrap the brown afghan around me. It's always cold in the house. I try to breathe out my irritation, because I can already tell I'm being standoff-ish, and I don't want to hurt her feelings. I want to tell her about Eli, ask for her advice, but she'll make it weird and so

I just stuff it down deep and change the subject altogether. "It was an audition party. I'm trying out for the school musical." I hold up my hand as her mouth drops a bit. "Don't make it a thing."

She puts her laptop on the coffee table. "But this is huge, Olivia." She tries to compose herself. I've seen her do this a hundred times when she thinks I'm being skittish and close to running off to my room. "I'm saying it's a big deal, because you're so talented and I always thought you'd make a great performer if you only..." she pauses, and I know she's debating finishing that sentence "...came out of your shell."

It really sucks when everyone who is supposed to know you the best thinks you're this hermit who can't let loose and have fun. My mom, Dré, and Eli, they see me like the bartender did. I'm surprised they aren't stockpiling cat litter for my future fortysomething cats that will eat my corpse when I die old and alone.

I just nod my head and turn on the TV, because telling her I'm not in a shell will trigger her taking me on a trip down memory lane where she points out every moment she thinks I've been *shy*. I'm not shy. I'm just weird—and I like deep conversations instead of chatting about the weather. I like friends I know instead of people I don't. I like long car rides going nowhere instead of parties where the music is too loud to even think.

I like those things. Eli likes those things. We are like the same person, so how can't he see how much I really want him to want me?

CHAPTER 9

It's Sunday night. I'm standing in line waiting to buy my movie ticket, and I have to let yet another couple skip in front of me because we can't figure out which movie we're watching.

This is why I hate hanging out with other people. If it were just Dré, Eli, and I, we'd have settled this in less than thirty seconds—mainly because Eli always picks the best movies. But Dré's invited half the band—okay, like three other people who aren't *uncool*, but it changes the dynamic.

There's Kara, Alexandra, and Tyler. It's not like I have a problem with them—except I do. Kara rode with us, which I didn't know was going to happen, and she sat in the back with Eli, chatting him up the entire ride.

She's still chatting him up about some dumbass movie she saw the other night, while we're all trying to figure out what to watch *now*. It's a choice between horror and action, and honestly, I don't know shit about either of these movies and this is a waste of precious homework time.

Dré nudges me with his shoulder. He's got his hands stuffed in his pockets because it's abnormally chilly tonight; he hates the cold and will literally huddle like a penguin for the tiniest bit of heat. I'm cold, too, which is another reason why Kara needs to shut the fuck up so we can pick a movie already.

Tyler's taller than all of us, and his voice is incredibly deep for a boy who plays a soprano sax. "I'm down for the horror. I know the ladies might get scared, but we're here for y'all." I'm rolling my eyes, because he and Alexandra are one dark room away from sealing the deal on the heavy flirting they've been doing since band camp. In fact, I can't figure out why Dré invited them since they're clearly making this a date, and Kara obviously thinks this is hookup time.

I purposely tap Eli's shoe, because now he's telling Kara about some stupid video game as if the rest of us aren't freezing right now.

He looks at me and raises a bushy brow.

"Which movie?" I say. I know I sound like a bitch right now, but he's the one who convinced me to come tonight even though I have math and history *and* I need to finish up reading for English. I thought he was going to… I don't know, use this opportunity to make something happen. I'm so stupid.

"Whichever," he says, like a chipper fucking bird on a spring morning, before turning back to Kara.

Kara leans into him. "I'm so cold. I pick horror. I'm a total wuss though."

"Well, that's fucking brilliant." I can't believe I said it out loud. Everyone is staring at me, and Kara's one of those simple bitches who wears her stupid, easily offended emotions on her face, so I course correct. "I was talking about something else—something I just saw." No one believes me, and I know it was a sad excuse, but...whatever.

The rest of us agree to watch the horror if not just to get inside, and we split up to save seats and buy concessions. I'm in line with Eli and Tyler when Tyler hands me money so he can use the bathroom.

Eli's fidgeting. He knows I'm mad but probably won't say anything about it, because he's not the confrontational type, and that drives me up the wall. So, I don't say anything either.

I order a bunch of stuff for Dré and me and go to the butter station to grab napkins and straws. Tyler comes out of the bathroom in time to take some of the popcorn and drinks just as Eli starts grabbing napkins.

I honestly don't know why I'm so bothered. I'm not his girlfriend. Obviously he's allowed to talk to other girls—or flirt—or whatever. I just don't understand why he's the way he is with me if he's going to turn around and chat up wide-eyed, blonde, bobble-head-looking-ass Kara.

I also hate that I'm mad at her. She doesn't deserve that, but that doesn't mean I deserve to feel this way either. Ugh.

I'm shoving napkins into my too-tiny pockets when Eli laughs.

"That...doesn't seem like it's working."

I hate that I agreed to carry all this shit back for these ungrateful punks. This is supposed to be a fun movie night but carrying this crap when I have piles of homework at home is not fun. "Well, unless you have a bright idea, I can do without the commentary."

He sighs, and I know I'm pushing him away, but I really do want him *away* right now. I don't like feeling like this. I need to get over him and move on. He's made it clear that he's open for business. *A girl gave me her number.* Like I fucking asked.

He's walking toward the theatre, and I'm walking behind him—how can someone be so familiar and yet so completely foreign at the same time? Right now I feel like I don't know him at all. Like our time together has been a figment of my imagination, because why else would he string me along just to flirt with another girl in front of me?

Everyone has picked seats in the middle of the theatre, and there are two open seats between Kara and Dré. I cringe, because, despite it all, I'm relieved that I'm going to be sitting next to Eli. I'm clearly one of those people who likes pain, because Kara's face lights up as she calls Eli over, holding out her hands to help him with the popcorn.

I plop down next to Dré and hand him his popcorn. I put the soda between us realizing I forgot to get my own. As I get up, with a hard exhale, he pulls me back down.

He's looking at me like he can tell I'm a few seconds from Hulking out. "We'll share."

I nod, staring at the screen, because I feel like I might cry. And I feel like an idiot for putting myself through this. The previews haven't even started, and Dré pulls out his phone and shows me funny cat memes. He does this when I'm upset, and I wonder if he knows.

He shoves his phone in my face as a cat readies itself for a jump and completely fails. I smile, but I kind of feel like that cat. Like, since the summer, I've been readying myself to jump into some kind of relationship with Eli, and just when I was about to take the leap…*splat.*

The movie starts and I'm already over it.

Eli leans into me as he pulls a box of M&M's out his pocket. "Hey, I got you these." He hands me the box, and I want to chuck them back in his face, because he's doing it again. Making me feel special. And I have no idea what this means, because now he's leaning back in his chair and laughing at something Kara says.

I'm telling myself that I'm a super jealous, overreacting asshole when light flashes on the screen and Kara jumps and grabs Eli's hand. I spend the next several minutes waiting for him to pull his away…and he doesn't.

He just sits there with Kara clutching him, and—fuck it.

I can't sit here watching this. My stomach is turning, but if I leave, where will I go? Dré is my ride home—but I can't stay here.

I get up and leave.

I know it's petty, and I'm completely ruining the evening for everyone, but I *can't* sit there and watch that. I'm his best friend, I know everything about him, but clearly that's not enough.

I'm not enough, which means he's just not attracted to me—he's attracted to white girls like Kara. What else could it be? That is the biggest difference between us and I can't even hate him for having a preference—and I get that all of America is conditioned to love skinny little white girls, but this is like a blade in the heart, because he's my best friend, and apparently anything more than that is beyond his imagination. Yet there is this pathetic part of me that still wants to believe he might like me. I'm such a fucking loser, and I can't stand myself right now.

I'm in the arcade room, sitting in a *Jurassic Park* game, when the curtain opens and Dré sticks his head in.

"Everything okay?"

I look at him and hold up my phone. "Got a call."

He nods. "Sure. I call bullshit, but sure." He doesn't have the grace to let me save face.

"I don't like horror movies."

He scoots in next to me, and the screen flashes over our faces. "Yeah, it's stupid. We should have gone to the one about—I don't know what any of these movies are about." He starts laughing.

The thing about Dré's laughs is they're kind of contagious, so I smile a little. We're quiet, staring at the flickering Start screen, when he says, "You've got to stand up for yourself."

I don't know if he's talking about Eli or about picking the movie, so I just say, "Everyone wanted to watch the movie, and I didn't want to stand outside anymore."

He lets out a small breath and looks at me.

I keep my eyes on the flickering screen. I'm not going to admit to him that I know he's probably talking about Eli. I don't want to admit that I have feelings for Eli, let alone acknowledge that Dré can tell—which means Eli can tell and is clearly trying to show me he isn't interested.

Dré gets out of the booth and walks around to my side, then pulls my curtain back. "Let's crash another movie."

Honestly, I just want to sit in this little *Jurassic Park* booth and turn into a puddle of pity, but Dré's already waving me out, and next thing I know we're walking into a theatre as cars are blowing up. Even if I feel like complete trash, at least I feel like trash with a friend who isn't going to let me wallow in it.

I'm adding another thing to the Fuck It list: *5. Stop crushing and move on.*

CHAPTER 10

In normal Tuesday fashion, Mr. Kaminski is yelling at Aaron because he's playing the timpani with the cover on. We're thirty minutes into class, and this kid still hasn't taken the cover off the timpani. Mr. Kaminski is about to blow a blood vessel, and while he's chewing the rest of us out for being subpar and an overall disappointment, he's got spit flying from his mouth, and us flutes are on the front lines.

I'm not moving an inch, because I didn't practice over the last two days, reserving that time for going over lines and the songs for the musical auditions. Eli and I haven't practiced together since the whole movie thing three days ago. He's been acting like everything is normal, which is normal for us—ignoring all the problems until they just go away—but auditions are coming up Friday.

I catch Eli staring at me for the third time today, and he

looks away like he did every time before that. Sometimes I wish he'd just tell me he doesn't like me so I can set some boundaries on how to be platonic friends. Like no staring off into the distance at me while we get verbally accosted by our band teacher.

Mr. Kaminski storms into his office after telling the clarinets not to play if they're just going to "shrill about!" I think that's a fair assessment, considering they did get a tad screechy—especially Kara. And that's not jealousy talking; the girl is tone-deaf and plays on cracked reeds because the idiot has yet to figure out not to chew on them.

I've packed away my flute and am putting it in my locker when I catch Dré a few lockers down looking at Eli. He's got his brow raised, and Eli's shrugging. They do this. Silent speak. It's a coded language they use when they don't want me to know what they're saying.

Before long, Eli's leaning against the flute locker next to mine. "Still mad at me?"

I almost drop my lock. "Mad at you?" I try to act all chill, like I didn't storm out of a movie because my not-boyfriend was holding hands with a girl who can't change her reeds to save her life.

"Yeah. You haven't been talking to me. So I assumed you were mad at me."

Assumed. You just assumed. "No. I was busy."

Eli looks down and then up at me ever so slightly, which means he doesn't believe me but he's not going to push it. He wants us to patch things up and move forward. Forever forward on the road to nowhere.

But I'm an adult these days and doing the Fuck It thing,

which means not holding grudges against people who don't even know why you have a grudge. I'm going to be the bigger person. I'm going to be so big that I blot out the fucking sun.

"I'm not mad, Eli. I've been stressed. I got hit with two papers and a test all at once." Not a lie.

He reaches out and pulls a curl from my bun, as if I didn't spend a significant amount of time this morning getting it just perfect. Cool. Now I'm going to spend the rest of my day with a lopsided bun and one whack-ass curl dangling from it.

I grab my book bag as Dré saunters over, running a hand through his hair. "You two good or whatever? I'm tired of walking on eggshells."

I shoot Dré a look that just makes him laugh, and Eli rolls his eyes.

Dré is as unfazed as ever. "I need to copy math homework. Whose turn is it?"

I push past Dré, and Eli and I walk to lunch, leaving him to follow.

"I'm serious, guys. I cannot go to Nova's class without my homework, the lady already threatened to hit me once. I'd tell admin, but she's old and black, so you know they won't do shit."

I glance at Eli. "My money says she hits him. I saw her smack a teacher with a folder once." It's easy to be the bigger person when you miss the guy who has your heart on a string. Actually moving on isn't as easy as writing it down on a piece of paper. It's not a to-do-list item, or as simple as saying yes.

Eli's smiling, and I can't help but think it's extra wide because he's relieved I'm no longer avoiding him. I exhale and give him a small smile. I've got bigger problems than crying over something I should have known was a nonstarter. Bigger things…like getting up onstage in two days and hoping to god I don't make a complete fool of myself.

Maybe the only way to move on is by simply putting one foot in front of the other in another direction.

CHAPTER 11

I worked with Al again, the day before auditions, and he told me if I got nervous to imagine everyone naked. I told him he was old and a cliché, and here I am trying that shit out because I'm nervous as fuck. We're all sitting in the auditorium, and there have to be thirty or more kids here. I'm between Dré and Eli, and Kai keeps glancing back at me from two rows up. He's giving me those dimpled Hawaiian cheeks and I am melting, because both Dré and Eli have noticed but they're pretending not to.

Or I'm overthinking it.

I'm overthinking a lot of things right now. Mrs. Gunta, the drama teacher, is onstage talking with a senior about lighting and music. She hasn't even acknowledged the rest of us poor souls who are about to pee on the stage because the anxiety is real.

I catch a glimpse of Cleo working with the curtains—I guess she's not trying out for a part. Now that I think about it, she hasn't been cast in a production since we started high school. She was always cast in plays in middle school, and the family was dragged to each and every one of them, including this weird space thing they did about a dog on Mars.

And then it dawns on me. Maybe Cleo's never been cast because it's just *that* hard. Cleo's very talented, and if she's not even bothering to try out, what the hell am *I* doing here? And why don't these people look as terrified as I feel?

Actually, everyone else looks bored, and the freshmen keep placing bets on which senior will get a leading role. They've even gotten bored. My leg is bouncing like I have to pee, and they're chewing gum and taking selfies like it's any other Friday.

Eli puts a hand on my leg. "You're ready."

A laugh erupts from me and I can't stop. This is the moment I die, I'm sure of it. I've gone over lines and songs a thousand times yesterday alone, not to mention I've been practicing so much I'm even singing in my sleep. I *know* I know the lines. I know the song, too, and I'm not that bad—the problem is doing it when it counts.

Mrs. Gunta taps a mic and a *boom* sounds. "Yeah, turn it down a little, Joshua. Cleo, dim the houselights. Good. Can everybody hear me?" Her voice is a mix between a 1920s jazz singer and the Wicked Witch of the West. The stage brightens as the lights above me dim. This is really happening. "Welcome to auditions. Everyone is here for *Othello the Musical*, right?"

All the drama kids are cheering and whooping, and a few

of them are even doing a short chant. Lennox is one of the chanters, and I'm wishing I was sitting next to her. Maybe that sureness could rub off on me.

"We'll do boys first. Ladies, I know, bummer, there are so many girls to go through, but I think we all can't wait to see who's got what it takes to be our Othello." The girls are all whooping now, and I realize I'm clutching my book bag like it's my oxygen and I have two busted lungs. I could really use a little extra O2 right now. "We'll do the lines first, then the singing. It's going to be a long night, so buckle up and get ready to belt. Auditions start now. Everyone, you know what to do."

"SMASH IT," everyone except Eli, Dré, and me yells. They're all applauding again, like we're on a talent show and Mrs. Gunta is Ryan Seacrest.

Eli squeezes my leg, but there is nothing he can do right now to make that *I'm going to pee* feeling go away. I know I don't have to, because I just came from the bathroom.

Oh. My. God.

Fuck this Fuck It thing.

One by one, the boys are called up to the stage. I think she's going in order of the sign-up sheet that was passed around. Kai's in the middle of the pack, and the guys that have gone before him were pretty good but nothing spectacular. The applause everyone gets after though—every single one, no matter how shaky someone was or how obviously nervous—*everyone* applauds like it was a performance worthy of a Tony.

Kai's onstage delivering his lines, and I know immediately he's not going to get the *supportive* applause. He's going to get whoops and cheers because he *earned* it. He's got bass in his voice, and it takes up the whole auditorium. He paces the stage like a lion on the prowl, and he—and I mean this in a good way, because he's doing Iago's soliloquy—looks and sounds like a son of a bitch. Like a guy who would manipulate you into smothering your wife.

It's creepy. He's *so damn good.*

I, too, stand up and applaud when he's done, and then we're back to people doing their best but nowhere near Kai's delivery. When it's Dré's turn, he gets onstage, and I realize I've never seen him practice or even heard him talk about practicing. I get that secondhand embarrassment, because I'm almost sure he's going to fail. He can sing his ass off, but just because he's good at pretending to be the cool guy doesn't mean he can act.

But he starts, and he's not bad. I'm squeezing the arm of my chair, but as every second goes by, I'm feeling proud. *That's my friend.* He's doing the thing, and he's amazing. Not as amazing as Kai, but better than most of the drama kids.

Eli's the last boy, and though we've practiced together a thousand times, when the light hits him, it's like I'm seeing him perform for the first time. He rivals Kai, and he's reading the Othello part. I thought that was a ballsy move, but now I realize every time he practiced with me, he must have been holding back.

My friends aren't just rock gods. They're amazing, talented guys, and I can't believe it's taken me this long to see the depths of their talent. Even though they've never done anything like this before, they didn't hesitate to try. They've got this hunger—this fire—to get up and perform, and they don't let anything put it out. No wonder they laughed when I said I was going to audition.

Like Kai, Eli gets applause because he deserves it—but even as I clap my hardest, my stomach churns. Girls are next, and though there are a ton of us here, we draw straws and I'm last. I swear I'm going to shit bricks when my time comes.

I go to the bathroom anyway; nothing comes out, and by the time I'm back, five girls have gone. *Five* girls, Dré tells me.

There are maybe fifteen left.

Eli tells me that, of the five girls, only one was really good, the black one with the braids—Jackie, the vlogger from the party. Lennox is onstage now, and she's kick-ass. I didn't expect anything less.

Time blurs, and then I hear my name. When I say my stomach fell out of my ass, I mean it. I trip over Dré's feet exiting our row, and a few kids behind us whisper. They probably aren't talking about me, but it doesn't matter, because I feel like they are.

I make my way to the stage, and I can't even make eye contact with Lennox or Kai or anyone from the party, even though they're whooping and clapping for me. I hear Eli and Dré shout in unison, "You can do it!" I'm trying to remember the other shit Al said about breathing through nerves, but the light hits me and I panic.

It's hot, and I scratch my face and chuckle like a deranged chicken. Mrs. Gunta says, "When you're ready." I can hear her, but I can't see her with the light in my eyes.

Ohhhh. Fuck. Fuck. Fuck. Fuck. Fuck.

Okay.

Do or die.

Now or never.

Someone whispers something in the wings, and I swear, if it's Cleo telling me I'm embarrassing the family, I'll just die.

I look over.

It's Lennox. She's peeking her head out of the curtain. "Mrs. G. Can I borrow Olivia for like two seconds?"

Mrs. Gunta *mmm-hmms* into the mic as I walk to the wings. I don't know why Lennox called me over, because I swear to god, I WILL NEVER WALK BACK OUT ONSTAGE.

As I'm walking, I realize she might be trying to spare me from embarrassment. What if I have a giant period stain on the back of my jeans? I don't feel like I'm on my period, but sometimes it comes out of nowhere, and that is some shit that would happen to me.

"O." Lennox pulls me farther into the wings. "Breathe out your mouth. You look like someone shoved a dry tampon up your ass."

"What?" I can feel my eyes bugging out.

She pinches my cheeks, and I wince. "Yeah, I know it hurts, but it will keep your mouth from tightening and being all nervous." We did warm up exercises as a group, so I get what she means, but…Christ. "You're not nervous. You're excited. You're about to rock this."

She's my Bob Marley angel, but I'm kinda wishing she was the real Bob Marley and just blew a weed cloud in my face, because these positive words alone don't help.

I go back out onstage, and I get another round of applause. This time I laugh and wave, because, *fuck it.* Eli's right. *We're all scared to fail or scared to admit we're in love. We're all stupid and smart all at the same time. Being brave enough to do it anyway is the difference.*

This is my open door. This is what I've been wanting to do ever since I can remember, and I'm here and scared, but ready to be brave enough to do it anyway.

I stand in the middle of the stage and take a deep breath. I've got nothing to lose. So I start, and all those hours of practice take over. I'm doing the only monologue that was offered in the girls' audition packet—Desdemona's. At first my pacing is off, but I fix it, taking the exaggerated breaths where I'm supposed to. Speeding up where I'm supposed to. I take time to think. I let my pleading words stretch and flow.

It goes by fast, and by the end I've forgotten there are people in the darkness. It's not me in my room pacing the floor. I'm onstage.

And then the applause starts.

The roar is unanimous, and I don't know if it's support, or if they think I'm hot stuff. I get the same applause everyone got—but my god, does it feel good.

By the time the singing auditions are about to start, I'm high off the generous compliments I'm getting. Kai gives me a hug and says, "Damn, you're talented, too. I told you, you make me nervous."

I smile and say something back about how amazing he was, and Dré's the first one to give me another bear hug. He's going a mile a minute about how I was born to act, and I still can't tell if they're just psyching me up, or if I was that good. I was there—I know it was good—but I was also not there. I was in the story. I was *in character*. I see what people mean when they say that now.

I'm sitting next to Eli when the first guy goes up onstage to sing. "You were better than when we practiced."

"So were you," I say.

His eyes flicker to Kai, who's giving me a thumbs-up again. "You've got a fan club." He says it like he's borderline irritated, and I'm not going to lie, that takes my high to another level. It's petty and it's greedy, but after the Eli and Kara hand-holding fiasco, I want him to see how wanted I am.

I give Kai my best smile. The one where I bite on the corner of my lip and *smise*. Yes, I am giving him my best Tyra Banks, and I'm not ashamed of how good I feel when Eli takes a big breath and pulls out his phone to do who cares what.

Kai's as good a singer as he is an actor, and of course Eli and Dré do well. The girls start, and this time I see Jackie perform. She's amazing. I wish I'd seen her deliver her lines. When it's my turn, I'm not as nervous as before. The *I have to pee* feeling is still there, but it's mostly butterflies now. It takes everything in me not to close my eyes, so I stare into a really black part of the auditorium and let the lyrics go.

I start off small and, even though I promised myself I wouldn't close my eyes, I do. There is a part of the song where I'm begging this guy to stay, and I can't do that with everyone looking.

I get more applause, and the spotlight turns off and the houselights come on. I can see everyone standing, and I'm grinning so hard I'm showing all my teeth. Even Cleo is clapping from the curtains, and for the first time, she's smiling with her teeth instead of that weird, tight-lipped thing she usually does with me.

Mrs. Gunta waits until I'm back in my seat before closing out the auditions. "You've all done a marvelous job." She pauses and raises her clipboard to read something. "I've got a few decisions to make, but the list will be up Monday morning. Remember..."

"No showboating!" everyone except Dré, Eli, and me yells.

Lennox and Kai invite me out—and everyone else, all these drama kids travel in a pack—and the invitation is extended to Dré and Eli, too.

I'm not used to this. Usually I'm the extra wheel in the Dré and Eli show, but this time they're *my* plus one. We go to a pizza place on International Drive, the traffic and neon lights adding to my buzz.

My mom calls me to ask how the auditions went, and I swear everyone at my table can hear her. She's screaming like I got a part, this is so embarrassing, but everyone is smiling and Rodney is saying, "Yaaasss, Mama James," from behind me at the other table. I don't tell him my mom's last name is Johnson. The moment has passed, and that's weird. So, I hang up with her and eat my pizza between Dré and Eli. Lennox, Javier, and Jackie sit opposite us.

Cleo is at a table with some other theatre kids I don't know, though there is this one girl I recognize from auditions. She was loud—but that's kinda all she had going for her. She's staring at me and saying something to Cleo, who then glances at me and shakes her head.

Okay, cool. I guess we're doing the *we're not really related* thing. I'm used to it ever since middle school when, once, I sat with her at lunch and she turned, looked at me, and dead-ass said, "Um, that seat is saved for my friend." Yeah, I'm not doing that nonsense with her again. Besides, thanks to her, I ended up sitting with the boy next door and his weird friend with the braces. The rest is history, so she can keep her friends; I'm just here for the songs and possible hookup with a hot Hawaiian.

Kai's laughing behind me. I was too chicken to sit with him; even though I'm pretty sure he was saving me a seat, I pretended not to notice. It's eating me alive, because I can't go on a date if I avoid the only candidate.

As I'm sitting between Dré and Eli, I realize this is where I *always* sit. Smashed between them like a sandwich. It's comfortable. We're sharing pizza even though we have our own slices. We always get different stuff and share bites. But right now, I feel like I'm relying on this. What if guys like Kai have always seen me, but I've been too smashed up to notice?

Like Al said, the opportunities are always there; you just have to take them. What if this is me staring through the window when all I have to do is walk through the door?

I go to the bathroom and check my face. I didn't wear makeup today, but my brows are on point, so whatever. I wash my hands and make sure there's no food in my teeth. To be sure, I swoosh water in my mouth, and when I leave, I go to Kai's table and sit in the empty seat next to him.

If I'm going to stand out, then I have to start standing on my own.

I don't know why my heart is racing—this isn't nearly as nerve-racking as getting up onstage.

He glances up with cheese caught between his mouth and the pizza. "Hey," he mumbles. He seems shocked but pleased. "How do you feel?" he asks after he's done swallowing.

"Pretty awesome. Even if I don't get anything, it was such a rush, I'd do it again." I'm not lying; now that all the nerves have gone away, I'm left with the euphoria of having done something worthwhile. Maybe this is how people feel when they go skydiving, except there's no chance of me crashing headfirst into concrete at the end.

Kai leans in and whispers in my ear. "You're definitely getting something." He sighs. "I swear I don't mean everything I say to sound so dirty."

I'm laughing. I catch Eli's eyes as I tilt my head back. I know I shouldn't think this way, but I feel like I'm doing something wrong. But he's not my boyfriend, and he was holding hands with that reed-splitting, clarinet-screeching Kara. So I give my attention back to Kai and let him keep it for the rest of the night.

I'm walking through the open door, and I'm not looking back.

CHAPTER 12

Monday morning, Dré, Eli, and I aren't the only ones crowded around the theatre. When the door unlocks with a *click* and Mrs. Gunta opens it, we all flood in. Everyone is quiet. All the drama kids go to the list, check it, and then leave. They don't say a word. When Dré, Eli, and I finally get there, my finger scrolls down the list…and I almost scream.

My name is there—next to Bianca. The whore. She's the smallest girl role, but I beat out so many other girls for this part.

Dré is behind me with his body pressed against me as he looks for his name. "Dude. I'm Cassio. Eli—Eli, you got *Othello*. Holy shit."

Eli stares at the board on my other side, and just under his name is Kai, who's playing *Othello*'s villain, Iago. "I don't know Desdemona," he says, looking at Jackie's name.

She must be a really good actress, because I really don't

see her as the kind of chick who would get smothered with a pillow.

Dré looks at him. "What does it matter? You're fucking *Othello*."

"Language, Mr. Santos." Mrs. Gunta leans against the wall next to us. "There is no showboating in my theatre." I look around, and we're the last ones here. Everyone else is outside shouting and talking a mile a minute. "Still." She's smiling at us now. "Congratulations. Very impressive auditions from all of you."

Dré's flexing, and she hits him with her clipboard.

"We have a lot of work ahead. Don't let *earning* the role be the best you do. I'll pass it along to an understudy in a heartbeat."

We're backing out and nodding as she waves us on. I'm about to burst. I. Got. A. Part. I even have my own song with Dré, and even though it's a small role, I am *in* the play. My name will be on the playbill.

Holy shit, I'm *in the play*.

I went from being nobody—to having my name on a *playbill*.

Eli pats my back, and I don't even have to tell him what I'm thinking. "And a star was born," he says and squeezes my arm.

Fuck cloud nine, I'm so high right now I'm in another solar system—until the girl from the celebratory pizza outing, the one who was talking to Cleo, walks past, saying, *"I can't believe the spaz who could barely get onstage got Bianca. I'm her fucking understudy. Can you believe that? I'm the understudy of the most basic of all bitches."*

She's around the corner and gone, and I don't think anyone else heard her; they're all still going on and on about the list—but *fuck that bitch*. I join Lennox as she's hip bumping me. I know I shouldn't let some nobody take me down a notch, but I can't help feeling like she's right. I barely got up on that stage—it took me weeks just to do that one small bit. I can't unfeel this dread coming over me. And to make matters worse, I'm about to spend the next three months of my life with that girl shadowing me.

ACT TWO

ACT TWO—Scene Three—
I'm No Angel

Desdemona (Cassio):
HE GAVE ME WINGS, BUT I'M STILL A WOMAN
HE GAVE ME WINGS, BUT I'M NO ANGEL (RIGHT?)

Cassio:
IT WAS ONE MISTAKE
BUT LIFE DOES A SOLDIER MAKE
I'M STILL NEW AT THIS, BAD AT THIS
I DON'T KNOW WHAT HE SEES IN ME
BUT I'M BEGGING ON MY KNEES FOR ME
BELIVE IN ME
COME ON, O
DON'T TURN YOUR BACK ON ME

Desdemona:
HE GAVE ME WINGS, BUT I'M STILL A WOMAN
HE GAVE ME WINGS, BUT I'M NO ANGEL
I'M FALLIN', JUST LIKE YOU
CAN'T SAVE ME, CAN'T SAVE YOU
HIS BELIEF IN ME IS THE WAY THROUGH
BUT I'M TERRIFIED THESE WILL LET ME DOWN

Cassio:
WAS IT THE FAME?
EVERYONE'S FINALLY SCREAMIN' MY NAME
WHEN DID I TURN INTO A CLOWN AND LET YOU DOWN?
I WAS GIVEN ALL THIS,
NOW I'M FLOPPIN' LIKE A FISH, OUT THE SEA

WHERE I CAN'T SWIM
NOT WITHOUT HIM

Desdemona:
HE GAVE ME WINGS, BUT I'M STILL A WOMAN
HE GAVE ME WINGS, BUT I'M NO ANGEL
I'M FALLIN', JUST LIKE YOU
CAN'T SAVE ME, CAN'T SAVE YOU
HIS BELIEF IN ME IS THE WAY THROUGH
BUT I'M TERRIFIED THESE WILL LET ME DOWN
IF I FLY WITH THESE WINGS, I'LL PLUMMET TO THE
GROUND

CHAPTER 13

I'm sitting in a circle onstage with the entire cast of *Othello*. Mrs. G—she looked at Dré, Eli, and I and told us to stop calling her Mrs. Gunta, because we were saying it wrong anyway. Okay, lady. I see you—is handing out a ton of papers. Our rehearsal schedule, the full script, our songs, and a notecard I'm putting my name, number, and address on. She's old-school.

I notice on the list of cast members that my understudy—now and forever known as *fuck that bitch*—has a real name: Angelina. She's sitting on the other side of the circle talking nonstop, and she's the reason I add a number 6 to my Fuck It list: *Don't let bitches try me.*

The only thing I know about her, besides the fact that she can't lose with grace, is that she's loud as hell.

I can hear her from the other side of the stage. *"Oh my*

god, basic Beckys buy a makeup set from Sephora and think they're witches." She's shoving her phone in this other girl's face.

She's the reason I don't have friends that are girls. It's the constant competition that drives me insane. I know I'm not immune to it; I'm still avoiding Kara at all costs, but that's because the guy I like likes her, not because she's got a vagina and breathes. I actually thought Kara was an okay person before the night that shall never be mentioned because it is still scarring me.

Guys are just easier.

Eli's on my right, looking over his lines. He's hunched over his paper like he's already committing the lines to memory. This year I only have band with him, but last year we had all the same classes. He's studious. The quiet, *I keep my book bag organized and take notes with pen and paper while wearing glasses* type. It's adorable.

Dré's on my left and has his hands behind his head and his legs stretched out with his papers on his lap. He's making faces at the redhead from the audition party. So far, he hasn't said anything to Lennox, who's across from me, next to Kai. She's making faces at me and wiggling her brows at Kai.

I don't know how she and Dré can be so cavalier. They had sex, and now they're acting like they don't even know each other. I want to know if they're still having sex, but asking Dré is out of the question, and Lennox will take that opportunity to take the topic way further than I want.

I'm not even sure I want to know.

The props and backstage crew go off into their own groups to sort out whatever it is they do. Mrs. G stands in the middle of the circle, and we all stand up with her: The roundtable read starts. We do weird breathing exercises and wiggle our mouths and bodies. At one point, I'm wailing like a siren, and we end the warm-up by massaging each other's shoulders. I've got my hands on Eli, and though I like it when he returns the favor, I kill all the Eli love bells by wondering what Kai's big hands would be like. I'm a mess—but this is healthy, getting over one crush by crushing on another.

We start the read-through.

These kids are in character even when we're just supposed to be getting a feel for the play. It's all modernized, but the essence is still Shakespeare, like in the audition packet, which is cool. But I was not prepared to read it like it's opening night. Keeping up with everyone's energy is hard.

Mrs. G ends rehearsal by telling us to practice and study our parts like our lives depend on it. And then she says it again, "But I don't need to tell you twice, you know what do to."

"SMASH IT," everyone yells. Apparently, it's the drama motto. It means to give it your all or, as Lennox explained, *make sure your performance blows the roof off this bitch.*

On the way home, I'm going over every moment I screwed up like I can magically change it. I fumbled almost all my lines, and I only have three scenes.

Everyone else just seemed to—get what they were doing? I don't know why I was the only one who sounded like a *complete* idiot. It's like everyone else went to some Disney acting camp and can just turn that shit on. Even Eli and Dré were relaxed with it. I've never felt more out of place in my life.

It doesn't help that I could feel Angelina's beady eyes on

me every time it was my turn to read. Like she was saying, *What did I say? The most basic of the basics.*

Fuck—how can something I've wanted so bad turn out to be so damn hard? I add a note in my phone to add to the list on my mirror:

7. Find some fucking confidence.

"You just gonna ignore me, then?" Dré says. I'm sitting in the passenger seat, staring out the window.

"Huh?"

He's looking at me like I'm playing stupid, but I really don't know what he said. I'm using the mute button. Sometimes it just turns on by itself when I'm thinking. My mom has thrown so many things at me because of it. Usually a slipper. Nothing like getting a funky, decompressed, dingy, leopard-print shoe to the face to jar you out of deep thought.

"Big Hawaii," Dré says.

I roll my eyes and then wish I didn't. I don't have to know what he said to know *what* he's saying. Dré nicknames people for two reasons. Because he likes them, or because he thinks they're goofy and easy to make fun of.

Now that I think about it, no one really called me Liv until I met him. Now everyone uses it. It's like he baptized me in his over-the-top personality and made me anew. But I'm taking me back. I'm O now.

"I'm just sayin'. Y'all were talking the other night, you went to his party, and now he's looking at you like you a pig on luau day."

Did this motherfucker just call me a pig?

"You can't be into him, Liv." Dré's still going. If he weren't driving, I'd go full Hulk on him.

Eli and I don't fight. We rub each other wrong and dance around an apology until we're just cool again, obviously—but Dré and I fight. I'm talking my-fist-to-his-body action. I attack, and he runs screaming and laughing until I catch that ass and make him say uncle.

He's laughing now, and I know he can see the crazy in my eyes. "Why you mad?"

Eli's not saying anything. I don't know why I'm surprised. He never does.

This is why I don't—*can't*—be a girl around them. They find a way to embarrass me, and instead of feeling like an ugly duckling, I just get mad. "Fuck off, Dré."

"Oh my god. Liv, it's not that serious. I just want to know what you see in a dude that looks like he's about to dance with flames while playing a ukulele. And his hair though—"

Kai is hot. Dré's mad he's not the hottest guy in the room. Kai's a year older and bigger than Dré, in the *I'm strong and I look like a man* kind of way. Dré still has boy body, despite the muscles, and maybe he's feeling a little insecure. I don't know. None of that matters, because he's taking whatever his nonsense is out on *me*.

"Shut up." I turn back to the window.

Dré's reaching over, flicking my curls. I wore my hair out, with a flower clip pinning half of it off my face. Lennox kept pulling on the jeans my sister gave me, saying, *Got flowers in your hair and everything. Go get ya man, girl.*

"Stop, Dré. She's gonna hit you." Eli says it like we're his annoying siblings and he's stuck in the car with us.

Dré pokes my thigh. "Come on. I was joking." He always touches the biggest part of my body—hell, even my hair is big. I swear to god it's like he keeps me around for amusement purposes.

"Dré, just leave her alone."

Oh yeah, thanks, Eli. That's how you stick up for someone. Never mind you don't even care that Big Hawaii *is* into me. Fucking A.

"I'm trying to apologize. Liv." Now he's shaking my whole damn thigh as the car lurches to a stop at a red light.

I turn to face him. "What, Dré?" I get mad at him all the time, and I can't stand the fact that my irritation doesn't faze him. He doesn't ignore me until I get over it. He pesters me until I talk about it or see his side.

"I'm sorry." He taps my nose. "Seriously, sorry." He's close to my face and pinching his lips together between his teeth. The light turns green, but he won't move.

"Drive, Dré." Cars start honking behind us.

"Forgive me?"

He's *so* annoying. And, to be honest, cute. We can't be a thing—ever—because we're on some toxic-level shit. We'd be married, he'd cheat on me, and I'd set his clothes on fire. He'd threaten to jump off a highway bridge if I didn't forgive his cheating ass—I'm pretty sure that'd be our future.

The honking gets louder as more cars join in.

"Oh my god. Yes. Just drive." I roll my eyes and Dré hits the gas.

"I love you, too." Dré keeps looking at me sideways, laughing again.

Just as he's turning up the music and belting out lyrics in Spanish, I hear Eli mutter, "So fucking annoying."

I didn't start my Year of Fuck It just to be mocked for being *liked*. I know Dré's not doing it to be mean-spirited; teasing is his thing. But what is the point of saying yes to things that scare me if I'm going to turn around and let my friends put me down for it?

It's Saturday and finally a day where I can wear a sweater outside, walk down the street, and not catch fire. I made up my mind to do a thing my sister always talks about from the time she worked as a secretary at a therapist's office. I'm going to set some boundaries.

One Christmas, my sister attempted to mediate between my mom and my aunt, and I remember how she told my mom she should listen to Aunt Rachel and respect her opinions, even if she disagreed with them. But that didn't go so well, because my mom told Aunt Rachel she *respectfully* thought she was a cheap know-it-all. Aunt Rachel said my mom was bougie and her lace-front looked like a ratty dog.

We don't talk about that Christmas.

But I have high hopes that setting some boundaries about me and my dating life with the guys will go much better.

I'm opening the door to Dré's house—they never lock it; I swear to god if I never locked our front door, my mom would tear my ass up from Monday to Sunday.

Dré and Eli actually settled on doing Battle of the Bands, but only if they actually get a band together. Since the auditions for it start in February, the same time as our opening week for *Othello*, I have no idea when they're going to find the time to practice. Dré's cool with skipping out on school and homework, and, well, everything not related to whatever he's into at the moment, but I don't know how he got Eli to agree.

Inside, Dré's house is pristine, and it smells like amber. Gloria, Dré's mom, burns incense and essential oils nonstop. She's also into the furniture no one sits on. The sitting room, decorated in colors of brown, white, and turquoise, has never felt the presence of a living soul.

I find Gloria in the kitchen on my way to the garage, where I can already hear Dré messing around on the guitar.

"Que linda. Hey, baby. I haven't seen you in a minute." She stops chopping up avocados to give me a hug. It looks like she's about to make some yellow rice. I can spot a box of Sazón anywhere. "Want some chips and guac? I was making some for the boys. They've got people coming over for *auditions*." She thinks everything Dré does is cute and silly.

"Does it make me a pig if I keep it all for myself?" I didn't eat breakfast—too much effort.

Gloria pinches my butt—I've said it a thousand times, the Santoses are handsy people. "Avocado is that good fat, baby. Makes you juicy. Eat it all."

I love Gloria. She's my second mom. She's the first person to cheer me on when I'm running through the house about to throw down with Dré. *Get him, baby!* To be honest, she and my mom are a lot alike, and it's not weird to find Gloria at my house with a bottle of wine and food.

The big difference though—Gloria never calls me fat. She says I'm thick. It wasn't until sometime last year that I started trying to figure out what that meant, because, for forever, I thought it was a nice way to say fat. I found a whole world of girls online that look like me—models. They've got big thighs, breast, ass, and a waist like me. But there are girls with way more body than me who are sexy and confident—maybe it's not about body as much as it is about attitude—so I guess I could be kinda sexy like them, too. It's just hard to remember those girls when my mom watches me eat a waffle-bacon-egg-with-a-little-bit-of-that-maple-syrup sandwich and says, *Damn, if you made better choices, you could lose those ten pounds.*

I'm sitting at the counter putting back chips and guacamole like it's my last meal when Gloria sets the rice to simmer. "Oh, congratulations."

I'm chewing and trying not to look like a pig. "Hmm?"

"On the play. Your mom said you got a part. Dré was telling me about the auditions. He's proud of you." Gloria's smiling, and it's that *you're good for my son* smile. She's banking on us for the long haul. I'm talking she's openly discussed throwing us a beach wedding. She said she was joking, but only because Dré yelled at her and threatened to sit on the *nice* couches.

It all started on Dré's last birthday. Every year on his birthday, I make him something stupid. Last year I used all our movie stubs and photobooth pictures to make his card, and I wrote a really basic poem in it. It was funny, and he keeps it on a string, hanging on his wall above his dresser.

She said it then—*Ustedes son perfectos. Y'all are so cute.* And then I knew she meant it like we're two halves of a puzzle. We kinda are—but Dré's this wild half that drives me crazy. We're straight passion. We laugh and we fight. There is no in-between. He also doesn't talk about what's in his head.

When he's pissed—my god, it's like he'll just force himself to be happy so he doesn't have to acknowledge the problem and talk about it. It's different than Eli's avoidance though. With Dré, it's like he's scared to be anything but what he thinks you want to see in him—like he never stops performing.

I'm pretending the guacamole is too good to comment when Eli's dad shouts from the front door. "Gloria!" He's got an adorable accent, and everything he says sounds kind and gentle.

"We're in here, Yosef." He comes in with a box of tools, and now Gloria's hugging him instead of me, but her hands are lingering and I try not to stare. The Santoses are handsy, but Yosef's a married man, and I can't imagine Eli's mom would be cool with her man coming over to fix the single, sexy Puerto Rican lady's...whatever.

"Olivia!" he says, smiling. Eli's got his hair and his big smile. "I hear congratulations are in order." His hand is only just now leaving Gloria's back, and I know I'm reading into this, but all of a sudden, I'm full and ready to take some chips and guac to the garage to share.

"Thanks, Yosef."

He pats my shoulder and says my name again, in that way that I know means he's going to say something important—or at least something he thinks is important. He does that a lot. "You're a talented girl. This is just the beginning for you."

I hate this kind of attention—I know it's the Year of Fuck It and I'm supposed to learn to take a compliment. But god, it's so embarrassing it hurts. I do what I always do to release the tension in my head—I reach up and pat his shoulder, too.

"Thanks, dude. I'll remember you when I'm famous and too rich to remember things like people and names."

"Oh?" Yosef laughs, and I swear as I take the food out to the garage that his hand has moved back to her waist and—holy fuck.

I know I'm putting more into it than there is. If they were cheating, they wouldn't do it in front of me.

CHAPTER 14

Band auditions are over, and we're in Dré's room. He's copying Eli's chemistry homework while I straighten up his stuff. He's got books and papers on every surface, a ton of clothes on his bed, and wires everywhere. Eli's organizing old aux cables, new ones, and a laptop cable—Dré is the most unorganized person I know.

Except for his desk—that's always in working order, as if a nuclear blast happened and his desk was spared.

The mess is worse than usual now that they've been doing more gigs, and Gloria won't let him out of the house again until the room is back to normal-messy and his homework is done. Which is where Eli and I come in. I know it looks like we're his personal slaves, but this is how we keep Dré from being a complete delinquent who lives in a dump—and unlucky for me, whoever provides the homework gets out of the heavy cleaning.

Hence why Eli gets to wrap cables on the bed while I make sense of the papers Dré has stuffed in his bookshelf. Most of them are sketches—doodles of people or places I've never been. Talent rolls off him in insufferable waves. Tidying is helping me work up my nerve to this conversation we need to have about me—and boys—and them not being dicks about me and boys.

"So," I start and then stop.

Dré's chewing on his pencil when he looks up from his desk. "Huh?"

Eli pulls out an earphone and eyes me.

"Nothing." I'm such a punk. I don't know why this is so hard to say. Maybe because I should have said something in the car. I've waited too long, and now it's weird.

Dré shrugs and points his pencil at Eli. "Brah, you fucked up on the question about molecular bonds."

Eli leaves the wires to hunch over the desk and they argue about electronegativity.

I need to boss up. Channel my inner Beyoncé. Tell these dudes what's up. I'm reaching under Dré's bed to collect all the stray clothes when I touch something hard and...crunchy?

I scream, pulling back my hand, and out comes a crusty hand towel. I know what it is. I'm gagging and running to the bathroom to wash my hands and my soul.

Dré's laughing and Eli's choking on a laugh saying, "Dude that's nasty, use a Kleenex like the rest of us."

I go back in the room, wearing yellow cleaning gloves from under the bathroom sink and point at Dré. "Fuck your laundry and fuck your messy-ass room."

Dré's shoving the pencil behind his ear, and his brown

cheeks are tinged red, so I know he at least has some shame even though he's laughing. I notice the towel is gone. Dré holds up his hands in surrender. "I'll do the clothes and under the bed. I promise, no more surprises."

I'm still eyeing him, because, *ew.* But I take off the gloves and work on organizing the books on his bookshelf. Dré used to read a ton of fantasy, and I used to borrow his books and never return them—probably have more of his books than my own, but since he's too busy to read, he's never complained about it or stopped lending them to me.

He and Eli go back to arguing over molecules and the weight of elements until Eli throws his hands up. "I don't complain when you fuck up all the answers on the history homework."

Dré sighs, squishing his face like he can't compute. "Who gives a fuck about history? That shit is subjective at best. This is factual. I can't argue my way around a wrong decimal placement."

"Dude, don't complain when you're copying off *my* homework."

Dré laughs, but it's the mean one. "Oh, okay. Thank you for passing along shoddy work. My humble apologies."

Eli shrugs and puts his earphones back in. He lays back on the bed, scrolling through his phone. The fact that he's not wrapping wires is his silent and passive-aggressive way of winning. They've been really irritable with each other since they couldn't agree on anyone during their band auditions. To be fair, everyone sucked, and they're holding another audition tomorrow, so it's not the end of world. They just need a drummer and, if they can find one, a bass player.

But since Dré's being an unrelenting asshole and I'm still salty about the *towel*, I say, "Don't be a douche."

Dré's still scribbling on his paper, but he throws me a glance as I put a few of his sketchbooks on his desk. "Those don't go there." He points at the bookshelf, but it's full so I don't give two fucks where they go as long as I'm the one cleaning.

I flick the back of his head, and he flinches. "Did you not hear me? Don't be a douche."

He's got a small, tight smile on his face. He's mad about something, but because he's not the kind to talk things out, he's just staring at me like he wants to say something slick instead.

But then, he looks at Eli and then back at me. "He won't give on anything, Liv. It has to be his way or nothing. If he doesn't want to do Battle of the Bands, he should just say it."

And here we go—World War III all over again—and here I go, sliding into the middle like I didn't learn anything from the YouTube debacle. Back before ninth grade, they fought over whether we should post our Harry Potter skits online. Dré wanted to, and Eli was against it. I didn't care, as all the shots with me were a tad fuzzy and no one would ever recognize me.

Dré called Eli a punk, and Eli said Dré was a self-obsessed wannabe. It was two weeks of hell, but finally they got over it—by ignoring it long enough and realizing we had two months of summer and only each other to make any fun of it.

I lean on Dré's desk looking at Eli. He's got this look on his face like he's still arguing in his head.

"Technically…" I say, but as soon as Dré's glare shoots up at me, I want to just plug in my own earphones and wait it all out—but something is different now than it was that summer before ninth grade. Dré's got more friends than just Eli and I, and he might choose to be with them instead of us. "Okay, hear me out."

He frowns, but he's listening.

"Eli did say he didn't want to, and he's doing it because you want to."

Dré lets out this breath like he's been waiting for me to say that so he can tell me how wrong I am. "He said he wanted a band. I didn't. *I* compromised."

Eli pulls out his earphones again. I have suspicions he was listening the whole time, and when he looks at me, I know for sure the earphone thing was a ruse. "Like *I* compromised with doing cover songs."

Dré's back to that tight-lipped smile where he pretends he's being civil but things are about to get ugly. "I'm sorry I want us to be famous and not infamously whack."

Eli sits up. "Fuck you, Dré."

And here we go.

"Eli, you won't write anything that actually beats. I told you, we can do one or two slow-as-fuck songs, but people want to bump, not cry." Dré's looking at me for backup, and I get what he means, but Eli looks like he's just been backed into the corner and might start firing from all ends.

I hold up my hands. "You guys are just different." I rub my head because this is about two seconds from going to the place where they start attacking each other's taste in music, and there really is no going back from telling Eli his playlists are trash, so I physically stand between them so they can't stare at each other. "Different isn't bad. You want a band.

You want to do covers. You want originals, and you want to grow the audience."

"Thank you, Captain Fucking Obvious," Dré says.

"Don't talk to her like that."

Dré smirks. "Oh, you wanna bring Liv into this, too?"

I don't know what the hell that means, considering he's the one who brought me into this in the first place, but they're both being petty, so I flick Dré hard on his arm because he's a dick, and I hold up a finger to Eli. "Chill. My point was you can find a way to make it all work. Instead of approaching it like a war, look at it like a puzzle—like a way to make the best thing out of a bunch of ingredients."

Eli's got his arms crossed. "I can do that. The question is can *Dré* do that."

Dré looks from Eli to me and back to Eli for a long time. The silent code, where they leave me hanging in the balance of what *could* happen and what I *hope* happens.

Dré lets out a small breath and leans back in his chair. "I'm flexible."

"We're good then?" Eli says.

Dré rolls his eyes. "We're always good," he says, but he looks at the floor when he says it, like he's too embarrassed to be kind. These two are so fucking dramatic I can't stand it.

I move from between them. I feel like my mom, because I've got a hand on my hip and I'm pulling this face that I know is the exact face I see when she's sick of my shit. "Good," I say. "Now finish your damn homework so we can do something today."

I didn't spend all last night writing a paper just to spend today cleaning Dré's room. We're supposed to go to a dinner show—the Medieval Times Dinner Show. I got four free tickets last year for playing Christmas songs with the flute quartet. They're about to expire, and we need something not school related to do.

Low-key—I'm excited for it. I love dinner shows; they're always extra as hell and sometimes the food is bomb.

Both Dré and Eli are looking at me, and they start laughing.

"She's going so hard for this medieval shit," Dré says to Eli.

I point out that half the books on his bookshelves are about elves.

"That's not the same thing," Eli says. "Elves can exist outside of the medieval *I pee in a pot and bathe once a month* era."

"Well, fuck you both, I can leave you here and go by myself," I say, offering Eli aux cables. There are so many, I can't believe Dré even needs them all.

Eli's up and taking the cables from me. "You can't leave us. We'll disappear into the black hole that is this room without you."

It's lines like *that* that pull me into Eli's game of *does he or doesn't he?* The rational part of me knows he means that in a very platonic way, because Dré and Eli are like oil and vinegar—they don't mix, but with the right tweak they make magic. But the totally-lost-my-shit *in love* part of me wants him to mean something way more. I'd blame Eli, but he's always been like this and said stuff like that—it's me who's making everything out of nothing.

"Besides all that," Dré scoffs, "I'm your ride." He waves his paper in the air. "And I'm done."

We all spend the next twenty minutes speed cleaning, then while Dré changes out of his sweats and T-shirt, Eli and I wait outside. It's starting to heat up again, a last-ditch effort for the sun to fry us before it sinks into the horizon. My sweater has become a tad uncomfortable even though the leaves are falling off the trees; as I sit on the porch, I crunch a few with my shoe.

Eli sits next to me, and before I can ask why he's leaning toward me all slow and intense-like, his eyes go from focusing on me to my hair, and he pulls out a piece of paper from my curls. "No one escapes Dré's room unscathed." He holds out the paper between us.

"Nope." I'm doing something weird with my eyebrows—they're jumping up and down, and I should have more control over my own facial expressions, but apparently I really am the most basic of the basics.

"I meant it," Eli says. He's back in his personal space and staring at the road, or the house across the street, I can't tell. "We're shit without you."

I pat his leg, because me doing that is normal and also because I'm the thirst queen and I love touching him. "Yeah, all drama queens need a steady Eddie."

He laughs. "I don't know what that means."

I laugh, too, because neither do I. I just needed to say something to ease the tension building in me. He's always telling me he needs me, but does he actually *want* me?

Eli stares at me, and I think he's about to say something, but Dré busts out of the front door jingling his keys and the moment is lost.

Florida tourists are predictable, and the ones staring wide-eyed and taking selfies in front of everything at Medieval

Times are no different. We're waiting in the lobby for the show to open its doors. There is this woman with a British accent—her cheeks are red, so I know she spent all day at one of the parks—who is waving her family from one suit of armor to the next, calling everything *ghastly inaccurate.*

The woman's trying to get her daughter to hug a knight for a photo when the girl says, "Boundaries, Mum!"

My stomach turns. I know I need to do it. I need to draw a line in the sand about me and Kai. I don't know how I'm going to do it, but I turn around and clear my throat.

They don't even notice.

"Guys." I should have practiced what I wanted to say, because I'm already drawing a blank.

Dré's attention falls to me, and Eli turns to look at me.

We're staring at each other—actually, I'm swallowing spit and shrugging my shoulders while they're trying to figure out what's wrong with me.

"Okay," I blurt. "If one of us likes somebody, we shouldn't be dicks about it."

Eli makes a face, and I realize he has no idea what I'm talking about because I just dropped this out of nowhere.

Dré bites his lip, and I think he knows. Then they're looking at each other.

Oh. My. God. I don't know why I do things like this. Why didn't I just leave it alone and ignore it, like we do everything else?

Dré nudges me. "Okay. If you like Kai, I won't be a dick about it."

I can't make eye contact. I can barely keep my mouth from making this grimace I do when I'm super uncomfortable. "I didn't say anything about Kai." My eyes dart to Eli, and I have never felt more betrayed by my body parts. "I'm just saying we shouldn't do that. Code of friendship or something."

Eli is still doing something weird with his face, and I can't tell if he has gas or thinks I'm being stupid. "Sure," he says, like he's still trying to figure out what I'm even talking about.

Dré laughs. *"Code of friendship?"* He looks at Eli. "I told you she's going hard about this Medieval Times shit."

The grimace is changing into a scowl, because now I'm getting mad. "It has nothing to do with Medieval Times." I know he's about to start another round of *crack jokes on Liv*. I put myself out there, and this is what I get. A friend wouldn't treat me like this. A friend wouldn't even need me to say *don't be a dick*.

Dré puts his hand on my shoulder. "Liv, I'm saying I get it." He takes a deep breath, and I'm waiting for him to tell me I'm being dramatic or overthinking everything. "And I'm sorry."

Oh.

I'm speechless.

Now Dré's waiting for me to say something.

"Thanks." I look at Eli, and he's gone from that weird face to his eyebrows up in his hairline as he stares at Dré.

That, Dré's response, was incredibly mature, and because I'm incredibly immature, I murmur something about kitchen wenches coming out for photos and turn away. I'm so used to fighting and thinking the worst of people that I don't know how to accept—*this*. I am both full of shame and pride, because I chose my insecurities over my friends. But I'm proud because my friends, despite me, won.

I'm watching a guy take a selfie with a kitchen wench when

my eye catches on a purple tent and a woman staring at me from inside. She's a tarot card reader.

She waves me over, and I look between Dré and Eli. They're both on their phones, and because I'd rather slip away than continue to acknowledge how massively insecure I am, I head to the tent.

Why the hell not? Old me would have shaken my head and smiled like a freak, hoping the woman would stop making eye contact. But I've never had my fortune told, and now is as good a time as any.

I'm a new woman. Out here setting boundaries and saying yes to spending my money on nonsense.

"Hello, pretty girl," the woman says. Her accent is thick and—unplaceable; I don't know where she's from or what she might be, and everyone here is in character, so I can't tell if hers is real or fake.

"Hi." I have this uncomfortable smile plastered on my face, because I might be a new woman, but I'm still as awkward as a naked baby bird. I sit on the little folding chair.

"For you, I do this for free." She's already shuffling her cards between her ringed fingers. She's got stones everywhere. On her fingers, on the table, around her neck.

She sets the card deck down and pulls out a pendulum and mumbles over it as it stills and then starts swinging by itself.

Now, I'm not super religious. My mom stopped taking me to church once a year on Easter when I turned ten. I don't think witchcraft is the work of the devil—but when I say that pendulum started swinging on its own, I really mean I'm checking over my shoulder for Voldemort and all his Death Eaters.

She looks up at me and smiles. "Be calm. Your energy is pure but it is clouded."

Yeah—okay. Like I know what that means. I'm not going to complain though. She said she was doing this for free, and hanging to her left are her prices. Normally she charges fifty dollars for a reading. Maybe this is one of those *get you hooked on magic* situations. The first reading is free, but after that, it's twice the price. I'm a hundred percent judging me for getting my life read by some strange woman with a double coating of eyeliner.

"Ah," she says, tapping on the deck. "I knew this was for you." She starts flipping the cards over.

Death.

I knew this was a dumbass idea.

The Hanged Man.

I should just get up and run now.

The Chariot.

She looks at me as she flips the fourth card over.

The Devil.

I gasp. Heathen that I am who hasn't been in church in seven years and uses the Lord's name in vain like it's breathing air—I *know* this woman is doing that dark magic.

She laughs. "Don't be worried. This is a beautiful reading."

I don't know how to explain to her that what I'm seeing ain't beautiful. "I don't want to be rude but—I'm going to die, probably by hanging or getting dragged by a horse, and the devil's going to take my soul. I don't see the beauty in that. If anything, your cards might be a little racist."

She strikes a match, and I jump. "Don't be so silly. Those who do not know always think the worst." She lights an incense stick, and the smell is a mix of flowers and earth. "You, I can tell, are someone who thinks a lot but does not *know*."

Did she just call me stupid?

She taps the Death card with her free finger. "In your recent past, you have let go of someone you used to be." She moves to the Hanged Man. "In your present, you have a new perspective on life. This is the time to build upon what you have laid to waste."

I nod like I get it, but she doesn't seem to care whether I understand or not, because she keeps her eyes on the cards with her brows furrowed.

She taps her finger on the card with the chariot. It's very Roman—very *Othello*. "You have great determination. It is your strongest attribute, but make sure to be kind. Because such stubborn determination to get where you are going can trample those in your path. For better..." She looks at me. "And for worse."

Does this woman know about my list? Does she know that I've been trying to change my punk-ass ways? Is this one of those moments where the vague message applies to you because it applies to everyone? I can't tell, but I need to know more.

She picks up the last card. The Devil. "This is you. Don't be alarmed. It is a warning. When we are scared, we lose ourselves in limiting beliefs. Stay true to yourself and you will overcome these limiting beliefs you have about yourself." She looks over my shoulder, raises a brow.

I turn around to see Dré and Eli standing behind me. They've both got smirks on their faces, and I know they're thinking of all the ways to rag on me for doing this. I narrow my eyes at them before turning back around.

The woman makes a strange sound, something between a sigh and a laugh, and flips her deck to show the card at the bottom. "I thought so." She shows it to me.

The Lovers.

"You're a rare bird, love. To be surrounded by such love—love that will last a lifetime." She winks and stabs the burning end of the incense into an ashtray. "Sometimes my guides send me messages, and my only job is to pass them along. To you, they tell me, you know who you are. Now…believe in you, even when it feels like no one else does."

The doors open for the show, and the lady waves me away like I can't get up fast enough. My cheeks are burning. "Thank you." I really wish she hadn't done the last bit about the Lovers in front of Dré and Eli.

Eli. Of all people to hear that.

The three of us file in with the crowd entering the arena. I'm between them again, and even though Dré's still got that smirk on his face, he's not saying anything.

I look at Eli.

He's looking at the floor when he says, "Consulting the cards for love advice? You're full of surprises these days." He laughs, but I know he's being nice.

I'm over Eli. I'm over Eli. I'm over Eli. At least, I'm pretty sure I'm over Eli.

Dré elbows me out of my silent psychobabble. "I'm not surprised at all. You are who you've always been."

I meet Dré's eyes. At first, I thought he meant that I haven't changed at all—that I'm still the girl he laughed at on the stairs because I wanted to audition for the musical.

But…he's got this look in his eye, and I feel like he *sees* me. Like maybe he's always seen me, and he's just been waiting for me to come out and show everyone else what he sees.

My heart speeds up. I can't be the girl who likes both her best friends.

As we cross the threshold into the dim area, Dré taps my nose.

I can*not* be that girl.

But I think I am.

CHAPTER 15

I'm in the band room after school, locking up my flute before I go to another read-through rehearsal in the theatre. Mr. Kaminski is kicking out a bunch of girls who aren't in band but followed Dré in here.

"Keep your fan club in the courtyard, Mr. Santos," Mr. Kaminski says as he ushers the last girl out the door.

Dré's wearing shades, and I want to gag because he's also got on jeans, a white T-shirt, and a gold chain. I don't know how he manages to look this full of himself, but he does. "My bad." He's walking over to me while waving at Mr. Kaminski, who's taken to spying out his office window at the rest of us.

Mr. Kaminski's slowly losing his mind. We have a concert coming up, and in his quest for perfection, he never took into account what he actually has to work with.

Don't get me wrong. There is a ton of talent in band—but

talent and focus aren't the same thing. However, I can't talk, because I'm passing up practicing tonight for homework and theatre rehearsal. I haven't gone over my concert pieces all week—but at least I'm not the only one.

"Liv. I need your help." Dré's got this sheepish grin on his face, which means he's up to no good, but I don't have time for his antics. Between now and the next hour, I have an entire history chapter to read and summarize.

I briefly thought maybe I had caught feelings, because Dré has this way of looking deep into my soul, but— I need to focus. I just went down a horrible spiral with Eli; I'm not doing that with Dré. "Nope." I grab my book bag and head to the table to start my homework.

Best thing about being in band is unlimited use of space after school. The library closes right after the final bell— which is annoying as hell—and administration always walks around kicking us off campus, telling us not to linger. But there is always something going on in the band room, so it's always open. Today it's jazz band practice.

"You don't even know what I'm going to ask." Dré sits next to me.

The jazz band teacher is different than Mr. Kaminski. He starts skating in the middle of the room while everyone is setting up. He's so old but so into it that he looks kinda cool.

"I don't need to know. I'm busy."

Dré leans on the table with his elbow and puts his hand on mine. "But I need you." He's making eyes at me like I'm one of his groupies.

I move my hand away from him. "Not working."

"Works when Eli does it." Dré's staring at me hard, but I refuse to acknowledge that. Fuck him. Seriously.

The jazz band starts giving announcements, and it's fairly quiet in the room so I whisper, "What do you want, Dré?" Because he's *still* staring at me.

He opens his mouth, and he's trying so hard not to smile. "There is this girl…" This is why I was dumb for even *thinking* about Dré in that way.

Nope. Never. Not that kind of friend. "I am not helping you get a girl."

He looks offended. "Um. No."

The jazz band teacher looks over as if our whispers are disturbing the sound quality of the room.

I wait until they start playing before looking at Dré. "Then what does this girl have to do with me?"

He's got this hysterical look on his face, like he knows I'm going to flip out. He licks his lips and stifles a laugh. "I need you to—help me get *rid* of her."

I blink, and then, because this is absurd considering I'm trying to get an education and balance my own fucked-up love life, I laugh. "No."

"Liv." He's moving in closer now, and the actual hysteria is coming out. "This chick is blowing up my phone, and she won't go away. I even told her I'm not interested. I stone-cold ignored her for a week, and that made it worse."

I do feel sorta bad, because I know Dré's not the ladies' man everyone thinks he is. He's actually really nice—maybe a little too nice. He's only ever had two girlfriends, and both relationships lasted no longer than a month. I think the girls he attracts are the kind that like guys who are total dicks.

And Dré's more of a wears-his-heart-on-his-sleeve-*if*-he-gives-it-to-you type.

Still. "Dré, you do realize that if I don't do the history homework, neither of us gets credit for it?"

He pulls out his phone to show me the countless messages this girl has sent, and when he stops scrolling, I see her name. Karma is a bitch, and I feel kinda bad for taking pleasure in this, but the girl in question is Angelina.

"That's my understudy."

He nods. "Yeah, no shit, Sherlock."

I glare at him. "Do you want me to help or not?"

The music stops and the jazz teacher has his hands on his hips. "Can you two take this—" he's waving his baton at us like it's a wand "—to the practice rooms?" It's not really a suggestion so much as a command.

This is mortifying. I hate getting kicked out of places, and when I'm with Dré, it happens way more often than not. After I've packed my stuff and we've crammed ourselves into the last practice room, he shows me the messages again.

A part of me wants to revel in Angelina's embarrassing thirst, but then I just feel bad. She really likes Dré. She also has a few self-esteem issues, because when he didn't respond for a week, she still kept sending daily messages asking how his day went.

I hate that I feel bad for this bitch, but being a good person is nothing to mope about. I hand the phone back to Dré, because I'm still tempted to message her something mean and it's better if Dré does this anyway. "You never told her directly that you're not interested."

He looks at me like I'm the dumbest person alive. "I kept her on Read for a week."

I shrug. "Well, how did that work out for you?"

He's rolling his eyes as he hunches his shoulders. "Point taken. Then what do I do?"

Someone walks past our practice room, and they do a double take when they see us in here. These people are always searching for gossip. It's kids from the choir, and they use these rooms to hook up, so no doubt me being seen in a tiny room with Dré is suspect.

Reason number two why I can't entertain the way my heart skips when Dré's arm brushes up against mine. The gossip would be overwhelming.

Dré's looking at me, and I realize he's waiting for my answer.

"Tell her you appreciate her messages, but you don't want to lead her on and you're not looking for a relationship."

Dré's tapping away at his phone but he says, "That sounds weak as fuck, but whatever."

"That's called maturely handling a situation, but I can understand why it's a foreign concept to you." As much as I complain about Dré teasing me, I am relentless when it comes to getting in my jabs, too.

Dré looks up and lets out a snort. "What's that shit your mom's always saying? Pot calling the kettle black."

This is the third or fourth time I think he's indirectly bringing up my feelings for Eli, and Dré is the last person I want to know because he'll make it all much worse. Instead of taking the bait, I open my history book and start reading.

In between sentences, I can hear a horn, sweet and clear.

It's Eli. He has private lessons today, and even if I didn't know that, I'd still know it was him just by the way he plays. Perfectly.

Dré's leg is touching mine, and I feel like the messiest bitch alive. Why do I have so many feelings right now? I always thought that nonsense about teenage hormones was bullshit, but I'm starting to feel like this is what the old people are talking about.

After a few minutes of reading, listening to Eli's lessons, and losing all my sense, I get a phone shoved in my face.

Angelina responded. Wow. I was just trying to be a friend. You're so full of yourself. It is what it is, homie.

Dré's shaking his head. "How did she go from calling me 'music bae' to 'homie' in the space of three messages? Tell me that's not crazy."

I give him back his phone. "She's just trying to save face." I can't believe I'm defending a girl who called me basic. Worse, I have to see her in less than an hour.

The three of us walk into the theatre through the wide-open back door as a bunch of the cast and crew filter in and out. I see Kai with a bag of McDonald's, talking with some people I don't know, and he winks at me.

He hasn't texted me yet, and I haven't texted him, so I don't really know where we stand, but when he looks at me, I feel like I'm the only person in the room. *This* is the guy I should be paying attention to, not Dré or Eli. Maybe I should text him and set a date—but I don't want to come off as desperate.

Seeing all of Angelina's texts has me anxious. I don't want to be the girl he asks his friends to get rid of.

Dré claps me on the back and drops his arm around me. "Need some water?"

I look away from Kai. "What?"

"You looking thirsty as hell." He laughs at his own joke, and I shrug off his arm. My. God. I don't even know why I'm friends with him. He drives me up the wall.

"*Code of friendship*, Dré."

He's shaking his head. "This doesn't count. I'm not being a dick. I'm trying to be supportive. This is me being supportive."

I narrow my eyes. I've got a list of things to call him ready in my mind, but Angelina walks by, and we both kind of freeze.

Eli elbows Dré and snickers, and I'd have snapped at them, because she's clearly trying to act unbothered as she swings her tiny hips onto the stage to sit with her friends—but as she sits down, her loud-ass voice carries back to us: "*…basics.*"

I want to run over and roll her off the stage. *Fuck it*. I'm not sticking up for that asshole.

I leave Dré and Eli to their own devices and find Lennox. She's one of the first girls I've met who I just feel comfortable around. That, and she's actively trying to help me fix my complicated yet nonexistent love life.

"O," she says from the gallery. She's sitting with Jackie and Rodney, and they're all waving me over.

"Get over here, Miss Bianca," Rodney says. He's snapping his fingers at me, saying, "Work. Work. Work." He's more extra than a RuPaul drag show—his words, not mine. He looks behind me at the stage and rolls his eyes. "Oh my god. Angelina is over there running her mouth again."

I turn around, and sure as shit she is. She's got her phone out, and she's talking shit about some girl's picture. I shake my head. "I really don't get why she's such a bitch."

Jackie laughs, and it's so loud. All these theatre kids are projectors. It must be a trick of the trade.

Lennox looks up from doing her homework. "Yeah, if there's any drama, she's at the root of it."

"Every. Fucking. Time," Rodney says and gets up. "But I'm a messy bitch, and I want all the drama." He's walking through the aisle, singing her name.

Jackie's still cackling. "Rodney's so fucking stupid. I love him." She turns to me. "Now spill the tea. You haven't been here for more than five minutes, and she's already pissed you off."

I sit down, debating whether I should be yet another source of gossip or if I should listen to my inner Jesus telling me to mind my own damn business.

Jesus is ringing, but I'm not picking up the phone. Not today. "Well," I start, and a smile creeps onto my face. I low-key love the euphoria that comes with ragging on Angelina, so I tell them what she said about me after auditions, and because I have no self-control, I tell them about the messages to Dré.

Lennox hits Jackie, who's howling about the *left on Read for a week*. She twists her dreads up into a bun and starts packing up her homework. "She's clearly got nothing going on, which is why she stay in other people's business. But that doesn't excuse what she said to you. Just ignore her."

Jackie pulls her legs up into her chair. "For real though. She knows she barely got the understudy role, and she's just salty about it. She's always got criticisms but none of the credentials to back it up."

I look toward the stage just as Angelina tosses her hair back, still talking a mile a minute about who knows what now, but the tea must be hot, because Rodney is sipping it up.

Behind them, Dré and Eli are onstage doing some weird choreographed fight. We haven't blocked anything for the play, and by the laughing fit they're having, I know they're totally improvising. Soon we're all watching them, because they've started rapping and stage fighting, and it's actually kind of funny.

Jackie pulls out her phone. "I might be able to get this in this week's edit before I upload. Vlogging gold."

I can't help but smile, because this is the magic Dré and Eli make together. Whether they're onstage singing or just messing around making each other laugh, they're captivating.

Angelina's the only one pretending not to notice that they're putting on a whole show, and they don't stop until Mrs. G comes out and claps for our attention.

"Thank you, Mr. Santos and Mr. Peretz, for that thrilling reenactment. But it's time to get to work."

So, it's the Year of Fuck It, and this is the first time I've actually been excited to say *fuck it* to an invite. I'm at the mall with Lennox and Jackie. This is ten levels deep of dorky, but I've never been shopping without my mom, and I refuse to try things on when I'm with Dré and Eli. I have the feeling they'd leave me and I'd have to spend thirty minutes walking around this big-ass mall trying to find them again.

Jackie is vlogging and the camera is in my face. "Go ahead, girl, tell us who you are."

I can't look in the lens, because this is weird. "I'm O." I don't want her weird internet people to know who I am.

She waits like I've got more to say. "Girl, you're more than your name. Damn, don't make me edit you out. You cute, and I can get some views with them cheekbones." She takes the camera behind me. "And that ass!" she shouts.

Lennox is laughing. "Leave the girl alone. Damn, Jackie."

Jackie's already got her attention on someone else. "Damn, that nigga fine." She says it so loud that the dude she's talking about looks at us. She smiles and waves. "Hey. I see you." He smiles—and she's not wrong, he's hot—but he's also laughing and embarrassed.

The thing about Jackie is, she's effortlessly confident—so confident that I get waves of secondhand embarrassment. She's also super black. She's from Atlanta, so she's used to being around black people all the time and she's never felt uncomfortable being black. Now, Lennox is half black, so I'm not uncomfortable code-switching around her, but Jackie just said *nigga* in the middle of the mall to a dude at least twenty feet away, and I swear I saw two white ladies clutch their pearls.

If I did that—especially with my family around—I'd have my teeth knocked out. My mom says it more than I do, in the car we be buggin' and thuggin', but we leave that shit behind closed doors. Still, I can't help but feel like Jackie being so unapologetic about who she is is something to be envious of.

She's looking at me and smiling. "You gonna get more jeans like that, right? They got that ass snatched." Of course I'm wearing my sister's high-waisted jeans again. I don't know where she got them, but Lennox and Jackie wave off my clue-lessness and take me in and out of stores carrying things that look like—*me.*

I haven't spent any of my work money in months—Eli and Dré always spot me because I'm not the kind of person who says no to free stuff—so by the end of the day, I'm down $500, but I've got all new clothes and even the right underwear. Yes, they made me buy new panties and bras, because apparently my kind of butt needs tangas and boy shorts.

We're in the car laughing because Jackie's telling us a story about a time she was having sex with a dude who fixed her wig as it kept falling off. "That's real love tho. I still talk to that nigga. I'd still be with him if I hadn't moved." Lennox and Jackie talk about sex so casually.

I keep thinking about what Lennox said, about my first time being *good* instead of special. I've got this image in my head of girls who have lots of sex—they either got daddy is-sues, or they're trying to fill some hole in their life. But Lennox and Jackie aren't like that. They're just having a good time and owning their bodies. They aren't a prize to be had by any guy. They're a prize to themselves, and they believe in getting want they want.

They're on birth control and wrap it up; they have sex with guys they feel safe with. I swear my mom's *talks* just left me feeling like I'm one choice away from being pregnant or used, but it doesn't have to be that way. I just don't know how to get from where I am to where they are.

Jackie and Lennox help me un-haul all my old clothes and hang up the new stuff. They're staying the night, and when my mom comes in, she looks over the clothes and gushes over

Lennox and Jackie. "I'm so glad Liv found some black folk. She was a lost cause, y'all."

They're laughing, but I remind my mom *she* was the one buying my clothes. I also know she's really in my room to make sure I haven't invited crazy people into her house; I get her nod of approval. She likes them—but she doesn't know just how different they are from me. I wonder if she's trying to pass the baton, because she doesn't know how to teach me the things they can.

Lennox is in the shower and I'm getting out some spare clothes for them to wear. This sleepover was super impromptu—I just didn't want them to leave. I look at one of the dresses Jackie picked out, a halter top, cinched at the waist and flared at the bottom. I told her it would bring too much attention to my stomach, but she yelled, loud for everyone in the dressing room to hear, *Bitch, there ain't no such thing as a problem area. Your body is beautiful, so fix ya warped-ass mind.* For a split second, while I stared in the mirror, I understood what she meant—I saw what she saw.

I want her eyes so I can see myself like that all the time— I can't for the life of me figure out why mine don't work.

She's at my window, peeking through the blinds. "Bitch, you ain't tell me you live next door to Othello."

I go to the window and open the blinds. Eli's staring at us and waving his phone at me. He looks amused.

Jackie pinches her lips between her teeth, her eyes glistening like she's about to say something I don't want Eli to hear or interpret. She whips her long hair over her dark shoulders. "Giiiiiiiiiiiirrrrrrl."

I'm looking for my phone in my purse. I've got a bunch of texts from Eli and—one from Kai.

Holy shit.

"You didn't tell me you live next door to Exotic Mulato."

A laugh bursts from my mouth, and I'm shocked more than anything. I don't even know what the fuck that is. "That is so rude. His parents are Israeli and Palestinian."

"Damn. I'd let him holy war up in me."

I don't even try to explain to her how fucked up that is. "It's just Eli." I'm texting him back, because he wants to know what I've been up to all day. I can't tell him shopping. This feels very much like an episode of *Queer Eye*, except instead of five gay guys, it's Lennox and Jackie, but I'm still the old guy with no fashion sense and a rocky marriage.

He's calling now.

Jackie is looking over my shoulder. "You like Othello, don't you?"

I'm laughing like that's the stupidest thing I've ever heard—except I don't say that, I just keep laughing. It's starting to sound weird. I'm the weird hyena from *The Lion King*.

Lennox comes back, drying her dreads in one of my old T-shirts. "Why does she sound like that?" she asks Jackie. Then she looks out my open blinds at Eli and waves. She goes to the window to open it, and I rush to close the blinds so fast that I end up smashing them into the window. I know that without that double pane keeping a lid on Jackie's loud-ass voice, she'll spill some truths that I can't put back in my box of secrets.

"I ain't gonna snitch on my bitch." Jackie's laughing and telling me to get away from the window. Somehow, I've admitted it without even meaning to—and then I'm confessing. I'm telling them how I don't know what Eli and I have, and I'm telling them about Kai—which they already knew—and somehow Dré's in the mix.

Jackie interrupts me. "You can't date somebody cuz they mama like you. Bitch, that's weak."

"I *don't* want to date Dré." I'm convinced my feelings are physical. His arm brushing up against mine gives me chills. But that's not emotional, it's hormonal.

"Uh-huh." Jackie's eyes are wide and she peeks through the blinds again. Apparently, Eli's given up on us. I text him some emojis that don't really make sense and say I'll call him back in an hour.

Lennox is lying on my bed, looking down at me. "You can fuck him though."

Why is she still on that?

Jackie chimes in. "That ain't a bad idea. Popping on that Puerto Rican papi." She's bouncing on one of my throw pillows and I. Just. Can't.

"Um, no. Lennox had sex with him." I realize maybe I shouldn't just throw out other people's business like that, but Lennox looks as unfazed as ever.

"So?" Jackie says. "Lennox has sex with everybody. She be reading people souls with her pussy and shit."

I am dead on the floor. Fucking dead. Send flowers and pour some whiskey on my grave. Jackie is so loud I'm legit hoping my mom didn't hear that.

"Oh damn, sorry," she says when I tell her to stop screaming about Lennox's soul-sucking hoo-ha.

"Besides," I say. "Kai texted me." I can't help the smile on my face. I'm looking at his text now: How you been?

"Damn, girl. You got three dudes checking up on it? You ready for that?" Jackie's taking my phone and reading the message.

I know she means sex. "I want to—and I want to do it without imploding my friendships." I give Lennox a pointed look.

Jackie nods. "Look, I know Lennox is a free spirit and all, but sex is big to some of us. So don't let none of these niggas pressure you into nothing you don't want." She's looking at me hard.

I gently slap her arm. "All right, Mom, Jesus."

"Don't be taking the Lord's name."

We go on for hours. I'm laughing and crying and Lennox is braiding my hair into a crown. It hits me again that the last person I talked with about my love life was Al—who I haven't seen in the past week. I really should have found girlfriends a lot sooner.

I get up to turn off the lights, and Jackie has claimed my bed. "Damn, girl. What's wrong with your cat?" Twinks is rubbing on Jackie's leg and doing the lawn mower purr and drool move. I don't have the heart to push Twinks away, she looks so happy and in love. Jackie starts petting her, rolling her eyes and claiming this is the most action she's had in months. When they're snuggled in, I turn off the light and lie down on a pallet of blankets and pillows on the floor next to Lennox.

It's quiet when we hear, "I'm a cute bitch." Jackie is talking to herself. "I'm a badass, smart-ass, boss bitch. I got bomb pussy."

Lennox and I are racked by another fit of laughter. "What are you doing?" Lennox says.

"My nightly affirmations. If I don't love this bitch, who will?" Jackie rattles off a few more while Lennox and I hold back more giggles.

"You right. You right," Lennox says. "Now shut the fuck up so I can sleep."

When they finally pass out, I send another message to Eli that I'm too tired to talk. I even leave Kai's message unanswered. *Leave them niggas hanging*, were Jackie's exact words. She said a busy bitch was a hot bitch—and, well… Jackie might be crazy, but she definitely knows how to get what she wants.

The thing is, I don't exactly know what I want anymore. This whole Fuck It list started out as me trying not to be scared of being myself, but the more I'm saying *fuck it*, the more I'm changing into someone new. And now I'm learning that I get to want things—and this new me wants to make them happen.

CHAPTER 16

I don't return Eli's call until Saturday afternoon, after Jackie and Lennox go home. I'm in front of my window while the phone rings, and he answers just as he opens his bedroom door.

We do this more often than not, so he's not surprised to find me staring into his room. He waves a set of keys at me just as I hear his voice. "Hey. Wanna eat?"

"Depends. Where are we eating?" He knows where doesn't matter, because he can see me grabbing my shoes.

"Cheese fries and shakes?"

I stop and look back out my window, checking to see if he's still there. He is, and he laughs. "What?"

"Well, that's my favorite, and when people offer to take me to eat my favorite foods, either the dog is dead or I'm moving to a new house." It really is my mom's classic move.

"Or maybe I have my mom's car, and I just want to have

fun before doing homework." Eli's backing out of his room. "I'll see you downstairs." He hangs up.

My mom is at the office today, so I don't have to tell her I'm leaving, which is a relief. She's one of those moms who has twenty questions even though she's going to say yes anyway.

When I get out the door, Eli's leaning against his mom's car with the wind blowing through his curls. He's still wearing the T-shirt he slept in, but he's put on jeans. I shouldn't know this. I shouldn't be checking him out, or looking at his arms and how deep pink his lips are.

He gets into the car and starts the engine before I slide in. "So, how was the sleepover?" He says it like I've hit a milestone and this trip is a mini-celebration.

What I want to say is that it was great. It was so much fun, and I no longer feel like I'm holding all these secrets on my own. Which is terrifying, but also liberating. What I actually say is, "Oh my god. Don't make it a thing."

Eli backs out. He's taking us on a smooth ride to my favorite burger place, Steak 'n Shake. I don't go for the burgers. I go for the cheese fries and shakes. They've got an array of shake combinations. But nothing beats old-fashioned strawberry-banana, except maybe cookies and cream.

"You know…" Eli says at a light and puts on his glasses. It's so damn adorable when he opens up his case and slides them on. I know this is the most mundane thing a person can do, but oh my god, it's stuff like this that turns me to mush. He catches me looking and loses his train of thought. "What?"

I realize I'm smiling—I look like an idiot—and I can't explain why, so I just shrug and look away. "Nothing."

He's smiling now, too. "Anyway, you don't have to front. It's cool that you're having girl time."

"Thanks, Mom," I say, still smiling. He has no idea it's because of him, and I'm okay with that, because this crush isn't going to last much longer. I've got plans for purging myself, but for now, I will enjoy the last day I crush on my best friend.

Eli gently pinches my thigh before putting his phone in my lap. "I made a new playlist. Tell me what you think."

We spend the ride listening to a mix of new songs he's found. They're all sweet, and my favorite kind of songs. Love songs. I get what Dré means about not wanting to play the kind of music Eli wants to write. They're best known for their upbeat covers. Music that gets people jumping. Eli likes songs that make his heart thump. I can't blame him for that. I do, too.

When we've ordered our food and have our shakes, I savor each sip—strawberry-banana. It's definitely a strawberry-banana kind of day.

Eli's laughing at me again. "You look like a kid."

Okay, first of all—he better watch it. It can turn into a chocolate day real quick if he starts slinging insults.

"Wow." He's taking in my squinty eyes. "Don't get mad. I just mean, you look so happy and blissful. Like a kid eating ice cream. It's cute."

The server drops off my fries and Eli's cheeseburger, saving me from having to deal with the *cute* comment. I used to like when he dropped a random *you look cute*. But I want him to find me sexy.

"So, what's up?" I say, because Eli must have something on

his mind. We don't normally do impromptu drives out of the way for Steak 'n Shake. It is *not* close to our neighborhood.

He's looking at his burger and messing with a few of his fries. "I wanted your advice."

Yep, I knew he was buttering me up for something. "Hence Steak 'n Shake."

He looks up, and his curls are so messy and silky, I could run my fingers through them. He really does wake up looking flawless. I require a slather of lotions and have to carefully braid or twist my hair in order to look semi-presentable. Guys have it so easy.

He chews on a few fries before he drops it on me. "Why do you think I'm single?"

This is the downside of having guy friends. They think I represent all girls. "Okay, that's a loaded question."

He's staring at me now. "Just your opinion. You won't hurt my feelings."

I laugh. "Why do you think I'd say something bad enough to hurt your feelings?"

He shrugs. "Because the answers involve what I'm lacking."

I shake my head, because he's just like Dré. They have a very skewed idea of how people see them. Or maybe what's skewed is how they see themselves. I don't know, but the fame really hasn't helped in the self-esteem department. "You aren't lacking anything."

He snorts like I'm trying to spare his feelings, and it's kind of maddening, because I want to shout, *I like you. Obviously you're single because you want to be.* But that's not going to help anything.

"I'm serious. If anything, you're intimidating."

He's about to argue, but I keep going.

"Girls see you onstage, they see your Instagram, or they hear about you from other people, and you have a larger-than-life persona. *That's* intimidating. Then when people get to know you, they realize that all that's—you know—not real. But it's a hard barrier to cross."

Eli eats a few more fries. "Okay, so what about after I've gotten to know them?" I can guess he means Kara. I notice she hasn't been as friendly with him in the past week. I haven't asked why, because honestly, I don't even want to talk about *this* with him, let alone why she's all of a sudden gone cold.

Maybe she liked the idea of Eli, not the actual person. And even though having this conversation with him kind of hurts, what's the point of being his best friend if I can't be a shoulder to lean on?

"Then she's not worth your time. Honestly, if she isn't into you by now, she's either an idiot or just not worth it."

"That's kind of harsh."

Yeah, defend the girl who drops you once she realizes the fame is all imaginary—that you're a real person and that's not as cool as what she expected. My speculations are rarely off. "I'm not saying she's a terrible person. I'm just saying she isn't worth *your* time."

He nods. "So, I just spend my life waiting for someone who is worth my time."

"Isn't that what we're all doing?" I take a long drink of my shake.

He picks up his burger. "What if we get along really well—isn't that worth fighting for?"

Maybe Eli and I are the same person, sad and pathetically pining after someone who just doesn't see us. "Maybe. Or maybe it's just a colossal waste of time." I can't help but think about the text I still have from Kai that I've left unanswered. "Maybe by not moving on, you're missing out on the people who actually want you the way you want them."

Eli looks at me. He's not just making eye contact because we're talking. He's looking *at* me. He's doing that thing he and Dré do, the silent speak. And though normally I don't know the language, the message is loud and clear this time: he knows that I'm really talking about me and him. I feel like he knows I'm telling him I'm moving on.

He nods and takes another bite of his burger. Chews. Swallows. "Maybe you're right."

I take a deep breath, because this *really* sucks, but it is what it is. Since he's still my best friend and that means more to me than anything else, I smile and tell him he's got ketchup on his lip.

We spend the rest of our time making small talk in between long silences and, in the car, I text Kai back.

It's time. I'm ready to let Eli go.

I'm outside in the employee parking at my job. It's the middle of the night, kinda cold, and my mom is late *again*. It's not like I could get kidnapped. The security booth is right behind me, and Al's sitting next to me on the bench—but damn, this woman really doesn't care about her *too curvy for khaki shorts* daughter sitting on a bus bench in the middle of the night.

This is Florida. People drive here in diapers to kill their

husbands. They take drugs and turn into zombies. They jump into whale tanks naked and try to have sex with orcas. It's not the best place to leave a kid stranded.

"You gotta cut her some slack," Al says. This is the third time he's sat with me, and I'm so embarrassed. I know he's doing it so I'm not waiting alone, but it makes me feel like I'm the kid with the irresponsible mom. What makes it worse is I'm black. Everyone expects my mom to be single and late. They also expect me to have siblings without the same father. We're checking off some boxes here, and I know I shouldn't care, but I really do. I want to be that special Negro. The one with the two-parent family, the kind who don't try too hard—you know, *Family Matters*, Winslow-style, not the Huxtables.

Even that sounds stupid. I just don't want people to think we're like this because we're black—but maybe we are. I don't fucking know, and I'm tired of thinking about it.

"Come on, kid." Al's handing me his bag of gummy worms. We had candy shop duty today. I've got my own bag of licorice, but again—I don't say no to free shit. "Adults are people, too, you know?"

I grumble. Al's right when he's preachy, but I can't admit he might be onto something when I'd rather be mad at my mom.

"You kids think we're perfect and infallible."

I raise my brow. "Do we?"

He laughs and snatches his gummy bag back. "I have a daughter, too. I told you that, right?" He's told me only a thousand times. She's in New York, working at a publishing company, and Al sometimes lets me borrow the books she sends him. "She was just like you." I've heard that a thousand times, too. He might be getting senile. "Always crucifying her mother for every little mistake." Al stops, and I know he's probably thinking about Veta.

We sit for a while, and I kinda wish we hadn't stumbled onto Veta. He's getting more and more choked up about her lately. I'd ask why, but I'm boss at avoiding things that make people uncomfortable.

"Good judgment—you listening, Livia?" Al's looking at me like *I'm* his daughter, and for a minute I think he might think I am. I swear, if this old man goes crazy on me, I'll lose it. He's the best thing about work. I can't have his ass catching dementia. "Good judgment," he says again, "comes from a string of fuckups."

When I think about it, that makes a lot of sense. Only when I constantly started having my ass handed to me did I realize that, if I just took the chicken out of the freezer *before* my mom got home, she'd stop yelling at me.

"Don't be afraid to make mistakes, Livia." My mom pulls into the parking lot, and Al nods at her car as she's whipping around the bend. "And remember, she's still got some to make, too."

I gather my stuff and say bye to Al. He's walking to his car when my mom pulls up in front of me. "Who's that?" she says, eyeing him like he's a perp on *How to Catch a Predator*.

"Good evening, *Mother*." I'm putting on my seat belt. "That's Al." I've told my mom about Al countless times. I don't think she listens to anything I say. She's always doing something else at the same time, saying, *Yeah, baby. I hear you.* But is she *listening*?

"I don't like you hanging out with old men."

"Oh. My. God." I don't say anything else or point out that Al's more reliable than her late ass. That will get my head mushed against the window.

She reaches into the back seat. We have this old Toyota. It's small, and my mom drives it like a bat out of hell. So when she reaches back to grab something, her boobs hit me in the face and I try to take cover.

"Jesus, Mom. Personal space."

She drops a bag on my lap, and she's holding back a smile as she puts the car in gear and whips us out of the parking lot. We're in third gear before we're on the street.

It's a gift bag.

My mom buys me stuff all the time. I'm spoiled, I won't lie, but I have no idea what this might be. I reach into the bag and pull out an *Othello* DVD—my mom still doesn't trust digital movies. There's also an envelope, and when I open it, I have to hold the tickets by the dashboard to see they're for the *Aida* Broadway musical that's playing over Christmas break.

My cheeks hurt, because I'm both smiling and trying not to smile. I hate this woman. She always does some shit to piss me off, and then she does really awesome stuff like this that makes me realize she knows my heart song. I know these tickets had to be hard to find and super expensive, because they're great seats to a show that is a month away.

"Mom." It's all I can say, because I'm starting to tear up like a little bitch. I hate crying.

"I've been looking for these damn tickets all week. I used a hookup. Don't even ask me how I got them, but *Mother* comes through, don't she?"

I'm hugging her arm, and she's hiding her smile, too. We're so lame. "I love you, Ma." I'm always judging everything my mother does, and sometimes I'm so busy judging that I don't see what she's doing for me.

My mom sniffles. "You're out here doing big things. I'm so proud of you. You know I always got you."

My eyes burn. Even when she's smothering me, I want her to be proud of me. It feels so good, knowing she's behind me.

CHAPTER 17

Thanksgiving is my favorite holiday. I'm too black not to love this day. My grandparents live ten minutes away, and all my extended family is in a 250-mile radius. Everyone from Miami, Jacksonville, and Fort Lauderdale comes to Orlando for Thanksgiving. I've got aunts, uncles, and cousins for days.

I'm at my grandparents', hiding in the garage with my granddad and great-uncles. The women are in the kitchen, and my grandmother gets a little uptight when things get busy, so I leave her to my sister, who is bomb at cooking and the perfect yang to my grandmother's yin.

Cleo's in the kitchen, too, and this is another way in which we completely differ. She's always been into being around the mother hens. I can't stand it; they fuss over everything and make me chop up the holy trinity—onions, *green* bell peppers, and celery—for days. What are the onions, bell peppers, and celery for? *Everything.* My family can't cook without them. Cleo's vegetables are always diced into perfect squares, and I don't have the patience to be criticized about my lopsided onions and funky-looking celery pieces.

The door to the kitchen opens, and my mom and Aunt Rachel come out to grab something from the deep freezer.

"Don't start, Rachel," my mom says between tight lips.

Aunt Rachel rolls her eyes. "Ain't nobody paying attention to you."

My mom reaches into the deep freezer and pulls out huge pitchers of mango lemonade. I love that stuff. Especially when it's chilled. "Green is not your color, yet you stay jealous."

I don't even know what set them off this time. It could be anything. Literally anything. Once it was who got my grandmother the lame Hallmark movie box set some years before. They both did—but did that stop them from bickering over this year's Mother's Day dinner?

They walk back in and the door slams behind them.

My granddad and great-uncles and I are sitting around a table playing poker for quarters. I sip a Coke as they pretend they didn't hear anything. In my family, we sweep things under the rug until we start tripping over the lumps.

My granddad puts his cards facedown on the table. He's good at existing in tension. A self-proclaimed shark, and even though *now* he's a straitlaced businessman, he used to own a grocery store back in the day and I think he was a *real* loan shark—possibly a bookie, too.

When we're sitting around the table like this and they're throwing out old stories, I get the sense that he wasn't so straitlaced back then. I dig it. The old man's cool. He taught me how to drive—lots of yelling and asking why I can't park straight—and how to shop for fish and buy odd stuff off the side of the road—my turtles were from the back of a truck and so was the shrimp he had three days ago. *He* taught me how to exist amid tension.

I'm waiting for the rest of my cousins to get here though, the ones I see only a few times a year. We get together, and you'd swear we all came out of the womb at the same time, hugging each other.

Keith and Kole live down South, and when they pull up, we take over the garage dancing and playing video games. "Shorty got skills. Now go put on a jacket. Walking around here like you grown."

I'm wearing jeans and a loose blouse. I do look good, but it's a family thing so I don't look *that* good. I smile anyway, because it's their way of saying I'm beautiful.

Denise and Emerald arrive, and the house fills to the brim with laughing, loud voices shouting stories on top of stories, and the fumes of okra and tomatoes, mac 'n' cheese, fried turkey, and ribs. I'm the freest I've been in a while. I'm me without thinking about it.

We're sitting around the kiddie table in the kitchen when I hear my mom at the adult table in the dining room talking about me being in the school play. I look at Cleo without meaning to, because I hear my granddad saying, *"Wait, I thought Cleo was doing theatre?"* and my sister is telling him to be quiet, because she, like everyone else with a modicum of social awareness, knows it's sensitive territory. The thing is, half the time my granddad can ride out the tension because he rarely has a clue what's going on.

I peek into the room and see Cleo's mom, Aunt Rachel, is gripping her fork, and I know it has nothing to do with me but rather the smug look on my mother's face, but it still makes me feel like I can't celebrate my success—like I have to keep it to myself for the sake of family dinner.

Cleo looks at me and then sighs. "Actually, Liv got one of the main roles. She beat out a lot of people. She's gonna smash it," she shouts for them to hear.

I blink and give a small smile to Cleo. I don't know how I feel about her being—supportive. It's too strange and new. If anyone would have told me Cleo was going to pay me a compliment—and now, of all moments—I'd have called them a dirty liar. It's not that I think Cleo hates me, it's just that she's been more distant than Twinks when I get out the vacuum. She barely talks to me during rehearsals—granted, we haven't had many—and I understand she's on crew and they've got their own stuff going on, but she walked past me onstage once and didn't even bat an eye.

So, to say I'm surprised that she thinks I'm going to *smash it* is an understatement. "Thanks," I say, and I really mean it.

She shrugs in normal Cleo fashion, and dinner moves on. However, when we get to dessert and it's just me and the cousins standing around the island grabbing seconds, Denise is egging me on to give them a sneak peek and before I know it, I'm out of my seat singing my audition song. It comes so easy, and it's fun. Everyone is looking at me like I'm the next Beyoncé—they're being so extra because we're family—but it feels so damn good.

Aunt Rachel gives me a small smile. "I'm glad to see you've

gotten over your shyness." It's a backhanded compliment, but I'll take it.

Even Cleo's smiling and giving me my props.

We're both packing away some of the food when I just blurt out, "So, I'm sorry if me auditioning made you uncomfortable."

Cleo looks up from wrapping up some turkey. She's got her mom's deadpan blank stare. "I don't own the theatre, Liv. It's cool." She stops for a minute. "Actually, it really did bother me at first. When I told you I'd help you with lines, you never took me up on my offer, and it made me feel—I don't know, like you think I'm not good enough to help. But obviously you *didn't* need my help."

Oh, I feel so greasy and wrong. "I thought you only offered to be polite." She *did* walk off before I could take her up on it.

She has a way of opening her eyes only halfway, and I swear her and her mother spend time in the mirror on this look. The *how to make a bitch feel dumb* look. "We're family. We're never polite."

"Well, if it makes you feel any better, I spent the weeks leading up to auditions completely freaking out." I'm scooping macaroni and cheese into a container when Cleo moves away from the counter and crosses her arms.

"No. It doesn't. I don't want to see you fail, and it bothers me that you think I do. I thought the bullshit between our moms was just between them. Not us." She's looking over her shoulder just like I am to make sure no one heard us. One thing about our moms is you can't call them on their bullshit, because they'll take all that pent-up sibling rage and wipe out any and everyone who tries to point out they have a fucking problem.

A laugh sounds in the other room. We're safe. I glance at Cleo before going back to packing away the mac 'n' cheese. This is the first time we've talked about it—well, at least out loud with each other. We normally just give each other looks and do our best to not be in the same room at the same time with our moms.

"Sorry." I don't know what else to say.

She's looking at the floor like she's choosing her next words carefully. "Just know I'm in your corner. And it's not the theatre department without drama. If you're not careful about who you're hanging out with, you can get swept up in a bunch of unnecessary nonsense. I just—I know you like Jackie and Rodney, but they're always stirring the pot, and I don't want you to get caught up."

Okay, that took a left turn. "Thanks. I'll keep an eye out."

As far as I'm concerned, they're not pot stirrers as much as a little loud and opinionated, which isn't a crime. But Cleo's still not really looking at me, and I can tell not going to her for "theatre advice" really hurt her feelings, so I placate her instead. "Any other advice? I can use all I can get."

She relaxes and starts scooping stuffing into another container. She goes into download mode and dumps a bunch of rules about never showing up late for rehearsals, never talking onstage during blocking, and the biggest sin, *never* drop character.

I'm on my second piece of sock-it-to-me cake when I hear Keith start up the Xbox in the garage. I really don't want to hear any more of Cleo's obvious tips, but then she says something that wakes me out of my impending food coma.

"Never date anyone in theatre. It's probably the best advice I can give you. You'll just end up looking like a ho with no class, and all your dirty laundry will be aired. It's unavoidable." She's raking a fork across a plate of half-eaten sweet potato pie when she looks up. "And no offense, but Lennox isn't exactly the best role model when it comes to not sleeping around."

So now my friends are loudmouth hos. Okay. *Tell me how you really feel, Cleo.* "I think sexual liberation is beautiful." I've never said shit like that in my life, but I feel like I have to say something. I can't let her think I feel like she does. I can't let her dump on my friends, who are so much more than some tired stereotype of what a girl can and can't do with her own body.

Cleo scoffs. "Whatever. I'm just saying you don't want to be the talk of the department, and thanks to me, you won't be." She's smiling. "You know, I'm glad we talked, because I've always felt like we should be closer."

I get what she means. It would have been nice to have someone my age to do everything with without that cloud of suspicion. *Is she trying to show everyone she's smarter than me? More talented? Faster?* Now that I think about it, we were hella dysfunctional growing up. But we can change that.

"Well, we aren't dead yet," I say, and we finish putting away the food before slipping out to the garage to watch everyone play games with glazed eyes.

Cleo and I will be fine…as long as she doesn't find out I plan to break a few of her cardinal rules.

★ ★ ★

As if timing couldn't be better to really mess with Cleo's tips for theatre success, a day later Kai messages me, asking if I'm free for a date. I have to admit, I thought he might have been blowing smoke up my ass, but he legit comes through with a day and time. He wants to take me to Jump Time—the trampoline place.

I'm not about to pass up a real opportunity with a guy because Cleo told me not to date anyone in theatre, so I hop all over it like he's the only puddle of water in the desert—which he kinda is. Plus, I finally get to cross off number four on my list.

I'm going on a freaking date.

I head outside early to avoid him knocking on the door—I refuse for it to be a whole thing with my mom—and just as he's pulling in, I see Dré and Eli walking around the street corner.

Eli's got his keyboard in his hand, so I'm assuming they were practicing for Battle of the Bands since they found a drummer, but they go from laughing to eyeing Kai's car.

Kai sticks his head out of the window and waves at them. "Hey. I didn't know you guys lived so close."

Eli points at his house. "I live next door."

Dré nods at Kai, and I'm just thankful he's not saying, *Sup, Big Hawaii.*

"Cool," Kai says.

The boys stop a few feet away. I'm standing between them and the car, and I know for sure I'm not making up this weird vibe. It feels like they're asking if I'm really going to get in the car with this guy.

"Y'all hang out now?" Dré says. He's got a smile on his face, but it's tight, and I want to know why they're making this so awkward and weird. Why, Lord Jesus, are they like this?

Kai looks at me. "Yeah, I hope so."

Dré looks at me, and I can sorta tell he's holding back some slick remarks, because he's tapping his thigh with his thumb. "So, you coming or going? We were gonna see if you wanted to come over and hang."

I'm staring him down, because I know that's a full-blown lie. Dré always texts me at least an hour before anything, because as our big blowup freshman year, when he showed up unannounced and complained that it took me forty-six minutes to get ready, proved, I need time to get ready mentally and physically before going anywhere with him. I got no such text from him.

Dré's staring back at me and laughs. "Chill. If you're busy that's cool."

Eli exhales and waves with his free hand. "Have fun." He looks at Dré and they do that silent code nonsense.

Kai's watching the three of us, and I totally get why he thinks Dré is a dick.

I can't stand this. "See you guys later," I mumble, and I get in the car.

Kai gives me a small, knowing smile as he pulls out.

We talk about safe, obvious topics, like whether we're ready for stage rehearsals to start next month. So far, we've done four roundtable reads, and we're supposed to have everything memorized for stage rehearsals, which are looming.

Kai's a safe driver, keeps his eyes on the road and both

hands on the wheel, all the safe stuff. Without eye contact, I just stare at the cars ahead as I say, "I am so out of my depth."

I have my lines memorized, but the songs need work—my song is pretty much a duet with Dré that we haven't practiced at all. Worse, when the understudies get a run-through, Angelina's version usually sounds better than mine—more confident—but I don't want to make the mood weird and self-pitying, so I keep that to myself.

"Don't sweat it. Everyone feels like that at first." Kai's focus is on the car behind us as he changes lanes. "Sorry, I'm still getting used to driving here. It's crazy."

I nod. But then add, "Yeah." Tourists make the roads a nightmare.

When we get to Jump Time, I'm not exactly sure what to do. Obviously we're here to jump, but I've got boobs. They aren't huge, but they will jiggle around if I start hopping around like Peter Rabbit. I've got on a hoodie, and I had imagined I'd just keep it on, but it's kinda hot inside and the more I think about it, jumping around in a hoodie is going to make me sweat like a pig wrapped in twenty blankets.

Kai's taking off his shoes and putting his keys in them. He takes my shoes, too. "You've got small feet," he says.

"Only compared to yours." He's tall and his feet are big—and I'm staring at his crotch because of that one saying and I think he notices, because he laughs.

He takes my hand. Oh. My. God. I'm on a *date*. He's holding my hand, leading me up the stairs to some crazy obstacle course. We pass that—thank god—and head to an extreme dodgeball net. The place is pretty vacant for a Sunday—at least, I assume it is. I've never been here before; maybe jumping isn't on trend.

"You ever play dodgeball?" He says it while picking up a foam ball. He's smiling deviously, and I run away as he pelts me with it.

"You know I'm competitive, right?" I say, picking up two balls.

He's already got another lined up. "You're already down by one." We chase each other around the pit. I'm so concerned with winning, I don't even care that I'm bouncing around in a tank top that keeps riding up. I'm giggling, ducking and dodging until he's trying to steal balls out of my hand. It's a smooth move, because he's holding me from behind, and then—we aren't jumping anymore.

We're kissing.

Hot damn. He's a good kisser. I haven't kissed anyone since the tenth grade, and that was all right…but I *know* this is good. He's got soft lips and a tongue that just knows what to do in my mouth. My throat aches—that aching that tells me I need more of this. I'm turning around into him and his hands are around my waist, and I don't care that I'm *that* girl, making out in a very public place. No one is around anyway—I hope.

He pulls away a little, and then we're right back in it. I don't know how much time goes by, but we spend it throwing foam balls and kissing.

I'm different with Kai. Free. It's not the same freeness I feel when I sing in front of my family—thank god, because I'm not trying to feel family vibes while we're locking lips. But I do feel a different kind of free. I'm a girl, and he's a guy who sees me as just that.

A full-on girl.

A girl he wants to talk to, kiss, and play with. But we're not playing like Eli, Dré, and I play around. We're not saying stupid shit. We're—I don't know exactly, but I really like it.

After Jump Time, we go to a taco truck. I kind of freak him out when I see it, because I scream, "We gotta get those tacos!" He's never been to this truck before, but it's a food truck you can only ever find by actually seeing it. They're the freaking leprechaun of taco trucks. The owners don't have social media or anything. You find the truck, and there's a pot of gold at the end—or is that rainbows? Whatever, these tacos are to die for.

I order us the fried chicken tacos—don't judge me, they're good and everyone thinks so, not just black people—two carnitas, and two shrimp. I pay, since he paid for Jump Time, and then we're sitting next to each other, bumping our knees back and forth. Eating tacos and flirting reminds me of that movie *Selena*. My sister used to watch it nonstop, and I remember thinking that thing Selena had with Chris Pérez was solid.

When Kai drops me off at home, there's no hesitation. He pulls up in front of my house, he cups the side of my face and kisses me. It isn't long and gratuitous, but I can feel the want behind it.

Hot. Damn. To sorta quote Selena, I could totally fall in love with this guy.

CHAPTER 18

I'm lying on my bed, making sure that really happened to me. Kai's body pressed against mine was euphoric, and if I close my eyes, I can still feel the warmth of his lips. He's so gentle and solid at the same time.

Twinks jumps on my bed, thoroughly ruining the moment with her pawing and drool, but my phone is buzzing in my hand anyway.

It's Eli. For the first time since I've known him, I don't know if I *want* to answer. Annoyed, I sit up and stare out my window, and he's sitting on his bed, too, blinds wide-open. We get horrible lighting as the sun sets, so his light is already on. We're staring at each other with our phones in hand. We're so creepy.

I turn on my lamp. The purple lamp shade is covered in

an orange neck scarf that I've never worn in my life. I grab it, needing something to fiddle with in my hands.

"Hey," I say. I feel like I've been caught, but he already knew I was going on a date. I think back to when I left, when I stalled because I was momentarily stuck between two worlds.

I chose Kai. Whatever. Why is it even an either-or situation? Friends or potential boyfriend?

Ugh. I feel like old me again, and not the cool middle schooler who didn't give two shits and did her thing. I feel like weird, super self-conscious me who wore khakis to a Halloween party—but the skin doesn't fit.

"How was your date?"

I grip the phone. Everything in me wants to scream and throw it. Why is he asking me this? This is the kind of thing Eli is good at—pretending there isn't this awkward thing happening *right now*. I know he feels it; his lips are kind of tight, and he's got his bushy brows raised like he's aggravated and *knows* something but won't tell me because *I, too,* should just *know it*. This is how all our non-fighting fights start. Except this time, I really have no idea why *he's* mad.

Maybe it bothers him that I'm not here to be his emotional cheerleader and boost his self-esteem while he waits for his real dream girl. But I'm tired of him toying with me and making me feel crazy for thinking there was *something* between us in the first place.

OH. MY. GOD. Nothing should be this complicated.

"Fun." I don't give him details, and he doesn't ask.

He just says, "I bet." And it's not like he's saying it with attitude, but it's how he's *not* saying anything else. Why the hell did he call me if he's not going to say anything anyway?

I don't even know what he's doing home right now. He's supposed to be with his mom; they always go antiques shopping Sunday evenings. It's weird. Mrs. Peretz has a freaky obsession for Spanish conquistador antiques, and she and Eli spend every Sunday in search of them like it's their church.

Almost every Sunday, that is—he's been practicing for Battle of the Bands with Dré for the last two Sundays. In fact I haven't seen Mrs. Peretz for a while now. Normally she's always in and out.

I remember the way Gloria and his dad were acting that day at Dré's house. I'm not going to bring that up. I'm so not getting into their family business, especially because it's probably nothing to begin with.

"Why aren't you with your mom?"

"I got to go." He hangs up. I'm still watching from my window when he gets up and closes his blinds.

Okay. Obviously, he's pissed that I'm hanging out with Kai. What was I supposed to do? Tell Kai no, because Eli's single and needs me to keep him from feeling lonely and unwanted by Kara, the girl who sucks up spit from her mouthpiece?

I've daydreamed this scenario more times than I'm comfortable admitting. Eli, struck with jealousy as another guy sweeps me off my feet. I didn't think it would actually happen, and I'd imagined it as a case of jealousy because he was in love with me, not jealousy because he selfishly doesn't want to be single *and* alone.

Fuck it. I've officially moved on.

I spend the night thinking about what I'm going to say to Eli the next day. But he doesn't call in the morning, and when I call him, he doesn't answer. I'm kind of freaking out. He *is* one of my best friends. And to be fair, we all have our selfish moments.

Losing Eli's friendship isn't the problem—that's pretty far-fetched and overdramatic—I just don't like this space between us. It hovers, ominous, like the hour before a hurricane hits.

He's not outside when Dré pulls in to pick us up, and he doesn't answer his phone or come out. He *does* text Dré. Not me, the one who called, but—cool. Cool. Yeah, that's cool. Anyway, he's staying home.

Eli almost never skips school. He has to be pressured by both Dré and me at the same time *and* bribed with pasta. So, when I'm at lunch, sitting on the big staircase with Dré, I can't stop looking for him in the crowd. I can picture him some-where, tapping his foot while casually scrolling through his phone and biting into a Snickers bar.

But he's not here.

I'm checking out every head of dark hair in the clusters of hunched-over kids eating and talking nonstop when I hear someone behind me.

"Hey, Dré. You gon' hook me up with that discount or what?" It's Oscar. He's in band, too, but he's like us. We're the kids who play instruments, but you'd never know it be-cause we don't announce it to the world. I don't care if peo-ple think I'm a band geek—that's what my mom calls us, but I don't even think that's a thing anymore—I just don't mesh with the vibe most kids in band put out. They're all way too happy to be there and think we're all one big family. They say things like, *Oh my god, you're my band mom.* No, bitch, I'm not.

Anyway, I'm staring at Dré, trying to figure out what the

hell Oscar is talking about. Dré works at the Kmart up the street, and he doesn't get a discount. Dré's gesturing for Oscar to drop it, and then I realize he's up to no good, because Oscar looks at me. "Yeah, brah. I'll hit you up later."

"What's he talking about?" I ask when Oscar's gone. I've got this weird feeling in my gut. More and more lately, he's been hanging around a bunch of people who are pretty much using him for his popularity, which is half the reason he never has time to do his own homework.

"Nothing." Dré won't look me in the eye, and when he finally does, he laughs and puts his finger on my cheek to turn my face away.

I slap his hand. "I'm serious." If he's stealing for his fake-ass friends, I swear I will choke the stupid out of him.

"So am I. When are we gonna practice our song?" I don't even have to say anything, because his shifty ass laughs again. "Damn, Liv. I'm serious, it's nothing."

I drop it. He's a vault. When he doesn't want me to know something, he clamps down on it for life. Besides, we do need to practice. Stage rehearsals start in two weeks, and I didn't need Cleo to tell me that Mrs. G isn't the kind of teacher you can screw around with. She's real respectful, but she'll also *respectfully* ask you to take your ass offstage and stay off if you don't take her craft seriously.

We make plans for Wednesday, but I change it to Thursday when I remember I have another date with Kai. Dré raises his eyebrows. "Big Hawaii, huh?" He has this really stupid laugh when he thinks he's funny.

I elbow him so he'll stop laughing. "Yes. He's cool, and I don't appreciate all the jokes."

"It's not a joke, Liv. I was calling him Big Hawaii before you even knew him." He's quiet, and then he's looking at me with relaxed heavy lids, classic *I'm bored* Dré. "If he makes you cry, I'll fuck him up."

Jesus.

"I'm serious. He might be big, but I'm quick." The lunch bell rings, and he's up and kissing my cheek before hopping off the stairs. He turns around. "I'm serious. I'll fuck him up."

I've been kissed by three different guys in two months. I don't know if my Fuck It attitude is leaking pheromones, but I'm kind of enjoying the attention. And even though Dré's annoying, he cares, and the look he gives me before disappearing into the crowd makes my heart dance between beats.

This time, Kai and I go to Disney Springs. We're walking around, eating gelato, when he leads me to a bench next to a fountain. We're people-watching and making up stories for them. One lady is a reformed CIA agent trying to get her life back after losing everyone important to her. And there goes a guy who loves dogs more than people. They bump into each other—it's going to be a rom-com. A montage of her having to find a place in her heart for his fifty dogs and overattached mother.

"So, what's your story?" I ask Kai. All I know is that his family moved here from Hawaii last year because his dad got a job doing something really boring at Disney. It pays a lot, but Kai and his sisters miss the waves.

I'm in awe. I live in Florida, but it's *Central Florida*. I almost never go to the beach, so I think beach life sounds majestic. He laughs when I say that. But he's not laughing *at* me so much as he just thinks I'm funny.

"I want to move to LA and try my hand at indie films." He pauses. "I know it takes hard work to get there, but why not?"

"No, I think that's cool." I really do, I binge-watch documentaries of people who follow their dreams, and I think it's the modern-day fairy tale. Then, *fuck it*, I tell him something I've never told anyone. "I want to work on the stage or on films—maybe composing musical scores."

Taking something that didn't exist and making it real—everyone is always looking for magic, but it's right in front of us. I know it sounds stupid. I just like everything to do with movies. *Especially* thematic soundtracks. I love the way music can completely change a movie. "Not to mention, Hans Zimmer has too much of a monopoly on the market."

"You're totally right. All the movies with his tracks sound the same." Kai takes my empty gelato cup and puts it in his. "I think you should go for it." He says it in all seriousness. There is no *yay! Follow your dreams* lameness to it. He's saying it as if I said, *I think I should try eating more vegetables*. Like it's something completely achievable. I wish it were that easy. I don't even know what specific thing I want to do, let alone how to make that a life path.

I'm around these people who are living their dreams. Dré and Eli with their music, Jackie with her vlogging, Lennox and Kai with acting. They're on the road to something amazing, and Kai actually thinks I can be one of those people. But if I'm honest, all I've ever done is listen to soundtracks when the mood strikes. Can I even call this a dream if I'm interested but not passionate like them?

I'm really good at school—I'm great at following rules and completing tasks—but following a dream? That's something I don't know how to do.

He kisses me, and this one is sweet and lasts only a few seconds. "Sorry," he says. "You have a really kissable face." And a few seconds later, I'm apologizing right back at him, because he *really* does, too.

CHAPTER 19

After being MIA for two days, Eli finally shows up at school. He didn't ride with us though. I feel like he's avoiding me because of Kai. Everything was fine until I went on a date. It's like he's making me choose: life in the shadows being his number one fan girl, or being with someone who actually wants to date me. Then again, it could just be he's afraid of losing me as a friend—the same way I sometimes get scared he'll stop being my friend if he gets a girlfriend.

After lunch, he walks me to my class, which isn't that special because our classes are right next to each other, but as I'm about to open my class door, he pulls me over to the lockers. We're standing in front of these matte, cobalt blue lockers not looking at each other, but standing close. It looks like a goddamn breakup scene—but he's not my freaking boyfriend, so this whole moment is ridiculous.

"Liv." I'm not looking up because he says it like he used to, I look up because he's saying my name like he hurts. He looks at me, but then his eyes dart away, and I think he might cry.

I don't know what to say. But my heart flips, because what if he actually is jealous? What if seeing me go on a date with Kai made him actually *see* me? "Eli," I breathe.

His face goes blank. "Sorry. For not answering your calls. I'm kinda dealing with shit."

Shit between us? Some other kind of shit? *Elijah* might as well mean *vague* in Hebrew.

The two-minute bell rings. "Can we talk later?" Eli asks.

I'd rather talk now, but... "Yeah. I told Dré we'd practice after school. After that, I'll text you?"

He runs his hand through his hair and is back to not making eye contact. "Yeah. Whenever." Then he disappears into his classroom.

I don't see him for the rest of the day, and after school, I catch the bus home and wait for Dré to get off work. When he doesn't show up, I blow up his phone for an hour before I give up on him. I call Eli, peek through my blinds, and nothing. Both of them might as well be together, giggling in my closet, watching me pace and curse their names.

That happened once, a long time ago. They were trying to make a prank video by scaring the hell out of me. My sister burst through my door with a mask on and everything. Thinking back on it, the whole thing was just creepy and traumatizing, and Amber really shouldn't have laughed as hard as she did.

I call Lennox, and she comes over to practice with me instead. She sings Dré's part, and when I feel like my stomach might cannibalize me, we raid my kitchen and make hamburgers and homemade french fries.

I make some for my mom and I can't wait to see her face when she realizes how thoughtful I am—I'm gonna rub that *ish* in her face.

"Kai told me y'all went on another date." Lennox hip bumps me. "He was grinning and all happy."

I can't stop smiling. "I think sex with him would be good." Lennox has converted me. I'm talking about sex openly now. The prudish side of me still cringes, but whatever.

Lennox cackles. "Let him tear that ass up."

"Oh. My. *God.* I can't tell you anything."

"I think you're right. He'd be good. He's kind." Lennox is simultaneously a young free spirit and the witchy old lady who teaches you how to make potions with dirt and bones. She hesitates though.

"What?"

"I have this weird vibe that it won't be him. It's going to be one of the two goonies you hang with."

I'm chomping down hard on my fries, because those "two goonies" are a sensitive subject right now. They literally just stood me up. Those assholes aren't even on the short list. Besides, Dré is—Dré. And I'm officially moving past Eli. I keep holding on to these glimmers of hope that I make up in my head and I. Am. Done.

Lennox smiles at my scowl. "It could be both at the same time." She's cackling, and I don't want to know if she knows what that's like.

"Not into it." Nope. Nope. I'm not some free soul-sucking sex spirit. I'm still me and not into that.

Lennox stays over and braids my hair again. If she wasn't here, I'd have wallowed and racked my brain trying to figure out what the hell is up with Eli and why Dré thinks I'm important enough to fight a dude for but not important enough to give me the time of day with something that *actually* matters.

With Lennox, I'm just a girl again. And being a girl is something powerful and good. I've gone a whole night without being consumed by the boys' bullshit. I don't know why it's taken me so long to realize, but Eli and Dré don't define me.

It's funny, because, in *Othello*, we play these chicks who get verbally abused, arrested, and murdered. Nothing in that play shows a woman's strength in saying, *No, I won't let you treat me this way.* Because the one chick who makes a stand *still* ends up dead. Maybe I'm reading too much into it. I get that I do that, but whether I'm right or wrong, I'm glad I have Lennox. She makes me want to stand up for myself and say, *I'm not taking this shit.*

And that's exactly what I'm going to tell them. I tried before when Dré kept teasing me about Kai, but now I realize it's about so much more than that. I've got to be my own person, and that means firm boundaries when it comes to how they treat *me*, too.

Lennox and I are on the couch watching *The Real Housewives of Atlanta* when I pause the show and say, "I'm a badass, smart-ass, boss bitch."

She laughs and nods. "Yaaas, bitch. Now press Play. NeNe's about to go off."

I ride to school with Lennox. I don't even tell Dré; I'll let him figure it out himself. But by the time I'm leaving band class for lunch, I haven't seen Dré or Eli, and neither of them have texted me to apologize either. I ask around—no one has seen them.

I refuse to text them first on principle, so the rest of the school day drags by, and then so does work, because Al and I are on different shifts again.

I make a plan. I'm going to confront them and tell them how I feel. First Dré, then Eli. I'm going to tell Dré he needs to respect my time. I'm going to tell Eli to stop using me as his emotional girlfriend.

I'm also going to do Eli last because, while I know I'm in my girl-power fury right now, I'm also still nervous about laying it all on the table with him.

The next day, I get up early and walk the few blocks to Dré's house. What I have to say needs to be said in person. I'm not going to hide behind my phone and get caught up in what his one-word responses mean. I don't care if it's Saturday and 9:00 in the morning. I march up to the Santoses' red door and knock. I've got a whole speech about how I'm tired of his shit and I'm not going to talk to him for a week. Complete silent treatment. I've never done that. I always cave after the first day.

Gloria answers the door and—she looks like a mess. That's saying a lot, because she's always wearing makeup, jewelry, and an outfit that makes her look ten years younger than she is. Today she's in yoga pants and a sweatshirt. She still looks cute, because she's Gloria, but damn.

I don't say that though. I just smile when she hugs me.

"I—I can't even say it." She calls Dré and the way she says his name is like she's cursing him. Dré is her only son *and* the youngest. She treats him like an angel who could do no wrong, so when I see Dré, I really have no clue what's going on, but it feels like someone died.

I immediately think of Eli, and I know I'm jumping to conclusions. I do that—think of the worst instead of being logical—but what if Gloria *is* cheating with Yosef and it came out? But why is *she* mad at Dré? Okay—chill.

Breathe.

Dré's at the door, and Gloria doesn't even look at him. "Tell your mom I have to cancel our plans tomorrow. I'll call her. But just let her know for me, baby."

I tell Gloria I will, but I don't think she hears me. She's back in the house, going up the stairs, and I guess Dré doesn't want to go back in, because he closes the door and sits on the porch steps.

He's peering up at the sky, biting his bottom lip. He looks like he hasn't slept, and his eyes have that eerie distant stare. He does that, when he locks himself off; he turns to stone and hides inside himself.

I just sit with him, because I know asking what's going on isn't going to make him say it any faster. He looks completely devastated—like he-saw-something-really-fucked-up devastated.

A minute goes by. I can't take it anymore. "Dré—"

"I got arrested."

This coming out of Dré's mouth doesn't make sense. He's not the kind of kid who gets arrested. He's flashy but not stupid—or so I thought. I don't get it—and then I remember Oscar and the *fucking discount*. Now I know why he stood me up, why he looks like he hasn't slept, and why Gloria was dressed like she'd been out all night. She was bailing her son out of jail.

A lot of words—mean, terrible words—are coming to mind, but I know Gloria's already said them all, because Dré looks destroyed.

I sit there, not saying anything—but I'm me, and I can't keep quiet, so I say, "I don't get it—" I have to stop, because I'm going to tell him all the horrible things he probably already knows, and Dré is the kind of guy who internalizes everything you say about him. "I don't know how to say what I feel without saying something I might regret."

He's squinting at some guy walking a dog down the sidewalk. "I know." His voice is low and empty.

I try to formulate the perfect thing to say. Anything to make him realize that he has the world in front of him and he's about to throw it away for some fake friends who don't give a damn about him.

He looks at me, his mouth pulling at the corners. "I don't know who I am anymore."

I'm stunned.

His eyes water, and tears drop to his cheeks and down, down, down. He doesn't make a noise. He doesn't shudder. He just stares at me and breaks.

I pull him into a hug. I've never seen him cry. I've seen him mad; I've seen him embarrassed. I went with him to his abuelo's funeral—he doesn't cry in front of people. Maybe right now, the last thing he needs is another person telling him how much he screwed up.

I just let him cry.

He sniffs, and when he pulls away, the only evidence of his

tears are his red eyes and the way his mouth kind of twitches. "When I'm onstage—I feel like me. But then there's all this shit that comes with it. People want to believe I'm this guy who's always *on*. Sometimes I want to turn off, but then who will want me?"

Me. Eli. I say as much.

He laughs.

"I'm serious. You think we care about all that? *You* are amazing. *You*. In everything you do—except school—but you're one of those few people who make up their minds about something, does it, and succeeds." I've always looked up to him, because he's always so *himself*. I think back to that night at Halloween. "Meanwhile, the rest of us are still stuck on whether we're wearing the right thing to fit in."

He wipes his face. "Yeah? I care so much about impressing people, I actually ended up in jail."

I grab his face with my hands and make him look at me, because this is the Dré who lurks in the darkness. The one who hurts himself before anyone else can beat him to it.

"You don't have to do all that. You're perfect the way you are." Lennox and Jackie are really rubbing off on me. "Only *you* don't see it." I feel like what I'm telling him is something we both need to hear.

He's searching my eyes to make sure it's the truth. He must find proof, because the hardness falls from his eyes, and then he leans in, and his lips softly touch my forehead.

I freeze.

It's not like before.

His lips linger, and when he pulls away, he tilts his head down to meet mine.

If I move, I don't know what will happen. We're at a bridge, and he might be asking me to cross.

His hand moves to the side of my face, and my eyes flutter as my breath catches. I'm stuck between moving back and leaning in—

Do I want to lean in?

My heart drums in my chest.

He pulls away and looks at me, and I sense he's trying to think of words to say.

I don't have any either. For once, I'm speechless and terrified, like the moment the roller coaster drops.

"Thanks." He pulls me into a side hug and rests his chin on my head. He's taking these deep breaths, like he's breathing me in, and I realize André Santos is someone I want to know for the rest of my life.

ACT THREE

ACT THREE—Scene Three—
Day and Night

Othello:
I'M SECOND BEST
LESS THAN THE REST, YEAH
I'M NOT THE MAN
NOT FOR HER PLAN

I'M AT A LOSS
ALL'S LEFT IS TO GIVE UP
I'M AT A LOSS
NEVER THOUGHT I'D FIND MYSELF HERE

I'LL SET SAIL
TAKE A NEW FLIGHT
LOVE WON'T LAST THE NIGHT
NOT WORTH THIS FIGHT

I'M AT A LOSS
ALL'S LEFT IS TO GIVE UP
I'M AT A LOSS
NEVER THOUGHT I'D FIND MYSELF HERE

Chorus:
(hums first verse)
NOT WORTH YOUR LIFE

Othello:
I AM THE SUN THE SUN IS ME
WITHOUT THE LIGHT AND BEAUTY
I AM THE NIGHT THE NIGHT IS ME
WITHOUT PEACE AND UNBROKEN DREAMS

Chorus/(Othello):
I AM THE SUN THE SUN IS ME (I AM THE SUN)
WITHOUT THE PEACE AND UNBROKEN DREAMS
(WITHOUT THE PEACE AND UNBROKEN DREAMS)

THIS IS YOUR PLIGHT (THIS IS MY PLIGHT)
THIS IS YOUR PLIGHT (THIS IS MY PLIGHT)
THIS IS YOUR PLIGHT (THIS IS MY PLIGHT)

Othello:
THIS IS MY DEATH, MY LIFE
I AM THE SUN THE NIGHT IS ME
WITH DISCORD AND FURY

CHAPTER 20

I give Eli another day to call or message or, hell, I'd take a carrier pigeon. I didn't have the mental space to unpack Dré getting arrested—and our near kiss—and whatever Eli's got going on all on the same day. So, I figure Sunday's a good day to corner him at Dré's while they practice for Battle of the Bands, but when I asked Dré if they were still getting together, he said Eli had skipped almost all the practices they had planned and he's been blowing off Dré's messages, too.

Dré wasn't too mad, because his mom pulled the plug on everything that wasn't school related anyway—no Battle of the Bands and no more gigs—but I'm seeing red flags.

We have an unspoken rule between the three of us. When someone wants space, you give them space. When I randomly got my period in school during seventh grade history, Dré gave me his jacket and the rule was established. If someone doesn't want to talk about the jacked-up shit they're going through, space is granted. No questions asked. In the eighth grade, Eli's first girlfriend cheated on him with this soccer kid. They were making out after school by the vending machines, and Eli needed a full week to brood before we were allowed to acknowledge what happened and openly give her dirty looks in the halls.

So, space. I get it—but as my mom and I eat dinner and watch a newest episode of *Real Housewives of Atlanta*, I'm not really into it. Not even NeNe Leakes can shake Eli off my brain. I'm thinking about him so much that, when I wake up at 2:00 a.m., I think I dreamed him screaming.

I lie still in my bed, heart racing. What if I didn't dream the scream? What if it was my mom fighting off a burglar?

I hear it again. It's definitely Eli, and his voice is full of such rage, I fall out of my bed, running to my window. His blinds are closed, but the light is on in his room and it's casting an off-kilter shadow on his window. But I don't think he's in there.

Yosef is yelling at Eli.

Then silence.

I grab my phone and text him, but there is no response or any sign he's read my text.

I'm standing in the middle of my room waiting for something, and then there's a crash that I hear all the way through the walls. I run to my mom's room, and if there is one thing I love about this woman, it's that she doesn't ask questions. I'm telling her something's happening at Eli's house while she pulls on her robe. "Be ready to call the police," she says.

My mom pulls her stun gun out of her dresser, and then I'm running down the stairs behind her.

She glances at me over her shoulder. "Nah, you stay here. I'm not having you caught up in whatever's going on."

But I'm already out the door. The screaming is even louder outside. We can hear them yelling at each other. I don't know what Yosef is saying, because he's screaming in Hebrew.

There's another crash.

My mom rings the doorbell, and she's got her hands on her hips. She's a lot better than I am at being calm when shit's hitting the fan. Once she went to her work friend's house while her husband was beating on her and said something to him that made him leave and not come back.

My mom's a rock, so when no one answers the door, she just goes to the back of the house like she's the damn police.

I'm following her, and I can feel my heart in my throat.

Yosef is rattling off Hebrew at the top of his lungs and then telling Eli to *"stop."*

Eli's chanting, *"Fuck you,"* over and over at the top of his lungs.

As we get to their sliding door, I see them in the kitchen. My mom opens the unlocked door and we get a full blast of their incantations.

Yosef yells, "I am your father. You won't disrespect me. It is not your place."

Eli throws a toaster at his dad's head but it misses and smashes into the wall. I jump and swallow my own scream. Eli's not violent. This guy picking up the waffle maker and flinging it at his dad is not someone I know.

Yosef bats the waffle maker to the floor and it cracks their kitchen tile. He closes the distance between himself and Eli and backhands him into the refrigerator.

I'm screaming and my mom's pointing the stun gun at Yosef. "That's *enough*, Yosef."

Yosef looks at us as if he has no idea how we even got into his house. He looks back at Eli and exhales, panting.

Eli scrambles off the floor and throws a wooden spoon at his dad's head.

Yosef just croaks, "Enough." And he leans on the nearest wall, staring at nothing.

"Take Elijah home." My mom is talking to me, but I can't move. The hate in Eli's eyes shakes me. "Go on, I'll be there in a little."

Eli sure as hell isn't coming to me, so I cross the kitchen, avoiding the broken bits of glass, scattered silverware, and chunks of porcelain from broken plates and bowls. "Come on, Eli." I have to grab his arm and lead him out of the house. He's not in his body; he's somewhere else.

I can't steady my hands. They shake as I pull him home and up to my room. I'm not sure what to do. I just walked in on a horror show. I want to know what happened. The Peretz house is the house of zen. Eli's not a fighter, because his parents never so much as raise their voices.

"Are you okay? Where's your mom?" I'm trying to remember the last time I saw her and—I can't. Leila's always in the garden or asking me if I'm hungry. I've been so busy with school and my own life crisis that I didn't notice I haven't seen her picking chili peppers and biting into them as if they aren't hotter than lava.

Eli slowly sits on my bed. He looks up at me. His face is red and already starting to swell a little where his dad hit him.

"Do you want to talk about it?"

Nothing.

"Do you want to sleep in my room?" I'm asking these dumb questions because I don't know what else to say.

He nods, and his shoulders slump like whatever weight he's been under finally broke him.

I've never felt more useless as I go to the hall to get the extra blankets. I've been thinking his attitude was about me—about him being jealous—and I couldn't have been further from the truth. I am such an idiot—stupid isn't even the right word for how I'm feeling. When I come back, he's sitting on my bed, staring at the floor. I start making his pillow pallet.

I'm shaking out a blanket when he tugs on the back of my shirt. I turn around, and he frowns as his eyes water. He rests his head against my stomach, and I hug him.

I feel every shudder as he cries.

My mom is standing over the stove cooking eggs, grits, and bacon. Eli's staying at our house for a few days, but when my mom tells me it's a favor for Yosef, I'm floored. If anyone *deserves* the favor, it's Eli. But I'm not going to argue semantics with my mom.

"It's not Eli's fault he got hit." I'm not acting like my mom's never hit me; she's slapped me before, thrown paper towel rolls at me, slippers, and she's threatened to beat me with about anything you can name. But she's never *hit* me like that.

I glance at the doorway, expecting him to come thumping down the stairs at any moment. I know he's asleep, but talking about someone when they're not in the room always makes me paranoid.

"He threw a toaster, a waffle iron, and from what it looked like, the whole damn kitchen at Yosef's head."

There's a reason. Eli's *not* violent. But my mom's making it sound like he's staying at our house until *Yosef* feels safe having him around.

"Y'all kids don't understand. Grown folk aren't perfect. We have emotions and hurt just as bad as you do. The only difference is we're also responsible for little mini-mes who are just as emotional and more like us than we expect."

She sounds like Al. "I never said you were perfect," I mumble.

She side-eyes me. "See what I mean? Being your mother doesn't make me immune to your picking. Sometimes it hurts more coming from you."

I roll my eyes. I don't know why she's making this about us. This really isn't about us.

"Yosef and Leila are going through a lot right now. Eli deserves to feel how he's feeling, but Yosef is taking a beating from his wife *and* his son. That's a lot for one man."

I'm seeing Gloria and Yosef and how they kept lingering so close, and it clicks why I haven't seen Eli's mom in weeks. *I* feel like somehow I'm complicit. "Did she leave?"

"Mmm-hmm," is all my mom is giving me.

"Why?" She has to know more than I do. She's damn near best friends with the woman who might have just broken up a marriage.

"Stay out of grown folk business."

I hate that. Grown folk put me in this business when they flirted in front of me and woke me up in the middle of the night.

"Is she coming back?" I push.

My mom looks at me. "It's none of my business. Go see if Eli's hungry."

He's still sleeping when I get to my room. My mom told me to make up my sister's old room for him, so I make sure the sheets on the bed are fresh and get him a towel. I eat breakfast, and he's still asleep when I get back upstairs. My mom leaves for work, and I tell Dré I'm staying home. I hate missing Mondays but I can't leave Eli.

Dré's typing a message and then nothing. And then again. And nothing. And then a message finally does come through. Okay?

I'm wondering what the messages he wrote and erased said, but I answer anyway. Eli had a fight with his dad. He's staying at my house until things cool off.

Should I come over?

I keep seeing his lips hovering over mine, and my stomach twirls.

No. He's not even awake and I feel like he'll just get defensive if we're both staring at him.

And I have no clue what Saturday was and can't deal with that right now.

lol. I'll call later.

Eli's *still* asleep on the floor of my room when I come in and sit on my bed. I pull out my homework; I have a pile of it that I didn't do over the weekend.

Eli doesn't wake up until noon, and then we wait until his dad's car is gone before we go over to pack some of his things. He's shoving clothes into his bag and doesn't say a word. There is this impenetrable force field around him. This is the storm I felt coming, and it might tear down everything in its path.

I go back home, leaving him to finish packing. Just when I think he might decide to stay at his house or run away or, hell, float off never to be seen again, he's back in my room.

"So, you know my dad's a cheating bastard?" His voice is grating and raspy as if his vocal cords took a beating from the yelling. These are the first words he's said to me since we were standing in front of the lockers, and again, I feel like such an idiot for making everything about me. I thought he wanted to talk about *us*, when really, his whole life was falling apart around him.

I just tell him a truth, because I feel like the bridge we used to have is about to get swept away, too. "I kind of saw him at Dré's and I thought maybe—he and Gloria were too friendly? I don't know."

He looks like he's going to throw more stuff, and this is the first time I've ever been afraid of Eli. Not afraid that he'll throw anything at me—but like I don't know *what* he might do. "You knew and didn't say anything?" He's shaking his head. "You really are full of surprises." His words are laced with something bitter, and I know he's in his feelings about his parents, but I can't help the way my face pulls as I think, *asshole.*

"What was I supposed to say? 'Eli, your dad's a cheater because he fixed Gloria's sink.' I had no way of knowing."

He doesn't say anything else about it and points to Amber's room. "Is that where I'm staying?"

"Eli."

He just stares at me.

Fine. "Yeah."

He goes into the room and shuts the door.

Fuck.

CHAPTER 21

A week goes by. Eli's still at my house, holed up in my sister's room. My mom doesn't seem to care that he doesn't talk or come out aside from meals and going to school—there's no reason she would. Eli's quiet and keeps to himself. I mind though—*because he's quiet and keeps to himself.* He's not talking to me *at all.* How can he not see my side? I gave it a week and was as patient as I could be, but this shit is getting old.

During the week, Eli made it clear he was in broody mode. Every lunch, he blasted music through his earphones and ignored us. One ride home, he slammed the car door and Dré cursed, "What the hell?" I casually brought up Eli having problems with his dad to gauge what Dré might be aware of. But he shrugged saying, "Parents can be dicks." It was obvious he didn't know a thing about Yosef and Gloria.

All week I made excuses with Dré as to why Eli has such

a piss-poor attitude. I can't tell Dré about his mom—besides the fact that it would be incredibly awkward, if Eli hasn't told him, it's not my place. And I'm not even sure that broke up the marriage—maybe Leila left before Yosef and Gloria started fooling around. I don't know—because Eli tells me *nothing*.

I try prying some details from my mom after dinner when I'm washing the dishes. I wait until Eli's done putting the food away and has gone back upstairs. "Mom?"

She looks at me from the fridge, where she's pulling out a bottle of wine. "No, you can't have any."

Ew. "I don't want your nasty wine."

She eyes me. "How do *you* know it's nasty?"

I roll my eyes. "What happened between Gloria and Yosef?" I need the deets, and I'm just dropping it on her because she'll dodge the question if I don't.

"I already told you to stay out of grown folks' business."

I drop the sponge into the soapy water and wave my hand toward the stairs that lead up to our bedrooms. "Well, grown folks' business is sleeping in the room next to me and hates me because I sorta saw them being flirty and didn't say anything." That's why I assume Eli has gone completely silent. I really don't know—I can't help but compare Dré having a crisis and opening up with Eli having one and deciding to shut me out instead.

My mom raises an eyebrow and mumbles under her breath. I catch the words *idiots* and *trifling*. "Look, nothing happened. Something *could* have happened—but nothing actually happened, and that's all I'm going to say about it."

I shake my head. "Well, if nothing happened, why did Eli's mom take off?"

My mom pours a glass of her dark red wine. "If you had a man—and something *almost* happened between him and a woman you know—would you congratulate him on not taking the plunge, or would you be pissed and come home to stay with me a while?"

She has a point. She walks into the living room to sit behind a laptop to work on a *Shark Tank* wedding as per the giant print title on the binder next to her, while I scrub a plate clean. I *would* be pissed—hell, I was mad when Eli, who isn't even my boyfriend, held hands with another girl. But as far as I know, Eli's mom doesn't exactly have a nonjudgmental family to go home to. Some of her family cut her off when she decided to run off with Yosef and get married.

She's Muslim, and the family dynamic is complicated. Eli's grandfather on his mom's side doesn't acknowledge his existence and—I hate to admit it, because it makes me feel all sorts of shame—I don't know a whole lot about Eli's family heritage. I don't know whether he wants to be Jewish like his dad or Muslim like his mom. We don't talk about it, because he doesn't like talking about it. I don't think he's ashamed of his culture, but I can imagine when your family is either actively ignoring your existence or talking crap about one of your parents, it causes a bit of confusion on which part of yourself you want to celebrate.

Or maybe I'm making a whole lot of assumptions instead of just asking...

I started my Fuck It list to change myself, but I didn't put anything on it about being a better friend.

When I'm done with the dishes, I go up and knock on Eli's door. He doesn't answer. I knock a little harder until he does. He's got his earphones in and they're blasting music. He doesn't even take them out of his ears.

"Can we talk?" I can't explain why my stomach is twisting. Why I'm so nervous just to ask him to talk to me. But he doesn't take out his earphones. "Eli?"

He sighs, pulls his phone out of his pocket and turns off the music. "Yeah?" His eyes dart everywhere but me. I get that he's mad about his parents, about staying with us, but I'm one of his best friends.

"I just wanted to talk...like about how you're feeling?" My mouth is dry and every word I say feels wrong, like I'm walking on ice that's getting thinner and thinner.

Eli's mouth tightens. "Fucking fantastic." Now he's staring right at me—daring me to ask another stupid question.

"I'm just trying to help."

The sound he makes is something between a laugh and sigh. "Because you can fix my dad screwing up my family?"

"That's not..." Who the hell is he right now? Eli doesn't do the mean, passive-aggressive thing—or so I thought. "Are you serious right now?"

He rubs his forehead. "Am I not allowed to process on my own, Liv?"

I fumble with the bottom of my shirt as my hands start to itch with irritation. I hate this—him being a passive-aggressive turd is unacceptable. But I'm not allowed to say that right now. Not while his whole life is falling apart. "Are you asking for more space?" I say with as much patience as I can muster.

"I'm asking you to just fucking stop. What's the point in talking about stuff that can't be fixed?" He raises his eyebrows for emphasis and then turns around and closes the door in my face.

Fine. Whatever.

It's hard to be a good friend when I'm catching grief about shit that has nothing to do with me.

The next day is a too-hot Tuesday, and the first day of stage rehearsals, and the marker of a regular rehearsal schedule. According to Mrs. G, *This is where it gets real.* Considering the intensity of the few read-throughs we did, I'm—shook. How much more real can it get for this lady? I'm sitting in the gallery, watching Kai onstage with Javier. Mrs. G is blocking act one, scene one. It's a nice break from going straight home with Eli. I get to breathe and focus on something else. I know that sounds insensitive, but he is suffocating me with his silence.

Lennox is sitting next to me and we're doing our bio work together. Our parts don't come onstage until act two. Mrs. G doesn't care if we aren't paying attention as long as we're quiet, so of course Jackie has already been kicked backstage. Dré's back there, too, somewhere, flirting with Steph, the redhead. He's back to normal, and maybe *too* happy since finding out Kmart's really bad at keeping track of their video footage. Without video evidence, they won't pursue his case in court—fingers crossed.

Anyway, that moment between us is so long gone and I can't even be sure it happened.

"What's up with Eli?" Lennox points her pen at him. He's leaning against the wall, watching what's happening onstage. "He's usually kinda—I don't know, upbeat for a mellow guy."

I *don't* want to talk about it. "No clue."

"Trouble in paradise," she says. I cut my eyes at her, and

she holds her hands up in surrender. "Okay, how about we take a break, because..." she waves her hand in my face "...this just got a little too intense for me."

She wants to help paint props, and I'm all for it, because, even as I get up, I can see Eli looking at me. And no, it doesn't mean he wants to talk. Took me a week to figure that one out. He just stares for a few seconds before looking away, as if I'm the one ripping up his perfect two-parent home. And of course, I'm not allowed to tell him not to take it out on me, because he, according to my mother, *just needs time to process his feelings.*

It's almost exactly what he said to me, which makes me feel like they're in cahoots—which I realize is self-centered and borderline lunatic. But seriously, if he looks at me like that one more time, I'll help him process his feelings all right.

There is a group outside painting set pieces. The paint fumes almost knock me off my feet, and Lennox hands me a breathing mask. I'm helping Jackie paint palm trees for our Cyprus scenes when she pulls her mask down and says, "You know what? I've been thinking, and *Othello* is racist as fuck."

Lennox shrugs, and Rodney, who's filming Jackie painting, throws in a "And homophobic. You want to tell me no one in this play is gay? It's the fucking Venetian army. *Everyone* is gay."

"You ain't never lied," Jackie says. "That nigga Shakespeare know he was wrong."

I'm adding some brown to my tree when I hear a kid next to me mumble, *"Christ."* And I know he's saying it to Jackie, and she hears it, too.

Now, I'm kinda saying the same thing in my head, because

Jackie says something is racist about every five minutes, but this guy is white and he's just asking for trouble.

"You got something to say, *David*?" She's looking down at him, batting her lashes whilst rolling her eyes.

David puts down his paintbrush and looks up at her. I don't know him that well, but he was at Kai's party and he's one of those guys who doesn't pick up on social cues all that well, the kind who overexplains when you clearly know what you're doing.

This isn't going to end well.

"I just don't understand how you can say the *N* word while at the same time calling someone out for racism. It's kind of problematic."

Jackie looks at me like, *Did this white dude just call me racist?* Actually, they're both looking at me, and I don't know why, because there is Lennox and a black dude behind me who deserve some of this *you're the other black person in the room. What do you think?* vibe.

Jackie doesn't need backup though; she just comes out of the gate hot. "I can because I'm black, bitch."

David shrugs. "Well, it's offensive. And it makes me uncomfortable."

Jackie laughs. "What? Me saying *nigga*? Nigga. Nigga. Nigga. Nigga. *Nigga.*"

Oh. My. God. Jackie is too much. She's not ghetto, but she can be ratchet as fuck.

The black guy behind me, Markus, sighs. "Yo, Jackie, chill. You're so damn loud. Just tone it down."

But that only adds to the dumpster fire that is this conversation. "You only saying that because you be sucking on white titty," Jackie spits back.

Too many people are laughing, and to be honest I am, too, but I look at David and I also get the nagging need to smooth things over. "I think you both have a point."

Jackie rolls her eyes and goes back to painting her palm tree, unbothered, and David bows his head. "Thank you," he says, but it's in that way that insinuates he's about to keep going to prove *his* point.

"Yeah, don't get ahead of yourself. I said you're allowed to be uncomfortable, that's it."

"You know what." Jackie turns around to face us. "I'm tired of being told I have to tone down my blackness. This is who I am. I have to be louder in order to be heard and seen. This is my first lead role in *four* years, and I've tried out for every single play we've had." She flicks the brush at the building. "And I'm pretty sure I only got this role because it's a rap musical and none of you white bitches can rap."

David starts to open his mouth, but she points at him. "Don't say shit. Until you're black and have a fucking vagina, you don't know *shit*."

I want to say that Jackie might be wrong in some way—but I know she's right. I'm the prime example that *being toned down* doesn't work.

I was so toned down I couldn't even put on a Halloween costume. I couldn't tell the guy I was crushing on how I felt. I can't tell that same guy that he's being an asshole for taking out his frustrations on me when I shouldn't have even been put in the situation to see what I saw.

Not to mention I get so scared of how others see my blackness that I get mad at my mom for being late. Jackie's expression of self might make people uncomfortable, but it's not fair to ask *her* to bend over backward so that everyone else feels comfortable. I've been bending over backward ever since I hit puberty and realized everyone saw my blackness before they saw me.

It ain't comfortable.

We all go back to working, and the vibe is kind of jacked, but soon it's time to go in to work on the musical numbers anyway.

I'm onstage with Dré, and Angelina is behind me just like David, Dré's understudy, is behind him. They shadow us, but David seems to be the only one who knows what a shadow is, because Angelina keeps bumping into me.

I'm trying to keep my cool, because I know she's doing it to be annoying.

Every time she steps on the heel of my shoe or elbows me, she drops an *oh, sweetie. I'm so sorry.* Or my favorite: *Watch where you're going, the mark is right there.* Yeah, bitch, I know where my mark is, thank you.

We're in the wings while Kai and Eli are onstage with their understudies, and we're supposed to be quiet and not talk, because this still counts as the stage to Mrs. G, but Angelina would talk her way out of a muzzle.

"Oh my god, David. I heard about what Jackie said. For what it's worth, I agree with you. She's so extra sometimes."

She's sitting behind me, so her voice is buzzing right in my ear.

I already told Dré what happened outside, because he wanted to know why Markus was mad at Jackie and what it had to do with "a white titty." Dré's a mess right now, because he thinks the whole thing is a big laugh.

Dré pinches my thigh. It's our way of laughing without being super obvious about it. He's looking up at the ceiling and biting his lips to keep silent. If Mrs. G hears us, she'll tear us a new one.

Angelina clears her throat and whispers loudly, "I'm sure *you* think it's funny, but it's not. What she said was wrong."

I can't stop myself. "You weren't even there. How do you know what she said?"

Angelina glances away from me before putting a smile on her face like she's about to answer a dumb question. "Everyone's talking about it. I didn't *have* to be there. Besides, David was, and I want him to know I understand his position."

Oh my god. I know she's not completely wrong. Jackie went way overboard, and David is kind of sulking because I think he was really offended, *but* something in me gets irrationally angry when this girl is involved. She's not the first person to say something slick to me—but I also don't make it a habit to spend ample amounts of time with people who call me basic and step on my heels.

I don't want to start anything—but I also don't like her, so... "The only position you need to figure out is where and when to walk onstage, thank you very much." It was low. And I don't care. If she wants to call me basic, she better figure out how to walk.

Dré lets out a laugh and I won't lie, it kind of gasses me up. My stomach is flipping, and I have to bite my lips to keep from apologizing.

Angelina doesn't say anything else, so I take it as a win.

Mrs. G calls everyone onstage for the party scene, and I'm in it not as Bianca but as an extra. Dré and I are in the back when he wraps his arms around me and shouts at Eli, "Yo, dude, she was literally taking shots at Angelina in the wing. You—"

Eli glances at us, and he gets this look on his face. I don't know how to explain it, because he's never looked at me like this before. "We're working." And he moves in between a few people to get to the front of the stage.

Dré watches him. "Seriously, what the fuck is up with him?"

I want to tell him—I do—but without all the facts, that could do more damage than create clarity. I just tell him what I can. "You know his mom and dad are having problems."

Dré rolls his eyes. "Yeah, but who doesn't have problems? That doesn't mean he has to walk around like fucking Eeyore."

Mrs. G whistles for our attention, and I shrug. Dré's kind of right, but at the same time—I know my mom's right, too. "He needs space to figure it out."

Dré's watching Eli, and I know he's trying to figure out how to make whatever is wrong right. He does that. He's not like Eli or me, who just wait for time to pass before we pick up again without solving whatever we fought about. Dré has to make it right then and there, because he doesn't like the uneasiness that Eli and I just put up with.

That's why we need him—he's our glue. If Eli and I were left to our own devices, we'd grow old never quite making up after some weird, long-forgotten argument.

"It'll be fine," I whisper before moving to one of the groups Mrs. G sorts us into. I need Dré to believe me so that I can, too.

★ ★ ★

When rehearsals are over, Kai offers to drive me home. Since Eli's already taken off with Dré and Lennox is giving me the wiggle eyebrows, I say yes. I don't want to go home to the fortress of solitude anyway, not with Eli brooding up the place. Whether he needs time or not, it's still majorly uncomfortable to be around.

Kai and I are in the student parking lot, talking and kissing, when he asks if I want to go on another date. I'm kind of wondering whether he'll ask me to be his girlfriend—and it occurs to me that maybe my problem is I'm kind of old-school. This is my moment to own it and just ask him to be my boyfriend—and I will.

Eventually.

Somewhere between the talking and kissing, we end up in his back seat, and the kissing evolves from me tasting his lips to craving something more. I'm straddling him, and I can totally feel everything he's packing. It was a good day to wear a skirt. It's loose and all the way up my thighs, where his hands are firmly planted.

We're breathing hard and the windows are getting steamy, and it's prime time for a *Titanic* reenactment, but suddenly he goes from grinding against me to lifting me *off* him.

"Fuck," he says.

Looking at his puffy lips, I'm really contemplating losing my virginity in the back of his car. It doesn't matter *where* as long as it's good, and I *really* think it'll be good with him. He kisses me again like he's thinking exactly what I am, but he pulls away, *again*.

"What?" I'm panting.

"I wanted to talk to you before we got this far."

Kai's a real gentleman, but right now I don't want to talk. I'm ready. Really, *really* ready. I've never been this horny in my life.

He's sliding his hand up my thighs when he lets out a breath. "Wow."

I'm so stunned by the brushing of his fingers over me that I snap my legs closed. "Sorry." I'm trying to open them again, but it's like getting ready to be tickled.

"I'm going to regret this—but we have to talk first."

I sober up a little and I'm sort of starting to freak out. If he tells me he has an STD, I'm going to weep as my V-card slides back into place.

He pulls his hand away and leaves it on my lower thigh. "I'm leaving soon."

Thank Jesus, he's not talking STDs or anything that would send me running to the hills, but I already know this. He's a senior. It's not exactly news.

"I'm not trying to get into anything serious. I want to keep hanging with you, but I know I'm leaving as soon as graduation is over—so—"

"So, you don't want a girlfriend." My stomach drops and I fill up with dread. I hear what he's saying, but it sounds like the *let's have sex and never talk again* spiel.

"I want—look, I tried a long-distance relationship with a girl back home. I got busy, she got busy, I ended up not calling because I didn't want to explain to her why I'd been busy—she's probably still pissed about it. The long-distance thing worked for a month before it just went up in flames."

He looks down. "I don't want that to happen to us—but I'm also really into you."

"Okay." I'm sitting up now. It's weird to have my skirt hiked up while we're talking about how shitty he is—or was.

"I just want to be honest. I really like you and I'm really attracted to you. I mean, you can feel that."

He's still hard, so I'm not arguing. I just don't get what the issue is. We don't have to keep dating after he graduates. We can date *now*.

He pauses. "I'm cool with us hooking up—but only if it's easy."

"No strings," I say.

"That sounds kind of like a fuckboy move. I want strings, but I want us both to be okay with those strings ending in a few months? I think it's better if we go into this as friends instead of trying to have something more."

I'm groaning in my head and wondering why this hot hunk of flesh is doing this to me. I want to say yes, but I also don't want to be someone's sex friend for a few months, then snip, snip: no more strings. Sounds like a sex toy—so… "Can I think about it?" I don't know what else to say.

"Yeah, for sure." Since the mood is dead, we get into the front seats, and he drives me home. He keeps trying to explain. "I just want to be up front."

I'm all understanding and trying not to make him feel awkward, but internally, I'm screaming. I kind of wish he'd just had sex with me and told me after. When I'm old enough to have hindsight, I'll probably be glad he didn't—but my hormones don't listen to logic.

Before I get out, he kisses me, and his hands linger on

my body. I'm tempted—*really* tempted. He's like hugging a giant teddy bear, but with muscles. And his fingers—I'm the only person who's ever touched myself there, and it *so does not* compare.

I fix my skirt and make sure my hair isn't too crazy before I go in. Kai waits to see me inside. He smiles and waves as I open the door. I try to convince myself that I can be the easy-going girl. That I can totally do the *we're not exclusive* thing. But that's a lie. I want someone to want me even if there are thousands of miles between us.

I'm a swan. Which is great and all, but what the hell am I going to do now?

CHAPTER 22

Eli's moved back home with his dad—his mom is still nowhere to be seen, and I don't know how he feels about that or anything. He didn't say more than three things to me the entire time he was in my house, no matter how much I nudged—or then *didn't* nudge per his rude-ass request.

Him needing space has turned into me wanting space from him. I feel guilty, because I'm supposed to be there for him, but how can you be there for someone who pushes you away?

He's not the only person I'm avoiding these days. I haven't answered Kai yet, and now that we have rehearsals every Tuesday and Thursday after school, I see him too often not to come up with something soon. I keep thinking that, if this wasn't my first time, I'd be okay with no strings. Like, I won't get attached if I don't have to think about him every time I think of my first. But it *is* my first time, and I want it to be good and memorable.

Lennox and Jackie are at my house for a weekend slumber party, and they both look at me like I'm stupid when I say it. Lennox shakes her head. "It really doesn't work that way. Whether it's your first time or your fifth, either you want to keep it casual or you don't. I don't think you do."

She clearly hasn't sat on top of Kai, because I'm tempted to keep it *whatever* just to do it again.

Jackie shrugs. "I don't know. I'm not into that casual shit. Either a nigga loves me or he's not getting this pussy."

"So, you're a swan." I explain what Al told me about mating for life.

"Bitch, I did not say I only ever wanted one dick in my whole life! I said he better be into *me* or he better keep walking." She's clapping at me for emphasis. Sometimes I feel like Jackie is used to fighting just to have opinions.

Lennox is lying on my bed like she always does. She's rubbing Twinks's stomach, which is making Twinks's eyes go crazy. "You're not the casual type. Just tell him no."

I start sorting through my flute music, pretending to finger through my parts. I want to tell Lennox she doesn't know what type I am, but she might be right. I don't know, I think my idea has merit. I can be casual with Kai as long as it's not my *first time*.

Lennox and Jackie take out their laptops to edit a film project for drama. I can't concentrate on the sheet music, and to be honest, it's showed in the last few weeks. Mr. Kaminski pulled me aside yesterday to ask if everything was all right with me. It's like he doesn't get that I'm in high school. I have shit to do. I also have a job and, you know, chores. Life is busy, and music isn't all there is.

But now that I'm sitting on my bed packing away my flute, I'm thinking maybe the problem is me. Maybe music isn't all there is to *me*. The more time I spend in theatre, the more I feel alive, and I never get that feeling in band. I mean, I enjoy *performing* in band, I enjoy that moment when we're all on the same wave and we're creating music...but that's about it. I enjoy all the in-between moments more in theatre than I do in band.

Lennox looks up and sighs for the tenth time in a minute. Her legs are sprawled on my purple rag rug and she spins the laptop toward me. "Guys. Look at this and tell me what you think. Your honest opinion. I can't tell anymore."

We watch the short film she's done. It's of her arguing with a puppet. It's funny, kinda deep when they get into the part about what makes us alive, and the editing looks way more professional than a school project. I tell her as much, but she shakes her head.

"Something's not right."

Jackie slams her laptop shut and starts massaging her temples. "You're fucking telling me. Mrs. G says she won't accept my vlog for a grade. She says that not all drama is theatrical. What the fuck does that even mean?"

Twinks is drooling on Jackie's legs, and I think they're becoming good friends, because she picks her up and starts hugging Twinks like her big fat body is a stress ball.

I finish packing up my flute and sit on the bed next to Jackie. "I take it the film projects aren't going well?"

They both look at me like that's not even the half of it.

Jackie puts Twinks down. "Like, for real, I love Mrs. G and all, but the bitch is backward. She thinks we have to do everything the way she did back in the fucking colonial days in order to have a career. And don't get me started on the fact that she doesn't think YouTube or what it takes for me to plan, film, and edit these videos is real acting. She thinks the internet has only done harm to the art and that I'm not serious and—" Jackie's starting to cry, but she's looking up at the ceiling to keep the tears from falling. "It's just bullshit."

She stands up and paces the room, and her hair falls over her shoulder, so we can't see her actually cry.

Lennox is grinding her teeth. "It is. I'm busting my ass on this, and I know no matter what I do, it's not going to be good enough. Like, what is the point of doing any of this if we're never going to be good enough?"

I've heard this before. Actually, I've heard it in my room before, when Dré and Eli tried to get Mr. Kaminski to add them to our last spring concert as their own act. Mr. Kaminski said it wasn't the time or place and that they had a lot to learn about musicianship before commanding a stage—and he still rides Dré's ass for not trying hard enough in class.

I won't let my girls give on up on their dreams just because our teachers are too old to get what's going on in the world around them. "To hell with Mrs. G's opinion. She might be our teacher, but she isn't the law."

Lennox shrugs. "But she's in control of my grades."

"Okay," I say. "But she can't be in control of how you see yourself. You know—you guys are so incredibly talented. Jackie, you have almost a million subscribers. That's almost a *million* people who watch you. Now—imagine what it will be like in five years or ten."

She looks at me, wiping her eyes to keep her mascara from smearing. "O, I get what you're saying, but I don't want to be a YouTuber for the rest of my life. I want to act. I want to be in movies, maybe direct and produce them."

I look between them. "You guys don't see it because you're *in* it, but what you're doing now, being *you* and not being what Mrs. G wants *everyone* to be, is how you get where you want to go."

It's like how Mr. Kaminski praises Zora for feeding off his every word and playing her part the exact way he wants her to—no deviation. We're playing out *his* vision, his dream. I know he wants us to grow and be better, but what about Dré and Eli? If they'd listened to him, they'd still be singing cover songs in the garage with just me listening while I do my homework.

"If you do it the way she wants, you'll get a good grade and feel like shit. If you do it your way and keep perfecting *your* way, you'll get harsh critiques, but feel amazing. You'll attract the people who love the way *you* do it."

Jackie's holding Twinks again and looking at Lennox. "This bitch needs an office. She's like a life coach."

It's not me. It's Dré—he was the one with the balls to do it his way. And it's Eli's dedication that kept them perfecting what they do. They're the reason I've got the guts to do this Year of Fuck It.

Then I realize—what does that say about me? I'm not that different from Zora. I go to class and play out Mr. Kaminski's vision—that is, I *did*. But now that I've been doing *Othello*, I've been living out my own vision of me. I know I've got a small role and I'm barely into rehearsals, but I'm really doing it.

I get goose bumps.

Lennox is reaching for her laptop again. "You're right. Mrs. G is going to shit on whatever I turn in, so I might as well do something I'm proud of, right?"

Jackie shakes her head. "But what about me? I can't turn in the vlog. A year's worth of work that I've put my all into that's probably more put together than what everyone else is doing—no offense," she adds to Lennox, "won't fly with her."

Lennox holds up her finger. "No, but you *can* make a film about *you*. Not *you*, but *Jackie the YouTuber*."

I pick up what Lennox is putting down. "Oh my god— like a biography. Like Beyoncé."

Jackie's smiling now. "Biiiiitch." She puts Twinks on my pillows and grabs her laptop. But before she starts typing up a plan, she looks at me. "Can we pause a second to acknowledge how our girl just talked us off a cliff though."

I shrug. "I mean, you guys talked me off the casual sex cliff, least I can do."

Lennox is pulling out paper and a pen. "Or we can make it a mini biography about O losing her virginity."

I pull out my math book. "And this is when I exit the conversation."

They're laughing at me, but it's better than when they were crying over their dreams, so I count it as a win.

They're deep in the zone with their respective projects, so I slip off my bed and pull my list off my mirror.

1. BE BOLD—DO THE THINGS THAT SCARE ME.
2. LEARN TO TAKE A COMPLIMENT.
3. STAND OUT INSTEAD OF BACK.
4. GO ON A DATE.
5. STOP CRUSHING AND MOVE ON.
6. DON'T LET BITCHES TRY ME.
7. FIND SOME FUCKING CONFIDENCE.

I've been pretty good about doing most of it. I'm actually proud of myself, but I'm adding a new entry to the list:

8. IT.

I'm not about to write down *Have sex*, because my mom could walk in and see this, not to mention I don't need Jackie snickering about how precious I am. But I'm ready.

I want to take this next step, and if putting it on the list makes that happen, then I'm underlining it twice. But I'm not exactly comfortable with the deal Kai's offering—so the question is, if not with him, then who?

I'm at rehearsals again, and before it starts, Cleo's waving me over to the curtains. We've been chattier, but…not a whole lot. But at least we're not actively avoiding each other.

"I heard what happened with Jackie and David," Cleo says and she's glaring around like Jackie's going to pop out of the curtains. "I told you she starts shit."

This is kind of old news by now. I don't mean because it happened a long time ago, more like because, between then and now, Markus was caught trying to have sex with his girlfriend in the changing room and that's all everyone has been talking about when Mrs. G isn't in earshot. "Yeah," I say, "she didn't really start that."

Cleo's shaking her head. "The thing is, everyone thinks you're a part of their little posse and, you know, *birds of a feather flock together.*"

Oh my god. Cleo is talking like our grandmother now, and I can't. I think someone told her she had an old soul once, and she took it to heart.

"Cleo, it's cool."

But then she does the slow eye roll, which means she's not done. "Well, remember how I told you not to date anybody here? Angelina saw you taking off with Kai, and Rodney's been talking about how y'all were all boo'd up at some party, and it's not looking good."

I'm not going to lie, I'm really irritated that Angelina is talking about me. And I *really* don't like knowing she's watching my every move. Kai and I were smart enough to wait until everyone left before we got hot and heavy, but I still feel violated.

Still, that's for me to be angry about. Cleo's looking at me like it's her problem. I don't get why she cares. She's trying to make me feel bad about my friends, about Kai, and there is literally nothing wrong in either of those departments. "I don't even know what you mean by *not looking good.* There is nothing wrong with me hanging out with Kai, and—maybe you shouldn't care so much about what other people think."

I'm saying this, but the me from the Halloween party is chiming in with *maybe I should.* Why can't I enjoy my life without other people having commentary about it? No. I'm not going back to being that sad bitch who cares way too much about how other people see her.

She sighs and throws up her hands. "I'm just saying maybe you should care a little more. It's *your* reputation." She sounds like my mom and I swear, as much as our moms bicker, they are the same person, because I know this is where Cleo gets the whole *protect your reputation* thing. "People know you hang around Lennox, and when you and Kai are the *last* to leave the parking lot, people talk."

"Then let them talk." I don't know how to express to her just how much none of this should matter—I mean, not really. What I do and with who is *my* business.

Cleo shrugs. "I'm just saying. That's all. Watch your back."

By the time rehearsals start, I'm thinking about going back to avoiding Cleo. She's probably more problematic than David, and considering I just heard him try to explain to Stephanie why tampons and pads aren't the most environmentally friendly products, that's saying a lot.

I'm looking around our circle while Mrs. G reads the schedule for today. It's so jacked up, but I feel like they're all thinking about me and imagining what happened between Kai and me. I look across the circle, and Eli's eyes move from me to Kai.

I know I shouldn't care, because nothing happened—and even if it had, I shouldn't be ashamed—but it's hard to actually take the advice to not care about what other people think. Especially when that person is Eli.

When we break to set up for blocking, Dré's giving me *the look*. The one that says I should just come out and say what's on my mind before he mines it out of me.

"People are talking," is all I say.

He sighs. "So. You like dude?" At least he's not calling him Big Hawaii.

I shrug. "Maybe. I don't know if it's going anywhere."

Dré's got a weird look on his face as we grab a few plastic oak trees to put onstage. "Then fuck what everybody else has to say. Just do you."

Markus calls him over to help find the helm of the ship.

Dré's right. As soon as I get home, I'm adding another thing to the list: *9. Fuck gossip.*

After the first hour of practice, Mrs. G has us pair off to work lines in different parts of the theatre. Dré and I are working on our scene in the sound booth. We can see everything from up here, and we've kept the light off, so no one can see us snooping.

When Mrs. G steps out of the theatre, we use the mic system to make demonic noises at David and Angelina. They have no idea where the sounds are coming from until Lennox points to us in the booth.

We lie on the floor with time still left on the clock until a run-through of act two.

"Kmart officially dropped the charges," he says. His voice is quiet, so I know he's just keeping me updated. He doesn't *really* want to talk about it.

"Thank Jesus."

"Yeah." He rolls onto his side, and his fingers graze my side. He's nudging me.

"What's up?"

Dré's looking down, picking at some of the wires on the floor. "Thanks." His eyes flick up at me.

I keep telling him that our friendship is unconditional, but I think it's going to take time for it to sink in. "You know what," I say, "I'm going to need something in return for all this friendship shit." I smile so he knows I'm joking.

He lies back again with his arms behind his head. "As long as it doesn't get me thrown in jail."

"*Dré.*"

"Too soon?"

"Too soon."

He's laughing that easy laugh, and I'm thinking maybe I *should* ask him to sleep with me. It makes sense. He's someone I trust, and I'd rather think of him as my first than a guy who told me I wasn't worth the long-distance heartache. I mean, it is the Year of Fuck It.

Plus—he'd never tell anyone. I'd never have to worry about it getting out. I don't think Kai would brag about it either, but I want a safe *first*.

"You could sleep with me," I say it before I can not say it.

His eyes go wide, and then I realize what a *massive idiot* I am. I just asked my best friend to sleep with me.

"I'm kidding." He's stone still, and I keep saying it. "I'm kidding. I'm just kidding."

"Jesus, Liv." He's not laughing, but he's not mad. I don't know what he is. I just know I'm a freak, and that was probably the dumbest thing I've let come out of my mouth since that time I told my sister I came up with the catchphrase Got Milk. I was seven, and I somehow forgot I'd picked it up from a commercial.

"Dré, it was a joke."

Mrs. G calls us all down to the stage, and I get up avoiding his eyes, because I think he knows it wasn't.

CHAPTER 23

Dré brings up the "joke" whenever we're close enough for him to whisper about it in my ear. *You want a slice of pizza? What else, a Coke, my penis?* Or like when I was at my locker and he snuck up behind me to ask, *Looking for my penis?*

It's not funny. He's not even clever with it. So, when he leans into me, in the middle of rehearsal and says, "You're begging for it," I scream at him. Loud. Everyone stops what they're doing, including Mrs. G, and stares at me. He was just saying *his line*. I'm supposed to say, *Just stay with me,* but instead I screamed, "Enough with your fucking penis!"

Mrs. G has me sit out, not for cursing, but for breaking character, and Angelina fills in as Bianca. Fucking great.

Dré doesn't say anything else to me for the rest of rehearsal, and it was an overall mess of a day. Everyone missed cues, and we all sang out of tune. Mrs. G yelled and said we sounded like feral cats. She wasn't wrong.

She schedules an extra rehearsal to punish us, and we do it all over again on Friday. I refrain from screaming at Dré, but we are completely out of sync, because I can't look him in the eye without knowing he's thinking of a way to make fun of me. It doesn't help that Angelina is having a field day with it. When I pass by the dressing rooms, I hear her retelling the story like everyone didn't already witness it.

Needless to say, I'm surprised to see Dré at my door Saturday afternoon. My mom is gone and I'm in the middle of binge-watching all the *Housewives* episodes I've missed. "If you say one more thing about your penis, I will chop it off."

Dré slides into my house as I swing the door closed.

"Lock it, we don't trust people around here," I say, walking back to my room. I don't even keep my show paused. I press Play as Dré sits on my bed and pets Twinks. After about five minutes, he closes my laptop.

"Liv." He's not laughing or smiling or doing his usual Dré business, and I swear, if he tells me he's committed another crime, I'm getting new friends.

"What?" I'm actually curious, because he still hasn't made another joke.

"I'm sorry." He's going to have to be specific.

I lean back against my headboard. "Oh?" I really like dragging out Dré apologies. They get more flattering the longer I hold out.

He takes a deep breath, and I realize he's nervous. Which makes me nervous. He opens his mouth to say something, but thinks better of it. "Okay, I'm going to do something and if you want me to stop, just tell me."

Oh. My. God.

He's got this look in his eye, and he's leaning toward me,

and though my heart is in my throat and my whole body seizes with panic, I'm not moving, because I low-key want to know if what I think is happening is happening.

And then he's kissing me.

It's slow at first, and I'm thinking he might not be as good as Kai, but then the kiss gets deeper. My hands are on his chest, and then my fingers grip his shirt.

He moves in between my legs and I'm trying to get over the shock of Dré being on top of me, running a hand over my boobs. I don't have the same cloudy lust I did with Kai; I'm kind of stuck in my head, because *it's Dré*, but I also feel kind of…at home. Comfortable.

Fuck it. We're doing this.

I let him take off my shirt, then my bra, and we're both down to our underwear and staring at each other.

His mouth is on my boob and just when I think I'm not going to get the lusty cloud thing, it's there—and I think it's there for him, too, because we go from these soft, deep kisses to pawing and moaning.

He stops to grab his pants and pulls out a condom. It takes him a while to rip it, and I kind of sober up a little. It's broad daylight, and I realize he can see all of me. I pull my knees as close to my chest as they get while he's putting it on and when he turns to look at me, he half smiles.

"I—" Dré stops. He's not speechless often. He's like me. We almost always have something to say. "Regardless of how this goes, I love you."

I'm not brave. I'm a chickenshit pansy because instead of telling him how I feel, or that I get what he means—we're still *us*—I say, "What the fuck is about to happen? Is your condom gonna pop off and blind me?"

"Jesus, Liv." My joke isn't releasing any of the tension. It only builds as he pulls my leg down and runs his hand up my thigh. His fingers slide over me and then inside of me as he's kissing my neck.

I'm not going to think about where he learned how to do this. It will ruin the moment. So instead I hold on to him and ride the wave that's climbing. It's *good*. All those pamphlets about not having sex or being terrified of letting boys put their hands in your pants… It's all a goddamn lie.

Maybe it's because it's Dré. I know him, and he knows me, and our hearts are beating at the same time as he lies on top of me. But it is better than good.

He's starting to slide into me, and even though he's going slow, there's this tightness and before I can tell him to pause, he's pushing all the way in and I yell, "Jesus fucking Christ."

"Should I stop?" He pulls halfway out, staring at me with wide eyes.

"No." It did hurt—but he also feels good. I didn't anticipate the crazy, intense goodness radiating in me.

"Christ, Liv." His voice rises an octave. "I thought I fucking broke you."

"Broke me?" A laugh bubbles out of me. Mainly because I feel kinda high. Like I could cry, because this is so crazy.

He starts laughing, too. "I don't fucking know. Jesus, Liv—*my god*."

I know what he means. I know why everybody talks about it now. I totally get it.

We're lying next to each other, naked and under the covers. I don't know why we decided to get under the covers. We've already seen each other naked. I've got my head on his chest and I'm afraid of what we're going to do next. It's like our nakedness left us overexposed.

I should have thought of that.

He's rubbing his thumb over my spine, and our skin is sticking from sweat. "Why are you so quiet?" Dré says. He's one to talk. He hasn't said anything in the last twenty minutes either.

"I'm thinking."

"About Eli?" He just drops it on me.

My mouth goes dry and I lift up to look at him. I need to know exactly why *that* of all things came out of his mouth. He sits up, and he's got on such a poker face I'm at a loss for how to interpret it. I settle on, "No." But I think I waited too long.

He lets out a long breath and rests his head against my headboard. He's looking down at me through thick lashes, and the lust cloud is completely gone. We're both sober as hell. "Because that's what you do. Remember the time we went to get ice cream without Eli, and you made me stop at the grocery store and we bought him a pint?"

I sit up. "This is *not* us getting ice cream, Dré."

He laughs. "Or the time we went to the mall without him, and you bought him that stupid shirt with the leaves on it." He's got a small smile on his face, and he's shaking his head. "It's obvious. The two of us never do anything together without you figuring out a way to make Eli feel better about being left out." He gently pinches my chin between his finger and thumb. "It's okay if you are. I'm used to it."

The *fuck*. There is a bitterness in his voice, and I can't tell if he's complaining about it or just stating an observation. "If you think that, why'd you have sex with me?"

Dré's taking deep breaths and I can't tell if he's shutting down or gearing up to tell me the truth.

My stomach twists.

"Because you asked me to." He's got the half smile on his face again. "And I love you. You're my girl no matter what. I'm always gonna be here for you. Whatever you need." He's leaning over and kissing me again, and I feel like there is something twisted about what we're doing, but the kiss is deep and his tongue is in my mouth like he wants more of whatever I have.

He's breathing heavy again, and it makes my stomach flutter. Next thing I know he's fishing in his pants for another condom, and we're wrapped in each other again. It takes him longer this time, and I'm glad, because it takes me a while to get Eli out of my head.

This time after we finish, we get dressed, because my mom's going to be home in the next hour. I'm looking at Dré, zipping up his jeans, and I feel like I took something from him.

I don't know any more if he meant he loves me in that unconditional, we'll-be-friends-forever kind of way, or if he *loves* me loves me and sees no future in it because of Eli. I'm thinking how Lennox said I'm not the casual type, and how I should say no to Kai. Now I'm wondering if I should have said no to Dré. He's still smiling at me, and I can't let him leave without knowing.

"Do you *love* me love me?"

He looks up, and he's thinking. I don't know how hard of a question this is to him, but the wait is killing me. "I don't know."

What. The. Fuck. *"Dré."*

He laughs, and I swear I want to hit him. He's being so cavalier about it. He sits next to me. "I love you, but I feel like I don't own you."

I don't even know what that means. "I didn't know the two were mutually exclusive."

"They are. When someone says they love you, it means they don't want you to love anyone else." This is about as open as Dré's been with me in his entire life. Then again, I don't ask him questions like this often. "I said it because I love *you*. Maybe I always have. But I like the way we are. We don't have to change it, if you don't want to."

"So, this was just sex for you?" I don't know what I want to hear from him, but I know I'm not getting it.

"No. I'm not dead inside. Jesus, Liv."

He's got this look in his eyes, and I know he's debating something in his head. I just want him to spill it, because we've been naked together. So there's no point in keeping secrets now. "Just say it."

"What?" He licks his lips.

"Dré." I don't even have to say anything else before he's laughing again.

"Okay. I'm happy you asked me. It means a lot." He kisses my forehead. "That, and you were in my spank bank. How could I resist."

And we're back to normal Dré. "Jesus."

"I'm serious. That waist, them thighs, and that *ass*. You have no idea how many towels have gone to—"

"JESUS, DRÉ." I'm thinking of the towel I found under his bed and I'm—sorta grossed out but somewhat flattered. This is weird.

"We just had sex—twice. How are you embarrassed? I can tell you these things now." He's massaging my shoulders as we head downstairs, and to be honest, I feel good. We did it. And *it* was amazing. *And* we're still the same. I mean, not exactly the same. But I don't regret this. I wanted good and memorable, and this is probably as good and memorable as it gets.

We go to the kitchen. I'm starving, and since he's looking over my shoulder, I can guess he is, too. "Thanks. For…" I gesture between us. "I could have done with fewer penis jokes though."

"I was nervous." He's grabbing straight lunch meat and cheese. No bread. Savage. "Can we agree not to tell Eli? He's been acting like a dick as it is."

Dré doesn't know all of what Eli's going through, and I still can't tell him. But I agree that we don't tell Eli about *this*. It's just our thing. Besides, it wouldn't matter to Eli, not as long as I'm still here to be his emotional pillow when he's done giving me the silent treatment.

There is a part of me, I won't lie, that does feel weird about how Eli is drifting further away while Dré and I are getting about as close as two people can—but I don't regret it.

We stop eating and stare at each other until we're laughing.

I don't regret Dré at all.

CHAPTER 24

We're supposed to be keeping it a secret. And at first, it's easy, because Sunday I don't see Dré, not in person. But by the time rehearsal comes around on Tuesday, he's touched me at least twenty different times.

Dré has always been touchy, but at my locker he rubbed my lower back. At lunch, he rubbed pizza sauce off my lip and his eyes lingered. I get it. I look at him a little different now, too. I see him without his clothes when he's walking or leaning on the props wall looking for his sword. But right now, as I'm bent over the table, trying to get my pencil that's rolled to the wall, he's behind me—all up on my ass—and because he thinks we're alone, he feels on my waist.

This is a *high traffic* room. "Not discreet," I say, nudging him off.

"Sorry." His eyelids are kinda heavy, and now that I know

what that look means, I'm thinking of all the times he's given it to me and I thought it was his *I'm bored* look. I really do not know how to read guys. I thought I did, but they're sneaky little bastards.

He's smirking with his hand back firmly on my waist, and he's sorta leaning in…and then I am, too.

"Y'all smash?" It's Jackie, and yes, she's loud as hell. Her voice echoes off the brick walls, and I can't figure out why I ever thought I liked either of these people.

Dré's pretending to pull something out of my hair—which is in a bun, so we look suspect as hell.

She's giggling now. "Fuuuuuuck. You did. I have a fuck-dar. I knew it. I can smell the sex on you."

"Jackie, shut the fuck up." We both say it just as I hear a big sigh as Eli walks in, grabs his book bag, and walks out.

She makes a face like *whoops*, and when we leave, Eli doesn't make eye contact with me at all. He hasn't in a long time. He's been eating lunch with us but keeps his earphones in, and honestly the "space" thing has gone on long enough.

Worse, we're rehearsing the scene where Iago (Kai) gets Cassio (Dré) to talk about fucking Bianca (me) while Othello (Eli) hides behind a curtain. I'm waiting to go out onstage and yell at Dré and throw a handkerchief at him. The understudies are deep in the wings, and thank god Angelina isn't shadowing me, because the tension growing between Eli and me is palpable.

Eli is in front of me, because we don't have the set he's supposed to be hiding behind, and Mrs. G has Kai and Dré do their part over and over again. Eli and I are pretty much going to be waiting for an eternity.

"How are you?" I ask Eli. It feels like forever since I've talked to him. I tap his shoulder, and he stiffens.

Onstage it's like nothing in the world bothers him—and lately, his deranged Othello has been kind of spot-on.

"Eli."

"I'm trying to focus, Liv."

"Right." I don't mean to sound like an ass, but I don't know why I'm getting this cold shoulder. All I did was stop him from potentially murdering his father with kitchen appliances. And I get he's got stuff going on at home, but he's not the first kid to have parents split up. I don't even have a dad.

I don't know how to get back on track with him if he's not willing to just—work with me. I gave him space, but now I don't know what else to do.

"Seriously, Eli?"

He doesn't turn or look at me or do anything to show he's listening.

"Fine. Shut everybody out. See how that works for you." I know I shouldn't have said it. But I'm tired of it. For some reason, this feels personal. He's still nice to everyone else. I get that he was mad about me not telling him what I saw, but *come on*. If he can't see that I was put in a really shitty position, then he's the ass, not me.

Mrs. G has Kai and Dré come to the wings and sit where Eli and I are. We're all on standby as she works another scene with Lennox and Jackie.

Dré's sitting next to me, and for once he's not feeling me up. Kai's not really giving me eye contact, and when he finally does, he raises his brows, like I'm some new kid he hasn't been introduced to yet. I know I've put off answering him, and now that I've had sex with Dré, I really don't think I could do the same thing with Kai. I don't know him well enough.

Sure, he's hot and fun to talk to, and he took me on two dates, but I wouldn't know what to do with him that moment *after* sex. I feel like all we are is the lust cloud, and when it's gone, we have nothing to fall back on. It'll make me feel empty, and I should probably tell him no instead of avoiding him.

I *will* tell him, right after rehearsal.

Dré leans his head against the curtain. "You know, I really don't know how anybody could believe I'm talking about sex. The shit Mrs. G is making me do is rated PG. I look more like I'm rubbing a towel between my ass cheeks than fucking you."

The way he said it, *fucking you.* It was kind of different than the way he said the rest of the sentence. Like he wasn't talking about character me, but *me* me. And it doesn't help that he *looked* at me with *the eyes* as he said it.

Eli's scrutinizing gaze slides over to us, and I know he heard it, too. He says something under his breath, but I'm sitting too far away to hear.

Dré heard him though. "You'd be surprised."

Dré and Eli lock eyes.

Eli breaks the silence. "Go fuck yourself."

"Nah, buddy. I already got enough ass on my plate." To everyone else, Dré looks like he's just joking—like he doesn't care—but I see the way his jaw is set like he's waiting for Eli to pick the fight so he'll be justified in popping off.

Eli looks at me, and I feel like I look guilty. I know they're talking about me.

"Dré," I hiss.

Then Eli tilts his head and looks between us. He's really taking me in for the first time in weeks. "You fucked him." He says it as a statement, not a question, and I'm about to deny it but I feel my eyes dart away from his face as I say no.

Kai's watching us, and he clearly doesn't know what we're talking about, because he says, "We haven't actually. You can chill." Kai gives a pointed look to Angelina, because he thinks Eli's talking about the parking lot rumor she undoubtedly started. Then Kai gives me a sympathetic look, as if he's sorry they're discussing something so private. So between *us*.

My throat knots as I give him a small smile and pray to god everyone just stops talking.

Eli laughs, and it's dark. He's back in the place I thought I dragged him out of. "I guess she didn't mention fucking Dré to you either?" He shrugs as if to say, *Tough luck, big guy*.

Dré squints his eyes. "You wanna go?" Dré switches to Spanish. He's much better at cursing people out in Spanish. At least, I think he is, because I never know what he's saying in Spanish. I just know that when he gets mad, he makes less sense, because he starts switching between languages.

"Try it," Eli says.

"Stop." Neither of them pays any attention to me. "*Stop.* Seriously."

Eli flinches away from me like my words have touched him. He gets up and moves as far as he can away from us. Dré leaves and—I don't know where he goes, but Kai is still there staring at me.

"Look. I've been waiting for you to get back to me—but how about we just call it a no?" He gets up and disappears into the curtains.

Perfect. I have no clue how to salvage this.

And then Angelina, of all the understudies sitting circled up on the floor, looks at me, jaw on the floor. "Damn," she says. What's worse is...she kind of looks like she feels sorry for me.

It's the day before we break for winter, and I'm sitting in front of the podium, as usual, as Mr. Kaminski gives us a speech on how we're all doing so horribly bad. He's not far off.

I keep trying to make eye contact with Eli, but he won't look at me. He hasn't talked to me or ridden to school with Dré or I since rehearsal last week. I get that he's mad, but honestly—I don't get *why*. He's taking out his anger on Dré and me, and he needs a freaking intervention, because this is the longest we've ever gone without talking since I've met him and it's starting to drive me crazy.

Maybe he feels like he's on his own little island and Dré and I are moving on without him, but it's not true—he just won't take any of the life rafts we keep sending out.

Zora's shaking a paper in front of my face as I watch Eli put his music in his folder and pick up his stand. "Earth to Ollllliiiviaaa." Zora can be so fucking extra.

I look at the paper. It's a sign-up sheet for the flute quartet, and it only has one name on it. Zora's. I don't have the time for the quartet this year. I didn't even like it that much last year. Playing Christmas songs on loop at the mall, or who-ever donates to the music program to have us, is a one-way ticket to lifelong insanity.

"I can't, Zora. I have musical rehearsals." There are plenty of other flutes to take my spot.

She's looking at me like that's not a legitimate excuse. "I know. I play in the pit."

It's totally not the same thing but I just say, "Okay," while packing up my flute. I've got my eye on Eli. I want to catch him before he bolts for lunch. I have no idea where he spent it the last few days, even though I followed him once. He changes locations, apparently. "That's good for you. Maybe you have all the time in the world, but I don't."

"I don't get it. You're in the music program, but you're spending all your time doing theatre stuff. Obviously, the problem is you think you can do it all. Life is about *choices*, Olivia. Choices." Zora's growling at me, and I swear this girl needs some kind of help because she's kind of tightly wound, but I *really* don't have the time for this.

I get up, shove my flute case in my locker—I don't even bother taking it home to practice anymore—and corner Eli at his locker. "Can we talk?"

He's taking off his glasses and putting them in his case. Locking his locker. Putting his glasses in his book bag—it's like I'm not even here.

"You're just going to completely ignore me? Do I not matter at all to you?" I'm starting to shake. I've spent almost six months fighting off a crush that has pretty much consumed me, so this silent treatment hurts more than when we were just friends.

I'm looking at the frown on his face, wishing I could somehow make him smile. I *want* to make him happy, and I know that's not my job. But I care.

He tilts his head, adjusting his book bag on his back, and then scratches at an eyelash. His eyes flicker to me and then back toward the floor. "Just not worth the time." And then he moves around me and heads out the door.

I just stand there, trying to control my breathing, because I'm stuck between following him, wrestling him to the ground and making him hurt as much as I do, and—crying. And I'm trying to blink back the tears because I *will not* embarrass myself by crying in the band room.

Dré is in front of me with his book bag over one shoulder. "What did he say to you?" He's looking at my face, and I can see he wants any excuse to fight. That's Dré—if he can't fix something, then he'll destroy it, but I'm not about to be his partner in crime.

"Nothing," I say low, between tight lips. I don't want anyone to hear the creak in my voice. Hell, *I* don't want to hear it because I can barely hold back the tears burning my eyes and nose. I don't know what's worse, being humiliated by what Eli said or being embarrassed by how it's made me feel.

I swallow the shame. If I really believe it was nothing, then I won't have to feel like this.

Dré gently grabs my arm, and I can see it in his eyes that he's not buying what I'm selling. "I get that he's upset. But if he makes you cry, it's over." He doesn't say anything else as we head to lunch, and I realize we're on the verge of World War III again, except I can't wait on the sidelines until it all blows over. Because now, I'm in it, too.

CHAPTER 25

It's Christmas break, but that means nothing to the theatre; we have practice three days a week. And we need it; I think we're giving Mrs. G an ulcer, so I'm not even going to complain.

I'm riding with Lennox and Jackie during a break to pick up the cupcakes and sandwiches Mrs. G ordered from the grocery store.

They're arguing about the jazz Lennox is playing. Jackie says it's that weird shit her grandma plays real loud when she's trying to be sexy for her granddad. She's gagging and begging Lennox to turn it off.

I need to tell them what happened—I'm surprised Angelina hasn't already spread it around. I keep waiting for the stares.

Fuck it. "I slept with Dré." I blurt it out so I don't psych myself out again.

"I told ya ass," Jackie says to Lennox. She turns around to

look at me. "Was it good? Please tell me he laid it down. I got on water-based mascara—I can't afford to cry over limp dick."

Jackie makes it both harder and easier to tell them what happened.

Lennox looks at me from the rearview mirror. "I told you he was a gentle lover."

I want to gag. "Please stop reminding me."

"Did you know that there is a matriarchal village somewhere in China where they share men? It's probably one of the most peaceful and powerful places on earth."

Jackie shakes her head. "Bitch, I ain't sharing nothing."

Lennox shoves Jackie back into her seat. "Put your damn seat belt back on." She looks at me again. "Why you look like that though?"

I tell them the rest of it. About Eli finding out but not really knowing for sure, and Kai. Lennox rolls her eyes and I'm waiting for the *I told you so*. It never comes, but she does share a look with Jackie.

Jackie looks back at me again. "Okay, all transparency. I knew that already. You know Angelina can't see some shit like that and not say anything."

I roll my eyes. *Great.* "Everybody knows?" I am not in the mood for this. Also—and I *really* hate this but—I feel dirty. Guilty, like I've sullied my good name now that people know I've had sex. I know that doesn't make sense, but it's how I feel and I can't shake it.

Jackie sucks her teeth. "Girl, you know like half the department has had some sex scandal that involves a lot more than you having sex with your best friend, probably in your room like some fucking ABC Family special." She's waving her hands around like she's batting away my insecurities. "Besides, I only know because she told Rodney, and he's not telling anybody."

I try to ignore how Jackie has guessed correctly how vanilla I am—it's nothing to be ashamed about but sometimes things just sting—and bring the conversation back to Eli. "Well, as comforting as that is, Eli's pissed."

Lennox is looking at me in the mirror again. "You're not responsible for Eli's feelings." That's all she says. I wish it were that easy.

I sit with it for a little while, because I *do* feel responsible. I know so much of what's going on and—when I think back on it, he's been there for me at all my low points, and the one time I was supposed to be there for him, I kind of sucked at it.

"So," Lennox says, "this mean you definitely don't have feelings for Eli anymore?"

I look out the window. As much as I want to say I don't, I just—can't. There is something that has me stuck on Eli, and I wish I could unstick myself, but feelings aren't that simple. "I don't know."

Jackie lets out a small laugh. "Girl, you are scandalous."

We get the food, and I'm carrying the cupcakes back to the car when Lennox grabs both my shoulders. "You are never responsible for someone else's feelings. Say it."

I mumble it back. It doesn't feel true.

"Say it louder."

"I'm not responsible for anyone else's feelings."

"Ever." Her dreads look light brown in the sunlight, and I've just noticed she's got a tiny nose piercing. It's rose gold and almost blends into her brown freckled nose.

"Ever." I wish I were as strong as her. She knows everything. She's kinda kick-ass, and I don't know where I'd be if we hadn't partnered in Bio II.

She hugs me and smells like flowers and fresh air. She really might be a witch.

I place the cupcakes on the table backstage, and after everyone attacks them like mannerless heathens, Cleo lingers by the table and I know she's going to start.

"What, Cleo," I say.

Angelina's snickering with her usual group by the wings. They're sitting in a circle, and I know they're talking about me, because Javier turns to look at me and snaps his head around really fast when I catch him. Fuck my life.

Eli's nowhere to be found, as usual. Don't know why I care. I need to stop caring so much about everyone else and just focus on myself.

"I didn't say anything." She takes her slow time getting a cupcake. It's not that hard. Reach in, pick it up, and go. I'm still getting a sandwich when she sighs again.

"Oh my god, just spit it out already, Aunt Rachel."

She cuts her eyes at me. "Don't call me outside of my name—especially when I haven't ratted you out."

I turn on her. "What is there to rat me out about?"

Then she rolls her eyes. "Girl, everyone's talking about how you slept with Dré."

I sit my sandwich down. "Cleo. Why the fuck do you care?" I'm at my limit with her morally superior lectures about who I hang out with and how I spend my time with *my* friends. I refuse to let everyone have an opinion about what I did.

Cleo's staring at me, wide-eyed. "I care because you're my family, and I'm trying to look out for you. Your name is coming up a lot, and you haven't even been here for a good two months."

I shrug. "And. What exactly is *your problem*, Cleo?"

She's staring at me, bug-eyed, and I'm aware that we sound just like our moms, but I really don't give a fuck because, to be honest, Cleo is a busybody just like nosy, always-has-something-to-say Aunt Rachel. "You want to know what my problem is? You literally just waltzed into my space, haven't put in any work, and you're all anybody has been talking about. Everybody knows we're cousins, so they *all* come to me to talk about you. Like I have the fucking tea."

I'm holding up my hands, saying, "Hold the fuck up," over and over because I'm still stuck on *haven't put in any work*. She honestly thinks I just *waltzed* into my role. Like I didn't bust my ass—like I don't bust my ass in every rehearsal? "I've been working as hard as anyone, and I don't even see why it matters so much to you. You didn't even try out for a role!"

It hits me. Cleo is jealous. She joined theatre and hasn't tried out for a single production because she's terrified of failing—and she's taking it out on me.

Cleo sucks her teeth. "You know what. I'm not doing this with you right now. You've clearly taken a page from Jackie's book, because you're making a fucking scene."

I want to tell her it's more than what she's done her whole time in the theatre program, but I stop myself. It's petty. She doesn't deserve that. I used to be her. Trapped in the shell of my mother and too timid to do anything that mattered—terrified of what everyone thought of me. She doesn't even see it, and she won't until she decides she's tired of it.

I just let her walk away and grab my sandwich. Shockingly, she's right about one thing. I caused a scene, because Angelina's eating this up.

She's got this smirk on her face, and all my petty is coming to the surface. The fact that Eli's still avoiding me like I have the plague, the fact that everyone is talking about me and my sex life because of this girl who can't shut her fucking mouth...

"You," I say. Now everyone *is* looking at me, and they know who I'm talking about, because I'm pointing at her. "The reason Dré slept with me and not you is because you're a pathetic piece of shit who doesn't know that when a dude leaves you on Read for a week, it means to back the fuck off."

"Olivia." Mrs. G is behind me, and I've never heard her say my first name. She always calls me Ms. James.

I take a breath before I turn around, because I know I went too far, but I'm not ready to admit it. Angelina deserved it. I might be messy, but she's fucking grimy.

"Both of you come to my office."

Angelina's slowly getting up, looking around like maybe Mrs. G means someone else.

Everyone is staring at us, and I still haven't turned around because I kind of can't face Mrs. G right now. I just yelled across the room that I slept with Dré.

He's staring at me still as stone, in the middle of chewing his food. He's got this look on his face like I've lost it and he wants to swoop in to save me, but there is no coming back from this.

"Now," Mrs. G says. I unfreeze and follow her into her office.

Angelina isn't looking at me. She's still looking around like she can't believe what's happening, and to be honest, neither can I. I just—saw red. No, that's a lie, I saw Angelina the bitch who's been talking about me from day one.

Mrs. G closes the door and sits in her chair. "Sit down." She looks between us and takes off her glasses. "I don't care what's going on. I don't want to know. What I want you *both* to understand is that we, as women, don't tear down other women."

I don't need this *hoorah* speech right now. I just want to go home and hide.

"In this industry, women are objectified, sexually assaulted, and forced to compete against each other for a quarter of the wages they pay a man. You will not disrespect each other in *my* theatre." She's looking at me now. "You owe Ms. Medina an apology. I won't make you do it, and I won't hover over you while you do it, because I think it should come from the heart."

She gets up and squeezes between her cluttered desk and the bookcase before leaving us in the room alone.

Angelina's still not looking at me or talking. She's just sitting in her chair and breathing like she's innocent and all of a sudden *I'm* the Wicked Witch of the fucking West.

I'm running my finger over my jeans when I say, "Look, I'm sorry I said what I said. It was a bitch move—which I don't think you're unfamiliar with."

She sits up and scoffs. "Are you serious? I've never said anything you didn't already put out there. What you did was beyond low."

I want to tell her she's a shitty person for consistently making me feel stupid. She tarnished a moment that meant a lot to me, yet somehow, I'm the monster for delivering a little bit of the karma she had coming.

But she's kind of right. What I did was low. I even dragged Dré into it, and even though I know he'll shrug it off because people talking about him is normal, it still wasn't right.

I turn to Angelina. If I'm going to tell her this, I want her to see my face. "When I got the part for Bianca, you didn't even know me, but you called me a basic bitch. Before that, I'd never done anything like this. This was—you have no idea what it took for me to get up on that stage, and you really knocked my confidence. And since then, you've been talking about me. You even talked about—my first time. Everyone knows something that was just supposed to be between me and Dré."

She's dodging eye contact, and her lips are twitching, so I know she feels bad. But she's still trying to skirt around it. "It's not like I was spying on you. I just told Rodney, and I casually mentioned to Cleo what I heard, and they haven't said anything. You're the one yelling about it like a fucking drama queen."

I just stare at her. "You guys were *just* laughing at me. I know what I saw."

Angelina rolls her eyes. "We were laughing because Cleo was chewing you out and you looked like you were going to throw your sandwich in her face."

Chills of horror run across my whole body. I'm such an idiot.

"But thanks, you literally just told everyone that I'm desperate and pathetic."

I keep staring. I don't think anyone has ever made her own up to her dumpster-fire behavior, because she's squirming and still dodging my shaken but steady scrutiny.

"Look, I'll just tell Mrs. G you apologized and we can let this go." She gets up and leaves the room.

I don't feel completely vindicated, but I finally got to hold up a mirror to Angelina, and now that she knows who she is, maybe she'll think twice about using my life for her entertainment.

When I leave the office, I feel wired.

Dré's waiting for me outside the door. Everyone else has already broken up to resume rehearsal. "You okay?" He's looking at me like I might start firing off again.

"I'm fine." I'm not but at the same time I am. There's nothing I can do about what I did except own it so—whatever.

He grabs my arm and pulls me into a hug, and I don't think I've ever needed one more.

Just as I start to feel a little better, Eli walks by.

CHAPTER 26

It should feel like Christmas. All the stores are playing the super festive Christmas songs; the streetlights have trees, menorahs, and sleighs on them. It's even chilly. I should be in the holiday spirit, but I'm not. I've been catching up on work hours and Al's in New York for the month, so life is both busy and a drag.

Gloria's having this Christmas Eve barbecue, and my mom drives us over because she doesn't walk anywhere. She says if it's not 60 degrees, she's driving.

I still have these cute braids Lennox put in my hair. She even added gold wire around a few, and I look pretty badass. She said I needed an adult hairstyle, since I was acting all grown and telling people off. Some of Dré's cousins are checking me out, so *grown* is obviously another word for *sexy*.

Dré grabs me something to drink and introduces me to a

few of his cousins from Puerto Rico. They're older and kind of slick. I'm about to tell them I'm jailbait when Dré puts his hand around my waist and asks me to help him in the garage.

I used to think I was a girl guys passed over. I was wrong. And it's not just the dress or the hair; I've gotten attention like this before. I just always do what I'm doing now—shy away. This kind of focus makes me nervous. I don't know why I don't like feeling pretty, but I want to be both hot and completely invisible. It's the same when Eli calls me cute or Dré looks at me for too long; I freeze and say something stupid to make it stop.

When people tell me I'm pretty, I feel like they're just being nice, or flat out messing with me. I make sure to take jabs at myself before they do. Maybe constantly doing that is more than a shield—maybe it's become a cage I can't get out of. A way of doing that thing Dré does, hurting myself before anyone can beat me to it.

Wow. I'm the girl version of Dré—sorta.

I smile at him, because maybe he's known that longer than me. "Thanks," I say.

"I'm not gonna lie, I don't blame them. You're filling out that dress."

"Dré." My stomach tightens around the flurry inside of me. I'm supposed to learn to take a compliment, but I'm still getting used to this new version of us. This new version of *me*. Confidence is key—so I'll just shove that crazy bitch, running around in circles like her hair is on fire, to the *far* back corner of my mind.

"*Liv*. I can tell you these things now." He hands me a guitar and kisses me. *On the lips*. "Spank Bank."

"I'm so done with you." I'm laughing, but I don't know what we're doing. I thought it was just a one-time—or a one-day—thing. But he just kissed me on the lips. "We need rules."

"Lame," he says, picking up wires for an amp. He and Eli are supposed to play Christmas songs after we eat—that's the tradition—but who knows whether that's a thing, given Eli's been as MIA as the feral cat I used to feed. "I was hoping to avoid that."

"Well, we need them." I start thinking. "No kissing."

"That doesn't sound fun. If we're not kissing, how do we get to the fucking?"

"We don't."

He pouts, but I don't think he's too bothered. He sits down on the amp. "Okay. One-time thing?"

"I think so."

He's staring at me, and I'm starting to realize we've leveled up as friends. Even though we're talking about sex more, I feel like I'm one hundred percent me right now. I'm *O* the girl—I'm also *Liv*. Hell, I'm not even glancing away while his eyes do that really sexy, soul-searching thing. He's been doing that for—years. *I* was the one looking away.

He picks up the amp. "All right. No making eyes at me then—those eyes." On the way out, he stops. "And while we're making a list, don't do that breathing thing."

He's ridiculous. "I'm not going to stop breathing."

"No." He leans into me and his mouth is by my ear. He kind of gasps and makes this raspy sound. It's kind of sexy. "You do that when we're on the phone, when I touch you, or when you're thinking really hard. Instant boner. In fact—

ninth grade, when we were in the practice room, you were helping me keep time, and I wouldn't pick up my trumpet. Yeah. Raspy breath boner."

I'm blushing—full-on white-girl tomato. I should get a medal for the level of eye contact I'm holding while acting super chill. "I'll try."

"Not too hard." He winks over his shoulder as we head back into the party. The crazy chick in my head is rolling on the floor and screaming.

Wow.

The food is delicious. It's always gorge-worthy. And Eli is still not here, so Dré asks me to sing with him. My mom pulls out her phone for video evidence because, in her words, "You're a whole new person."

But when we're in the middle of "Let It Snow," Eli waltzes up, jaw clenched. I see Yosef making his way to say hi to Gloria, and I wonder if he dragged Eli here.

He's not looking at me. He's staring at Dré. When the song is over, I try to talk to Eli, but he ices me out like I don't even exist. "I want my old guitar back," he says to Dré.

"Dude. It's in the fucking garage."

No one's paying attention to us, but Gloria comes over and slaps Dré on the back of the head. *"Language."*

Eli looks at her like she bought him a dog and set it on fire. "You're one to talk morals."

"What the *fuck*, dude?" Dré's in his face, because we have another unspoken rule: we don't trash-talk family. It's never needed to be said out loud. Then again, none of our parents have ever broken up the other's family.

"Your mom is a fucking home wrecker, that's what." Eli's

stepping up to Dré, and I don't know how I know this, because they've never done it before, but they're going to fight.

Dré punches him, and then they're on the floor hitting each other.

I'm screaming at them, both mortified that they're doing this in front of all these people and terrified because I can *feel* the anger rolling off them.

Some of Dré's cousins pull them apart, and his uncle stops the cousins from getting into the fight, too.

Dré's rattling off in Spanish, and Eli is fighting against everyone until his dad grabs his arm.

"Fuck you, Dré," Eli yells. He pulls away from his dad, and everyone gives him space as he heads for the door. I'm running after him, because he's spiraling. I'm not responsible for his feelings, but he is my friend. He's hurting, and if the roles were reversed, he'd come after me.

Dré's behind me and his mom's yelling at him to get back in the house. "Eli," he yells.

I don't know if Dré's trying to make it worse or not, but even I tell him to go back inside.

Eli spins on us. "Fuck you, Dré. You take everything away from me. You *knew* how I felt and you—the *one* fucking person."

Dré spits blood out his mouth. "*No.* I didn't. I'm not going to spend my whole fucking life *guessing* how you feel about everything."

"It was fucking *obvious*," Eli yells back.

Dré laughs, and it's mean and angry. "No. You don't get to do that. You don't get to put it on *me* to figure out how you feel when you never asked how *I* felt. So go fucking cry about it."

Eli looks at me, and he's shaking his head like he doesn't know who I am or where he is. He's backing away from us and down the street.

"Eli, wait." I turn to Dré. "Seriously?" And I'm replaying the words over and over in my head. *You knew how I felt…the one fucking person.*

He won't meet my eyes. "He talked about my mom." His two older cousins come out to check on us; they look up and down the street for Eli, and when they're satisfied he's gone, they go inside.

"I'm not going to leave him wandering the streets," I say.

"We live in the fucking suburbs, Liv." He sighs. "Want me to drive?"

I shake my head. I've got on flats, and Dré will only make it worse.

"We're cool?" he says to me. His eyes are searching me, asking if I'm cool with the fact that he sorta knew Eli liked me—and I don't know how to process that right now.

"Did you *really* know?"

He shakes his head. "I don't know. I thought, sometimes, yeah. And there was a time I thought you might like him, but then you started hanging out with Kai. He was talking to Kara. I didn't feel like I had to check in with him on whether it was okay or not for me to feel the way I do."

I'm standing in between them again, but they're going in opposite directions. I am an elastic band being tugged on both ends, and Dré doesn't want to let go. "How *do* you feel?"

Dré's running his hand through his hair and he looks up at the evening sky. I feel like crying, because I think he lied about it being okay for things to be the way that they are. For us to just stay friends. He lied, but I need that lie to be real, because even though I love Dré, all I'm thinking about is Eli, walking down the road all alone.

"It's okay, Liv. You can go." He goes back inside, and I go looking for Eli.

I'm running down the next block when I see him. He's sitting on an electrical box on the corner.

He sees me and starts cursing. "I can't." He's standing up and pacing, like he's some animal boxed in a cage.

"We don't have to talk. But—look, you're coming to parties starting fights and—"

He laughs, and it sounds crazy. I think he might be crying without tears. "Are you serious? She invited us like she didn't fuck my dad—then I see you and Dré singing some fucking Christmas song together. Since when do you sing at parties?"

He's picking at things that aren't relevant, but I take the bait because I'm petty. "What the fuck is wrong with me singing Christmas songs?"

"I just didn't realize your Year of Fuck It meant sing at parties and fuck everyone you know."

I take a step back. Shame coats my skin and I feel exposed and ugly—I don't even know how he knows... I've got the Fuck It list taped to the mirror in my room.

The list.

I don't even notice it anymore, but he must have seen it when he stayed with us. It feels like such an invasion of my privacy—and he just called me a ho—*fuck him.*

"Liv." Eli's looking at me now, and I see a piece of him surface. "Liv, I'm sorry—don't walk away. I'm sorry."

He grabs my hand, and I turn around and shove him. He

looks like he wants me to do it again. Like he wants me to hit him so he can feel something. Jesus—

"Fuck." He pulls at his hair. "I'm sorry. And I realize you have no obligation to me, but why—" He's staring at the sidewalk, and when he speaks again, his voice is broken and breathless. "Why not me?" He looks at me, eyes watering, and he rubs his face and the tears away. "Never mind. I get you don't owe me an answer to that. Fuck. I'm sorry."

My heart is in my throat. I—I don't know what to say. I've spent *months* hoping—*dreaming*—that he liked me. That he'd see me. "You like me?" I sound so stupid, but I need to hear him say it.

"Isn't it obvious?" His eyes are wild, and I want to tell him *obviously fucking not* but instead I walk over and sit on the electrical box. It's cold on my legs.

"You never said anything." My heart's squeezing, and it's hard to sort out all the thoughts in my head.

He lets out a breath that sounds like he's dying. "I sent you love songs."

My stomach twists and turns. "You send *everyone* playlists." And I didn't think I was special enough for them to *mean* something. He never *told* me they meant something. I wanted him to, I gave him opportunities to, and he never *said* anything.

"I sent *you* love songs. I *wrote* you love songs and posted them online. I called you every morning—I—Jesus Christ. What else was I supposed to do, Liv?" He says my name like it breaks him. *Liv. Love. Liv. Love.* It's all falling apart.

"You never *told* me, Eli." I'm replaying everything in my head. I *know* I'm not crazy. "You were holding hands with *Kara* at the fucking movies."

"She held *my* hand and I—you looked me dead in my face and told me to *move on*."

I'm yelling at him, because I'm *not* taking the blame for this. I'm not taking the blame for breaking my own heart. "I was talking about *me*. I was telling *myself* to move on, because you were hung up on Kara!"

He's running his hands through his hair, staring at me wide-eyed. "I was talking about *you*."

I'm shaking my head. I'm not crazy. "You didn't *tell* me, Eli."

"Did Dré tell you? Did he say it?"

He did. He does. I'm realizing that even Kai said he liked me. I've been told I'm cared about by everyone except the one person I most wanted to hear it from…but I didn't tell Eli either.

Eli's reading my face, but he's misunderstanding me. "So that's it. You guys are a thing."

"We aren't."

He shakes his head. "Oh, give me a fucking break. You put out and you're not even with him?"

I really don't give a rat's ass how he's feeling or if I was part of the problem, too. He just called me a slut—twice. I get up, and I leave him there on the corner. He's calling after me, but I don't care. I don't know if Eli's completely broken now, but I won't let him break me, too.

ACT FOUR

ACT FIVE—Scene Two—
Here I Come Reprise

Othello:
IT'S A SONG, IT CAN'T BE UNSUNG
MY LOVE, HERE I COME

Desdemona:
(HUMS) MY LOVE, HERE I COME

Othello:
WELL, THE WINDS ARE HERE, NOW IT'S TIME TO FEEL
THE CHANGE AND THE SHIFT

Desdemona:
CAN'T WE MAKE IT WORK OR WILL WE COMPLETELY
CALL IT QUITS?

Desdemona/Othello:
THE WIND'S A ROARIN', I CAN'T HEAR YOU, NOT THE
SMALLEST, LITTLE BIT

Iago:
MY PLAN HAS FOUND ITS PLACE IN THE BEAT

Desdemona (spoken):
I believe in Othello. He'll see that I am true
and that I always have been.

Emilia:
Men are beasts. You're too young to see it. But
they are all the same.

(Othello ENTER bedroom)

Othello:
EVEN THOUGH I'M SCARED, I'M COMMITTED TO THE
FALL
IT'S HERE AND NOW OR NEVER

Desdemona:
PLEASE REMEMBER OUR LOVE SONG

Othello/Desdemona:
I'M FALLING, BABY, I COULD DIE, I COULD DIE
I'M FALLING, BABY, I COULD DIE
I'M (YOU'RE) HURTIN, BABY, I CAN'T LIE, I CAN'T
LIE
I'M DYIN' DOWN DEEP INSIDE

Desdemona
THEN LET THE SONG BE SUNG

Othello:
MY LOVE, HERE I COME

Desdemona:
MY LOVE, HERE YOU COME

Othello:
MY LOVE, HERE I COME
MY LOVE, MY LOVE, HERE I COME
IT CAN'T BE UNDONE
THE LAST THING I HEAR
ARE HER BREATHS DISAPPEAR
SHE DIDN'T SCREAM OR HAVE FEAR
I CAN'T UNWIND OUR BROKEN TIME
MY LOVE, MY LOVE'S NO LONGER HERE

CHAPTER 27

The holidays are over. Christmas sucked balls, because I couldn't explain to anyone why I was completely vacant. I'll die before telling my mom that I got into a fight with Eli because I slept with Dré in an attempt to move on from the crush that turns out wasn't unrequited.

I also can't tell Lennox or Jackie, because I don't want to feel like sex with Dré was a mistake. I wouldn't have done it if I knew Eli felt the same way I did—but I don't regret it—which leaves me in this screwed-up quagmire. And then, my mind is stuck on what Eli called me. I know it's not true, but I feel the label sticking to me the way pancake syrup sticks to my fingers.

I saw *Aida*, and even Tony Award–worthy songs couldn't wash away what Eli said.

Just because he liked me doesn't mean I owed him anything.

Just because I had sex with someone I care about—someone who cares about me even though we're not together—doesn't make me anything but a girl with a body. I hate that, for a split second, he made me feel dirty. Like somehow I tarnished a prize that was *his*.

Fuck labels. No, really, I wrote that down on my list: *10. Fuck labels.*

But that label is keeping me up at night, because... I kind of believe it. I went from almost losing my virginity in the back of a car to actually sleeping with someone else—and I know I went into sex not looking for a relationship with Dré, but what the hell am I doing?

I keep seeing the way Eli's face pulled in disgust when he implied I was a slut. Deep down inside—*deep* in there, I know I did nothing wrong. I was there for him while his life was falling apart, and how was I supposed to know how he felt when he *never* told me?

Just because he liked me doesn't mean I owed him my virginity. It was *my* first time to have with whoever I wanted to share it with.

I'm not trying to make it all about me. I'm not, but there is only so much emo-fuckboy attitude I can take. If I could go back and do it over again, I'd have left that stupid crush to sizzle up in the summer sun. I'd stop picking up all those damn phone calls like a moron, because I refuse to be in love with someone who makes me feel like this.

I feel so *stupid* and now with school starting again, we have practice every day, on top of everything else going on in my life.

As far as my band director is concerned, I'm *just not giv-*

ing my all when it comes to music and—well, obviously. I'm a high school student with a lot of fucking extracurriculars that all believe they deserve my undivided attention. And guess what? No one gets undivided attention—not even me. I don't even know the last time I deep-conditioned my hair.

The third day into this bullshit and I've got more drama in my life than this theatre can handle.

I'm sitting next to Dré, pretending to do my homework. He's doodling on my binder—a cartoon version of me freaking out over said homework. I'd laugh, but I'm so behind on everything already that it isn't funny. Mrs. G doesn't believe in us having free time. She brought in a vocal coach yesterday, and the lady is coming back today to criticize me some more. *You're not giving him what he's giving you, honey.*

First of all, I'm not her honey. Second, Dré is ten times better than I am at singing, so of course I'm not as good as him.

Dré taps me. Mrs. G is calling us to the stage to practice choreography. I'm in four dance routines. The thing about having such a small role is I'm also an extra in scenes my character isn't in.

If I'd known this, I wouldn't have signed up to do this ridiculous musical, because now I'm getting onstage and I'm supposed to make eye contact with Eli as we celebrate the fact that he didn't drown at sea. Honestly, he ends up smothering his wife, and he's already called me a slut, so are we really happy?

Ugh. I don't mean that. I don't want him to drown in a make-believe ocean. I just want him to look at me so I can glare and tell him to fuck off.

I'm obnoxiously petty, but I don't care. He's trying to shame me and my sexuality. He's trying to un-liberate my lady parts because he didn't have the balls to make a move.

After an hour of yelling at us, Mrs. G sends the girls to get fitted. "Ladies, take this time to compose yourselves. If I pull out any more of my hairs, I'll be as ugly as a newborn baby."

I really think this woman might have a stroke. She's always yelling.

Lennox is in the big dressing room, getting her measurements taken by a lady volunteering to adjust some of the old costumes.

"She's always screaming and threatening us. Just get used to it." Lennox lifts her arms. "Why you got that look on your face now?"

I turn away from the door just as Eli walks by to get his sword from the props room. On his way back to the stage, his eyes flicker toward me, and I pretend not to notice. I don't tell Lennox why I'm slamming my books on a table while reorganize my book bag until it's just her and Jackie in the dressing room.

"He called me a slut."

Lennox raises her eyebrows.

"Which nigga?" Jackie says like she's about to step outside and fight whoever *he* is. She looks like she's trying to run down the list of this week's rumors to figure out if she already knows my particular situation. Angelina hasn't been running her mouth since I aired all her dirty laundry, and Markus was caught in the props closet with his pants down again, so people have pretty much moved on from me. Besides—no one knows what went down except Eli and me.

I tell them about the party. I leave out the fact that Eli called

Dré's mom a homewrecker and most of the argument. They don't need to know the gritty details, because to be honest, Eli and I still have that secret space. So I just tell them, "He asked why not him, and I told him because he didn't tell me he liked me. Then he asked if Dré and I were together, and pretty much said I was a slut for putting out but not being with Dré."

Jackie leans away from me like she can't believe it. "The *audacity*. Oh, hell no. Hell. No." She puts away her costume and puts her hands on her hips. "Your first time was beautiful and I'll be damned if we let that salty punk decide the criteria for you to share your body."

Lennox claps her hands. "Preach, bitch."

Usually I'm the first one to tell Jackie not to talk all loud, but the way she and Lennox are looking at me makes me feel good. It's better to be angry with two other people than just myself. We're like an unstoppable wave of girl fury.

We're halfway through January rehearsals, and I feel like we've hit an all-time low. It's almost 9:00 p.m., and Mrs. G is having Kai and Eli go over the same scene again and again. We have one other scene to get through tonight, but she won't move on until Eli gets this one right. It's already been an hour, and the rest of us are being punished for it.

"Mr. Peretz," she says, taking off her glasses. She only wears them when she's tired. I don't know why she's torturing herself; she should just call off this damn play and let us all get on with our lives.

Eli looks up at the ceiling before turning to her. A piece of me—the one that has known Eli for years and can feel his helplessness—feels bad. I knew from his body language the moment he got frustrated. He's stumbling over his lines and taking these deep breaths like he's trying not to lose it.

Kai's scratching the back of his neck, and even he's starting to lose patience with Eli. "Dude."

"I know," Eli says. "I know."

The whole auditorium is quiet. It's like we're all taking the heat right now—this is painful.

"Well, we're all waiting for you to show us that," Mrs. G says as he stares at the floor. She takes a deep breath. "I'm giving you until tomorrow. Whatever is in your head, get it out." She gestures for them to get offstage and calls up Lennox and Jackie.

"'Bout damn time," Jackie says. They've been giving Eli the cold shoulder since I told them what he said, but I can tell she's only saying it for my sake because her heart's not really in it. Neither is mine. When they pass Eli as he comes into the gallery with the rest of us, she says something to him, and he shrugs his shoulders and rolls his eyes.

He looks at me and Dré, and his face gets stone-cold again as he passes our row and sits in the way back.

"He's been acting like a little bitch. I get that he's pissed about us, but he was acting like this *before* that." Dré still has no idea what happened at Eli's house. He thinks Eli called his mom a homewrecker because Dré's dad's not in the picture and she's a big flirt. I don't have the heart to tell him, and it's not my story to tell anyway.

"Still not a reason to call me a slut," I grumble.

Dré looks at me. *"What?"* he whispers, because Mrs. G

might snap our necks if we make noise while Jackie's doing her monologue.

I never told him what happened with Eli and me, but I do now.

He looks back at Eli and puts his arm around me. "Don't let that shit get to you. He's taking out his little bitch feelings on you." He grinds his teeth and squeezes me closer.

I lean my head on his shoulder. I can feel Eli's eyes on us, and I know he's probably making up something in his head about what this means. But as mad as I am, I just want to cry.

CHAPTER 28

I'm trying on my costume with Lennox in the small dressing room. For a whore, Bianca wore an awful lot of layers. Fuck. I'm judging her the same way Eli judged me. She was probably just some chick who liked a guy and didn't wait around for him to finally pop the question before deciding to have sex—like that's a crime.

I'm starting to like Shakespeare less and less these days. "You know what," I say to Lennox as she checks the hem on her dress. "Dudes are the worst."

"Eh," she says, shrugging. "I think there are good people and assholes. Just have to figure out which is which."

I ignore her, because she's being way too rational and we still have an hour before we break for early dinner. I'm hungry and feeling a little self-righteous. "No, they think because they write you songs and hold some undying love for you, you owe them something."

"Undying love?" She kind of laughs and takes off her dress to put back on the rack.

"He didn't say anything. Ever." I'm thinking back to when he wrote me a song for Christmas in the eighth grade. Now that I think about it, it was kind of lovey-dovey, but it was also about friends on a road trip. We were so dead set on taking a road trip to Key West; we couldn't wait to get our licenses. We thought we were going to do a lot of stuff by this time.

But that was just the start of things—he started making me playlists in ninth grade. He showed me his poetry in tenth grade, and the more I think about it...maybe he's liked me even longer than I've liked him.

"We're talking about Eli again?" Lennox says it like I'm always talking about Eli—okay, I am. But I'm also stuck with him every day until almost 8:00 at night. We obviously don't ride to and from school together anymore, because he drives his mom's car now. Which makes me wonder if his mom is back home. Whatever. I'm not even invested. I don't care.

I don't.

"I was talking about Shakespeare," I say.

Lennox helps me take off my dress and puts it on the hanger. "So I was kinda talking to Eli yesterday in the wings. Did he *say* the word *slut*?"

First of all, why was she talking to our sworn enemy? Second, since when does one have to say it, as long as it's implied? "He said he couldn't believe I put out to Dré and we're not even together." I'm waiting for her to get back on the hate-Eli train, but she's still stalling.

"That's not the same thing," she says, putting my dress on the rack.

I'm about to hit Lennox over the head with a hanger, because she's lost her goddamn mind.

"O. Think about it from his perspective. He's liked you for years, writing you songs and doing sweet shit. Then you sleep with his best friend for fun—don't look at me like that, I agree there is *nothing* wrong with that—so it can also be inferred that he's simply *disappointed*. Heartbroken and really in his feelings about it? I mean, pick one, but whichever you pick is more likely than him simply calling you a slut."

"*Our* best friend."

She's looking at me like that doesn't matter, and I get that it doesn't, but neither does Eli's perspective. I'm not even going to waste my time arguing with Lennox, because she has that look on her little freckled face that says she thinks she's right, and she's *not* always right. At least not about this.

When I get home, I just want to shower and sleep. I have to read a book for English and learn new sheet music for band, but I think I might just drop out of high school after the play, because I am exhausted. *Fuck it*, not all assignments need to be done, and why do I always have to be the one ready in band class when half the other flutes still can't figure out how to tune their fucking instruments?

My mom calls me into her room. She's sitting up on her bed, surrounded by papers. The TV light flickers off her reading glasses. "How was rehearsal?"

I show her my most dramatic *I'm dying* face, and she pats the bed next to her. I kick off my shoes and climb in, curling up on her pillows and thick duvet.

"I think you'll be proud once it's all said and done." She's got her hair pinned up in curls, and even though she's got work stacked up around her and is probably just as tired as I am, she isn't pouting like me.

I let out a breath. "You're right." I indulge in her pillows a little longer, rubbing my face on the soft cotton.

"Stop rubbing your greasy face on my pillows."

I laugh. "Why you so mean?"

She smiles. "Hey." She hits me with a piece of paper. "How is Eli doing? I haven't seen y'all running around like usual. Gloria said Dré and Eli are still at odds, too."

I shrug. I've stolen a page from Dré's book; I'm a vault.

"What you mean, *you don't know*."

Technically I didn't say anything, but I do this time. "I don't know."

Her eyebrows go up and her mouth gets kind of small. "You haven't thought to ask?"

She has no idea how many times I've asked him since everything happened. I know she doesn't know why we're not talking anymore, but I'm mad at her for being mad at me.

"His feelings aren't my responsibility," I say. I feel a little good, because she's taken aback.

"So that's how I raised you?"

I mean, yes. I am who I am right now, so it's a dumb question, but I'm not about to tell her that. I mess up and roll my eyes, because I'm sleepy and dirty and I need to wash my hair. I don't have time for this.

She shrugs with her eyebrows way at the top of her head. "Whatever. Can't tell nobody nothing." I've disappointed her. Whatever.

I get up, but even though my mother pretends to acqui-esce, she doesn't really, because she's like me and we never stop talking once we think we're making a point.

"You might not be responsible for someone's feelings, but how you act and how you choose to behave says a lot about *you*. Your friend is hurting, and you know what his home life looks like right now. The choices you make can affect some-one else's entire life."

Oh. My. God. She always does this. She takes something small and turns it into something it's not. I just placate her with a bunch of agreements and escape.

I'm actually low-key pissed. Why is my choice to have sex with Dré tantamount to affecting Eli's entire life? Dré had sex with Lennox, and we're all friends. I'm still kinda grossed out by it and prefer not to think about it at all, but I'm not stomping around acting like Dré's virginity should have been mine. But somehow me sleeping with Dré is the equivalent of me cheating on Eli just because he liked me?

It's hypocrisy. I know my mom doesn't know she's making a double standard, but I feel like the world is.

CHAPTER 29

I'm sharing a cupcake with Dré. Mrs. G had some leftover in her office and we stopped by at lunch to get one. There was one left. Out of twenty. People are so damn greedy.

We're walking to our usual spot by the staircase, taking turns licking the frosting. It's kind of stupid. We're in competition to see who is the most generous so we keep taking these tiny bites.

Then he's trying to shove the whole thing in his mouth.

"DRÉ." I've got both his hands pulling the cupcake away from his mouth but he's stronger than me.

We're laughing, but I'm serious. If he eats the whole thing, I'm going to sucker punch him. I've been thinking about it all day—the cupcake.

"Okay, okay," he says. He takes a small bite and gives me the rest. "I was going to give it to you anyway, damn."

His hand is on my waist and lingering. I'm licking the icing off first, and he watches me with his hooded eyes. Lust cloud.

"Oh my god," I snap at him. "We have rules."

He smiles. "For the spank bank."

I pretend to be bothered but I'm laughing again. *Fuck it,* I like this confidence. I like not looking away. I'm getting better at enjoying the attention and letting it wash over me instead of deflecting it with dumb jokes.

We're sitting on the staircase and back to arguing about Marvel movies. Dré's super into Marvel heroes, and I like making up stupid fake-facts about them and defending them until he pulls out his phone to Google the truth. He always shoves his phone in my face like, *See. You're wrong. Ironman's father was the Stark who made Captain's shield. Not Dr. Strange traveling into the past. He's a magician, not a con man.* He gets so mad when I start laughing.

"Liv, why do you do that?" He pinches my thigh but it doesn't hurt. I'm wondering if he did it just to touch me there.

The time we spend together is what I live for these days. It's the only time I'm not actively thinking about Eli—or looking for his face in the crowd. He's avoiding us just as much as we're avoiding him; I can't tell if I'm mad or sad about it.

I don't like feeling anything about it.

Another day goes by and another until the need to get away from those feelings is what has me standing in front of Dré's house. We have the day off because it's a holiday, and even Mrs. G. doesn't make us rehearse on MLK Jr. Day. Dré answers the door still in his pajamas. We're both tired. He's been working really hard on the play, and I'm actually surprised that he's keeping up with schoolwork. I had to copy *his* math homework. I've really fallen on hard times. Returning his homework is the excuse I use when he opens the door.

But when I'm standing in his room, watching him put his papers in a folder, I'm at this do-or-die moment and I just say, *Fuck it.*

I hook my finger in his sweats and pull him away from his desk.

He's looking at me with sleepy eyes but waking up really fast. "We have rules," he says.

Fuck the rules. I don't want to keep thinking about Eli. I don't want to keep feeling bad every time I see him alone or remember that his blinds have been closed for weeks and weeks.

I do the breathing thing, and I see him going from Dré to *Dré* who's definitely lost in lust land. I feel like I have this power, an ability that has him entranced. I'm Black Widow, and the Hulk is putty in my hands.

His hands are around my waist and we're kissing before we get to the bed. The majority of me is enjoying this. His hands are all over me, and we're taking our time. The first two times were kind of hurried with lots of fast breathing and needing.

This time he's staring into my eyes and we're hugging and holding on to each other.

Then it hits me.

I just want him to hold me because I'm sad. And he is. He's holding me and kissing me and giving me so much more like he's saying it's going to be all right, and I can't tell if I'm making all of this up in my head, but it's kind of twisted and I feel—I just feel sad.

After, I wrap myself in his sheets and lie on his bed. I don't want to say anything yet, because I don't want to start crying and freak him out. I'm kind of freaking out.

I hear him sigh. We just lie there, not saying anything for the longest time before he rubs my back. "Why'd you come over?"

I know he's asking me why did I have sex with him again, but I don't know if he's asking because he regrets it, or if he thinks I want something more.

"To give you your homework back." I'm such a chicken-shit idiot.

"Liv." He pulls away and sits up. He's rubbing his face, and I feel worse because I think it *is* regret.

He regrets it.

The longer I lie in his bed, the worse I feel, so I just start getting dressed.

"Liv?" Dré's watching me; the look on his face—I don't know what it means. I don't know what any of this means. I don't know why I thought saying *fuck the rules* was a good idea, but now he's making me feel like it was the worst thing in the world.

"Liv, where are you going?"

"Home." I can't look at him. I can't stand to be in my skin right now. I *used* him—

He's pulling on his pants and trying to help me find my shirt. He finds it first, and when I try to take it, he won't let go. "Talk to me."

"I just wanted to fuck." The words are out of my mouth, and they aren't mine, but I can't tell him I'm here because I didn't want to think about Eli. That's twisted beyond belief. I can't tell him I just wanted him to make me feel good. I can't say any of that, because he'll hate me, and I can't take not having him, too.

His face drops and he lets go of my shirt. "Seriously?"

I shove on my shirt. "You said you're cool with just doing it and whatever." I'm breathing hard. I need to get out of here.

"So you used me?" He's staring at me, and I'm trying to figure out when Dré grew into the guy who's no longer a vault but open with whatever is in his head. When he became someone whose words could slice me open and gut me in an instant.

And when did I become the vault?

"You're the one who's into the casual thing." I get what I did was wrong, but some of this had to be mutual. It's not like he wanted to be my boyfriend after we had sex—twice. He's the one who's all cool with not owning another person.

"So I don't have feelings? You made rules and now you're crossing them every chance you get." He's trying to understand, but doesn't he realize even I don't know what the hell I'm doing anymore?

I don't know who I am anymore.

"Bullshit." All I know how to do is fight this. "You're feeling me up all the damn time. Touching me everywhere and always saying *spank bank*…" I feel the half-truths on my tongue, and I know he hears them just like I do. But I can't accept this ugly as all mine.

"Because I—I thought you liked it. I—clearly I was wrong." He runs his hands over his face and hair and paces to the window.

I blink fast. "You could've said no." Why didn't he? Why did he hold me and kiss me and— I can't breathe.

He squints at me, and there is this disconnect between us. I see it in his face. It goes blank, and it's like that rubber band holding us together snaps. I feel the break. "You can be so fucking selfish it's astonishing."

I can't stand the way he's looking at me. It makes me feel like everything we are is tainted and— I smooth my shirt over my body. "Good job on the big words." I don't know why I said that. He's not stupid. I don't know why I keep talking. My words and my feelings are the exact opposite of each other. One trying to defend the other. I can't make it stop.

"Fuck you," he says, and I leave.

I cry all the way home and in my bed, and I don't stop until I wake up in the middle of the night to close my blinds. Eli has his open, and he's in his room with the light on. It's almost midnight when he looks up at me as I turn on my light.

It's all coming at me like a wave, and I close my blinds before he can see me cry.

Right there on my mirror is the stupid fucking list, and I hear Eli in my head, saying, *I didn't realize the Year of Fuck It meant fuck everyone you know.*

I rip the list off my mirror, and then I'm screaming into my pillow.

CHAPTER 30

Dré's not talking to me. I tried to apologize in the morning before classes started, but he gave me the cold shoulder. I feel like we both said things that weren't okay, and I'm kind of irritated that I'm always the person to apologize first.

He called me selfish, and I've spent most of our friendship being *selfless*. I let him and Eli shine, and the moment I started doing my own thing, everything fell apart. I'm not getting cut any slack for making *one* mistake.

I shouldn't have used him to get Eli off my mind. I get that. But Dré knew it was casual sex. That's all it was.

After a few days of the cold shoulder, I start eating lunch and doing my homework by myself, because Lennox and Jackie are on the other lunch schedule. Rehearsals are packed from 4:00 to 8:00 at night with a thirty-minute break for dinner, so I spend my spare time studying with Lennox or Jackie.

We're in Lennox's car going to the McDonald's when Jackie turns around and sighs. "Okay, bitch. What the fuck is wrong with you now?"

They'd been talking about their film projects, which they turned in. I kind of drifted, staring out the window.

I shake my head, still looking out the window. What isn't wrong? I'm sitting fourth chair flute because even Spitty Patty, who sounds like her tongue is flopping around in her mouth, is performing better than me. I got a C on my history test, and I didn't read the book I have to write a paper on due tomorrow in English.

"Nah, bitch. You've been pouting and quiet for days, and I notice you ain't around your little friend." Jackie has a way of telling me my business even when I'm clearly not trying to share it. Cleo was right; the theatre department feeds on drama, and I can't help but feel like I was better off before I auditioned for this musical.

But *fuck it*. Keeping all this shit in my head isn't doing me any better either. "Dré's mad at me because we had sex again."

Lennox breathes out, puts her arm against her window, and rests her head in her hand. "I swear you like looking for trouble."

I don't know what that means, because I'm about the least confrontational person there is. I went to a Halloween party dressed as myself because I don't like attention. "How is this my fault?"

Lennox pulls up to the order box and orders our food. We

get our food before she says anything. "I told you. You're not a casual person. I'm not even sure Dré knows how to be casual—especially with you. It was a bad idea. I told you that."

"*You* told me to have sex with Dré." I get my large fry and Oreo McFlurry. I start scooping out the ice cream with my fries, and, I swear, something that is usually the gateway into heaven tastes like cold grainy crap right now.

"Because I was sure y'all would get together. And that was before I knew how deep this Eli thing went. *And*, if I remember correctly, we told you sex with Kai was a bad idea *because* you're not a casual person. To top it all off, you're not exactly good at giving all the facts. I always find out crucial bits *afterward*."

I eye her, because I've noticed she's been talking to Eli like he's a person and not a monster. She's kind of a hypocrite. One minute, I'm not responsible for his feelings, and then the next, I'm not considering them.

Jackie butts in. "Wait. I still don't know why he's mad y'all smashed."

"He thinks I used him for sex." I feel ashamed, saying that out loud. It's not like we're dating, so maybe we've been using each other?

"Did you?" Lennox asked.

It isn't any of their business. "He could have said no. I didn't force myself on him."

Jackie sucks her teeth. "Bitch, you're so wrong for that. Dré's a decent dude, I don't even know why he fucks with you."

"Shut the hell up, Jackie." I know my tone is off. She looks at me like she has to check that I'm actually talking to her.

"Bitch, I ain't Angelina. Don't come for me," she says, eyes wide.

"No, but you're still annoying. You're loud as fuck and I'm tired of your dumbass opinions." I want to get out of this car. I'm tired of them judging me. They're always talking about me and my problems. I'm conveniently reserved as the entertainment. The whole theatre department is probably laughing at me.

We're quiet on the way back, aside from Jackie mumbling under her breath when she turns up the music. When we're out of the car, Lennox stops me. "O."

It's getting dark outside and it's not even six o'clock. I pretend to be fascinated by the streetlights humming above us.

"You owe her an apology."

"I don't owe anybody anything," I say. I'm always apologizing. I'm always smoothing things over. I'm always the one keeping the peace. I keep the peace between Eli and Dré. I have to apologize to Eli because his family life sucks. I have to apologize for not waiting on him to tell me how he feels. I have to apologize for doing what Dré wanted to do anyway.

This is the Angelina shit all over again. I have to apologize for standing up for myself. *Fuck. It.*

Lennox stands there with her keys in her hand and her bag in the other. "Whatever," she says. Her green jumpsuit swishes as she walks away.

I'm sitting in the back row doing my homework, listening to Mrs. G lecture us about how we have two weeks before opening night, and we're still singing like somebody is shak-

ing a cage of freaked-out birds. I don't know how she knows
what that sounds like, but I'll take her word for it.

I'm trying not to catch her attention right now, because
she already spent an hour yelling at Dré and me for messing
up our number. I'm not feeling it. I can't fake it. I can't smile
and beg him to stay with me when it's so degrading. I hate
Shakespeare.

I have to become a whore onstage when I know my friends
are basically judging me for the same thing Bianca gets thrown
in jail for. I stand up for myself like Emilia stands up to her
husband, and everyone turns their back on me. Emilia—
news flash—gets stabbed, so fuck Shakespeare and his tragic
fucking women.

Mrs. G keeps telling us to use this opportunity to make
a statement about all the problematic issues, but I'm at the
point where I want us to do something different. Call the
whole thing off and do *Sweeney Todd* instead. It's a bunch of
weirdos murdering people and baking them in pies, what
could go wrong?

I also want to be somewhere else because Dré's walking
over to Eli, and he sits next to him. At first, they don't say
anything, but after a few minutes they're talking and then
doing some dumbass handshake.

I want to vomit.

Dré has sex with me, and all is forgiven, they're friends
again.

I have sex with Dré and I'm—I'm not Bianca.

I'm *Desdemona*.

My gut squeezes with horror. I'm stunned. I'm living in
some freak version of *Othello* where Iago ends up being a de-

cent guy, Cassio and Othello work it out—but Desdemona? She still ends up dead.

I'm up and running to the bathroom. I don't throw up, but I am crying. I feel like an idiot, because I'm bawling my eyes out into the sink while trying to splash cold water on my face to keep from getting red and puffy.

Somehow Eli has turned me into the monster. Everyone is mad at me. I've lost my two best friends, and they're happy to move on without me. Jackie and Lennox aren't talking to me. I haven't been to work in forever, so I don't even have Al. I have only this puffy-eyed girl staring at me in the mirror.

Cleo walks in, and I know God is up in heaven somewhere laughing, because *what the fuck.*

"Hey," she says. We haven't talked much since I pretty much told her to kick rocks and stay out of my business. But we're family, and family never stays out of your business. "Don't let Mrs. G get to you. You weren't that bad. I mean, Dré's not helping any, it's not all you."

She thinks I'm crying because I got yelled at. It's better than explaining to her that maybe she was right. Maybe I should have stuck to the shadows, because my life has never been worse.

I just nod. And wipe my face. I leave before she finishes using the bathroom, because there is only so much pity I can take.

At the end of rehearsal, we pick straws and Eli and I are left with the short ones. I've never known dread until this moment. It's not a dark cloud, it's a fist around my heart threatening to squeeze me out of existence.

We have to organize the prop closet. Now that all the props have been created, there are a ton to put back, so no one will trade with me. I try to swallow the panic that rises in my throat with every step to the props closet, but my hands are shaking as I open the door.

"I guess you're stuck with me," Eli says when I walk into the room. We haven't spoken in so long that he feels like a stranger. A stranger who's turned all my friends against me and smothered me out of existence.

"I bet you're all having a laugh about it."

He shrugs. "We only like to laugh at you on Tuesdays." He's looking at me, but I refuse to give him the satisfaction.

"Fuck you, Eli."

He groans. "Look, I'm trying, but you're not making it easy."

I gape. He's such a fucking asshole. "Well, I'm only a slut on Wednesdays," I snap back at him.

He looks confused and then his eyes go wide. "That's *not* what I meant."

"Fuck you. Really. Fuck you. I know what you *meant*." I actually don't know anymore but *fuck it*. I'd rather be safe than be the butt of the joke.

He looks completely offended. Like I should have thought his joke was funny—or been able to tell it wasn't a joke. Whatever. "It's not what I meant," he says, his voice getting louder. "I—fine. Forget it." He turns around and goes back to ignoring me.

My hands are twitching with energy, and my heart is thumping in my chest. I've thought for so long about all the things I want to say to him. All the hell I'd let him have when the moment came.

The gate floods open. "You're really good at that. The whole pretending to care and then cutting people off. Your family would be *so* proud." I never rehearsed *that*. I never once thought about bringing up his family's drama.

On both sides of his family, he has grandparents who either don't acknowledge his existence or barely talk to him at all. His mom talks to only some of her family here in America, and they always disrespect his dad in front of him. She's terrified of her family completely disowning her, so she doesn't stick up for Yosef or for half of what Eli is—I don't know, we almost never talk about it, and I never bring it up.

Except I just did.

He's staring at me. I expect him to say something about how my dad walked out on me, or something about me sleeping with Dré. I'm readying myself for anything, because I think the last plank on our bridge just snapped.

The anger fades from his face, and he's just standing there. He's so still I could blow him over. "I'm only going to say this because you were there for me at the lowest point of my life and because I know you—you're better than that."

He walks out and leaves me to finish the props by myself. I'm kind of glad he doesn't come back, because I feel so ugly I could die.

Before we all leave, we gather in a circle to close out rehearsal like we do every night, and when it comes time for

Mrs. G to tell us, *You know what to do,* she doesn't. Instead, she looks at each of us and says, "You guys can do better than this. We're not going to *smash it* tonight, because when you say it, I want you to mean it."

She walks away from us, and we all stand there, quiet, not meeting each other's eyes. Then we just walk away, one by one, because what else is there to do?

CHAPTER 31

My sister is home when I get inside. My mom thought it would be a fun surprise. I'm kind of stunned, because everything running through my head is making it hard to compute why she's standing in the kitchen making mashed potatoes.

"Hey, Amber." She's normally only home for the holidays or the occasional long weekend. I love my sister but I'm not in the mood to chitchat about how great Atlanta is or whether or not I've started picking out colleges.

"Hey, baby sister." She calls me that now. She didn't always. When we were younger, she called me things like Olive Garden and Fungus Freak—I used to love mushrooms. Now she calls me *baby sister*, and I think it might be because I'm getting older. Who knows?

She looks at me and then Mom, and then kind of nods her

head like she's making sure we didn't run anybody over on the way home.

Mom and my sister are now looking at me. I know Mom noticed how irritable I am because when she picked me up from practice today, she just turned up the music in the car and chatted about how hard it is booking an aquarium that lets people take their vows in a shark tank.

Amber sighs. "I'm just going to say it. What's wrong with her?" They do this—talk about me as if I'm not in the room. It's always been a thing, so I don't even care anymore.

"Puberty." My mom has been saying that for the last five years. Maybe this time she's right, because I've really lost it and I can't figure out when it all started to slip out of my hands. I've literally screwed my life into a catastrophe.

I sit at the counter and eat mashed potatoes and steak and pick at the green beans. My mom's already left to shower. Apparently ten o'clock is way too late for normal people to eat.

I bring Amber up to date about the play and rehearsals and leave out everything in between—which is pretty much my entire life since Halloween. It feels like a long time. Looking back, it's been about three months, but they've been the most intense three months of my life.

This is how we communicate. Updates between dry patches. I love my sister but she's twenty-six and in a world of her own. We have nothing in common except the fact that we're sisters. That's kind of comforting though, that two people can exist connected by such an arbitrary thing and still love each other—Amber makes a face and tells me to chew with my mouth closed because I look like a cow—*sometimes* love each other.

I'm in the middle of explaining my schedule when Amber interrupts me.

"So, I'm bringing my girlfriend down next month."

I'm not sure why that was important enough to interrupt my very detailed description of my daily schedule. Then I realize it's the way she says *girlfriend*. "Oh? Shocker," I say. I don't mean it to come out so sarcastic, but my sister's been gay for like—forever. But she doesn't think anyone knows. At least that I know of. She's always been super secretive about her friends, and she has these mysterious "best friends" who then disappear without a trace after a few months or years.

I don't know why she's always been scared to tell me. I'm notorious for not making people feel uncomfortable—or I was. I just figured, one day, she'd be old and I'd be old and she'd finally tell me she was a lesbian and I'd cackle an old-lady laugh and then die?

I don't know what old people do after they get old—besides work at Universal Studios and give advice to teenage girls who can go their whole life without doing anything bad and then royally screw it all up in three months.

I'm crying, and my sister is freaking out.

"Not because you're gay," I say between tears. "Because I'm a really horrible person."

It takes me a while to calm down, and then I start crying again, because I realized I totally ruined my sister's coming-out moment.

"You've been ruining my moment since you were born. I'm used to it. Besides, everyone knows I'm gay—I think I was trying to make it a thing because my friends keep telling me it should be a thing." She leans on the counter, watching me, and I realize I *really* don't know a whole lot about my sister. I think that I do, but I'm totally oblivious about everything going on in her life.

Dré was right. I *am* selfish.

She nudges me and hands me another napkin. "So. Why are you a horrible person?" She gets up and opens the fridge, and she pulls out an entire key lime pie. I could hug her. But I don't, because she hands me a fork and this pie is better than a hug. That's why she made it. She's always known how to show me she loves me, but what do I do to show her? I don't even know what she does for a living—I should, but every time she says *digital marketing*, I turn on the mute button like an asshole.

"You going to tell me or not?" she says, settling in next to me.

I start in on the pie because I don't know how to tell my sister that I appreciate her more than life itself right now. I don't know how to say anything but "Things happened, and now my friends all hate me."

Amber looks at me and rolls her eyes. "*Things* don't just happen." She sighs. "This is like that time I walked in and you were gluing hair back on to your Barbie and you said, 'It just fell out.'" Leave it to my sister to bring up the past while I'm drowning in the present. "Well?"

She's like a dog with a bone. When she grabs on to something, she won't let go, so I take a deep breath and pray this is exactly like the time she helped give my Barbies cute bobs after I hacked up their hair.

"I had sex with Dré," I say with a mouth full of pie.

She's nodding even as her eyebrows go waaaaay up on the top of her head. "Wow, this took a wild turn. *Your* Dré?"

"My Dré."

She smiles with gritted teeth. "How'd Eli take it?"

I'm gaping. Why is that her first question? Why isn't she asking how *I* took it? It was *my* first time, and she's asking about Eli. I say as much, and she's waving me off.

"Because Eli's been into you since y'all were running through the house acting like the wizards and shit. Y'all are weird as fuck, but I try not to judge." She's a bold-faced liar. She judges everything and everyone. But I don't say that. I just tell her the whole story.

Everything, and I leave no detail untold. I'm done with the whole pie by the time I'm getting to the part where I completely dragged Eli's family through the dirt.

She only stopped me when I talked about Gloria and Yosef. She was kinda shocked by that turn of events. She was also a little wary of Lennox because, though she thinks Lennox gives some good advice, my sister is just as much of a prude as I am. She comments on how I shouldn't pay Cleo any attention, because she's always been a tad stuck-up, and she thinks I should have snatched Angelina's edges, until I tell her about the part where I put her on blast in front of everyone, and then her jaw drops.

"Damn, Liv. You went HAM on that bitch." She's licking her fork. "Hate to tell you," she says, putting her fork in the empty pie container, "you should probably start handing out some apologies."

I groan. "I already sorta apologized to Angelina."

Amber sucks her teeth. "Ain't nobody talking about *that*

bitch. She asked for that. I'm talking about your friends." My sister has a way of puckering her lips that says if I don't take her advice, she's going to judge the hell out of me. "I'm not saying there isn't a lot of blame to go around. But is that really how you want to leave things?"

She's right. I can't help but think my Year of Fuck It needed to come with some cautionary notes. Like, *Don't say Fuck It to using one best friend to get over the other,* and so much more. And just because I didn't like *everything* about me before doesn't mean there was nothing to love.

I can't help but think about Jackie and her damn love affirmations, and Al telling me to do things *for myself.*

"Good judgment comes from a string of fuckups," I say. "Al told me that." I miss Al; he'd probably have saved me from half of the mess I got into—then again, I probably wouldn't have told him half of the crap I was doing, because he's *still Al.*

"Wait, who the hell is Al?"

"He's the old guy I work with."

"Oh lord. I can't. This is too much. It's two in the morning, and you have school. Go to bed and please stop talking to old men."

I cackle and my sister flicks my forehead. We don't really hug. We have other ways of saying I love you.

I do head up to my room, because she's right. I have a lot of apologies to hand out, but I have no idea where to start. The list is still on my floor—my room has been a complete mess since rehearsals started, so it's not out of place down there.

My once clean cream-colored dresser with the succulent that was supposed to make my space look chic and minimal is now covered in clothes that are either clean or dirty—I can barely make out my purple rug under the mess of papers I dumped off my bed a few days ago.

But all crumpled up on top is my list.

I pick it up and smooth it out. So much has happened since I wrote those first words, *Do the things that scare me*. I started this for myself—but I forgot to love myself in the process. I don't think I've ever truly known how.

I grab a pen. I'm not going to quit. I'm changing, and I'm fucking up, but that's no reason to quit.

11. LOVE FIRST—ESPECIALLY MYSELF.

ACT FIVE

**ACT FIVE—Scene Two—
Bedroom**

Iago: (Center Stage—freeze—spotlight)
The past is riddled with missteps, but I
regret nothing.

Dear Liv,
~~We need to talk~~

Dear Liv,
~~We both said some fucked up shit~~

Dear Liv,
~~I regret everything.~~

CHAPTER 32

It's one week to showtime, and Mrs. G is having conniptions. One of the mics is dead, three of the lights aren't working, a flute player is missing from the pit and the heat in the theatre went out. We've all got sweaters on over our costumes, and it's so cold my bones hurt.

It doesn't snow in Florida, but that doesn't mean it's not cold in February. It's 40 degrees outside and it feels lower than that in the theatre.

The HVAC went out sometime during school, but no one noticed until all the maintenance people left. Most of us are bunched together in the big dressing room for warmth between sets. Eli's leaning on the corner by the door, earphones in, eyes closed. Half the cast is on the floor, bunched together, talking quietly, while I'm in the back next to Jackie and Lennox, trying to work up my nerve to apologize to my girls.

Because I'm super classy and suave, I just blurt it out. "I'm sorry I was being a bitch."

Jackie turns around, and she's rubbing her bony arms. "Damn, girl, took you long enough." She smiles. "I wasn't even that mad. I just thought you'd lost your damn mind."

"I kind of did."

Lennox moves closer, too. "I'm glad you found it." She wraps her finger around one of my curls to fix it. "You doing all right?"

There are friends you make who don't deserve you, and then friends you make that you don't deserve. These two are the latter, and I can't believe I met them by chance. Then again, maybe nothing happens by chance.

I got to know them because I said *yes*.

"I had a pity party, drank too much iced tea, watched too many Spanish soaps."

Jackie is jumping up and down now, still rubbing her arms. "You know you didn't have the time to watch no damn soaps." Her face kind of lights up, and then she pulls her phone out. "BITCH." She's smiling from ear to ear. "I didn't tell you. I got my gold plaque from YouTube." She shows me the video of her unwrapping it and screaming. A million people think Jackie is bomb enough to follow.

I don't blame them. She's crazy talented. She's been living her own version of Fuck It, and more than a million people have showed up to love her for it.

She pulls a face. "I mean, Mrs. G still gave me a B on my project because it was vain, but she can't steal my light." She elbows Lennox. "This chick got the highest grade in the class though."

I'm so proud of them that now we're all jumping and hugging. Everyone else is staring at us like we're crazy, but a few join in, and then we're a room of about fifteen people packed in tight, hopping and *whooping* until Mrs. G comes in screaming that she can't hear the stage.

When she leaves, we all laugh quietly. It's funny—I didn't get the family feeling in band, but here I do. I spent so much time living a life that wasn't mine but was picked for me that I almost missed out on *this*.

I catch Eli's eyes. He looks down at his phone.

Lennox never misses anything. "Y'all should get on the same page."

"We need to find the same book first." I still can't believe what I said to him. I can't believe what I said to Dré either. I'd blame it on being momentarily possessed, but I know I said those things because I was scared of saying the truth; that I was in love and heartbroken.

I've been angry with Eli for not saying anything to me when I didn't tell him how I felt either. I wanted him to take the risk when I wasn't willing to. I'm a sucky coward—or maybe I'm a really good one. Either way, I'm scared we won't even make it to an apology. I don't see how he'll forgive me after I made him out to be some kind of monster.

Eli's last on my list anyway. I ranked everyone from *easy* to *holy fuck maybe I can still move to another state*.

Next on my list is Kai. He's been chilly with me since he found out I slept with Dré. In hindsight, I see that telling him I'd give him an answer and then hiding from him for a week, sleeping with Dré, *and* not saying anything at all was kind of low.

He was honest with me from the start, and he deserved that in return.

I try to catch him after rehearsal as he heads to his car. "Kai?"

He looks up and waves. "Hey." He's still actually really nice for a guy who was jilted. "Need a ride?" This would be easier if he'd followed that up with *Too bad* or *Then ask someone who cares*. But of course he doesn't, because he's Kai.

"No." I'm pointing behind me and just standing here like that was all I came to say.

He's scratching his head and looking around because he's too polite to point out how much of a weirdo I'm being.

"So, I actually wanted to apologize." Oh. My. God. I'm slapping my hands together and swinging them around. I never do this. I stop and try putting them in the pockets of my coat.

Kai, bless him, smiles and nods like he just realized he picked a crazy girl to get messed up with. "Nah, it's cool."

"No. You were really awesome, and I got— I was a virgin, and I think that freaked me out a little—the idea of casual sex. I really wanted to though." Fuck me. I have to stop vomiting words. "Have sex with you that is." Somebody gag me. I should have written out a script. I can't be trusted to improvise.

Kai steps over and gives me a quick hug. I think he's hoping I'll just stop talking; it's a very friendly hug. "Really. It's okay. Life is complicated. I get that. We're cool if you're cool."

No, Kai. No one *is as cool are you are. Jesus.* "You're—pretty awesome."

We're not hugging anymore, and he's opening his car door. "Sure you don't need a ride?" He's looking around again, but his concern mellows out when he sees Lennox. I realize I wasn't even pointing at her car before. I was pointing into the empty part of the parking lot, lit up by orange light and mist. Wow.

I wave him off with this weird smile on my face, like I'm the local, easygoing, chummy Girl Scout. I really need to work on this—*apologizing*. He's touched my boobs and way more, so I don't know why I'm acting like this but I can't shake the freak off me.

Lennox pretty much laughs at me. She didn't hear the conversation, but she asks why I was swinging my arms like I was getting ready for an Olympic swimming competition. Truthfully, I'd rather do that all over again than face the next person on my list.

Dress rehearsal is both super exciting and so anxiety filled, I keep going to the bathroom, thinking I have to pee. We're in full performance mode, running the show from start to finish, and Mrs. G looks like she might keel over. We're not doing bad, but we're not doing our best either. We keep making little mistakes here and there: a missed line, music delays, small stuff, but to Mrs. G, it's huge.

Dré and I are talking a little in the wing waiting for his cue. But the conversation is stiff, and this isn't the place I want to get into how sorry I am.

I don't get a chance to be alone with him until I find him putting away his costume. He sees me and makes this face, saying he recognizes my presence but he has nothing to say.

"Can we talk?"

He keeps his eyes fixed on his costume like it's going to fall off the hanger by itself, but after a moment he relents and looks at me.

"What I did—I wish I could take it back. Everything I said and what I did." By now I should be good at apologizing. My voice shouldn't shake, and I should be able to look him in the eye.

"So you regret everything?" He's picking lint off the sleeve of his costume. "All of it?" His forehead is creased.

"Not everything."

He's looking at me again, and I know he's going to make me say it.

"Not the first time."

He exhales and drops the sleeve. "Why'd you do it? Why'd you come over? I'm trying to figure out how we went from being cool and having our rules to you—you looked like you were going to cry." He paces the floor and messes up his hair, running his hands back and forth over it. He groans. "I don't get it."

I'm wiping away tears, because I know I don't deserve to have them, and crying is the kind of thing I do behind closed doors. But I feel ugly. Like what I did tainted me. I didn't want to be *casual* because I didn't want Kai to use me. Then I did the thing that scared me to my best friend.

"I'm sorry." I stop talking, because I can't between the sobs. My hands are shaking and I'm covering my face, because even I can't stand myself right now.

Dré's hands are over mine, and then he's pulling me into him. I can't stop sobbing. I'm getting snot all over his shirt. I've always taken Dré for granted—mostly because I thought he'd get too cool for me and stop being *my* friend.

We stand in the middle of the room until my breath stops hitching. I keep praying no one else comes in. A few people do, but as soon as they see us, they leave, and I'm glad my face is in Dré's chest and not exposed to half the damn theatre department.

He wants to know why, and he deserves the truth.

"I didn't want to be lame anymore."

His cheek is on the top of my head and I feel his "hmm?" as much as I hear it.

I tell him about the Year of Fuck It. I start with Halloween, and I feel like I've told this story so many times, but this is the first time I'm telling one of the people who's been with me through it all; someone who means the world to me. I can't remember why I didn't tell him in the first place. I feel like I haven't changed at all.

Dré sits with me on the floor, and he listens without saying a word.

"I thought I'd come out at the end of it this confident chick in control of my life. I don't know why the hell Shonda Rhimes was allowed to publish that book, because it ruined my life."

Dré laughs. "You weren't lame."

"I wore khakis and a hoodie to a Halloween party! That's as sad as it gets." I'm picking at my shoelaces, my face feels hot, and I sound weird.

"Yeah, but that's just *you*." Dré slides his hand over mine and intertwines our fingers. "If you had to go through all this to realize you're special, fine. But you were then, and you are now."

Christ. I'm crying again. I've always wanted a guy to tell me that. I've daydreamed all the scenarios, and in all of them I end up on cloud nine, kissing under fireworks—I watch a lot of rom-coms. I've got to get my shit together, because with my record of missing the mark on monumental moments, my wedding day will be in hell and I'll be surrounded by freaky bug-eyed dolls.

I've got the world record in puffy face right now. I'm not an ugly crier, but tears don't fall from my eyes in epically cin-ematic ways either. "I'm sorry."

"Stop apologizing. It's okay. I should have—I should have stuck to the rules, too. I love you, but I want you to be happy—that's not with me." His breath hitches, and then he says, "I knew you and Eli were into each other—I convinced myself you weren't. You were talking to Kai, and I figured I was making shit up in my head."

I meet his eyes, because I've been wondering for a while now... "Did you invite Kara to the movies to set them up together?"

Dré rolls his eyes. "Maybe. She heard me invite Alex and asked if Eli was going—which, obviously—and I kinda wanted to see if my hunch was right." He lets out a long breath. "I never knew for sure how he felt about you, and I would have asked, but we both know how that would have gone. It's just not fair that everything I do has to revolve around if Eli agrees or not." He looks at me. "I meant what I said. I meant *everything* that I've said. But most of all, I want you to be happy."

I squeeze his hand. I've never known what bittersweet meant until this moment. I've always thought of Dré as the cat that purrs one moment and scratches up my couch the next, but now that I think about it, he's always been in my corner.

He's always expected me to love myself. He didn't tell me he liked me—he told me he *loved* me. And I think he's telling me now that he loves me enough to let me go. "You're my best friend." I mean it. I've grown closer to him than I've ever been. It wasn't just the sex—that definitely changed things, but the more I'm changing, the less afraid I am to be honest with the people I love.

"Yeah." He holds my gaze. "I know that now. And I'm cool. No matter what happens."

My body kind of shakes and my breath keeps skipping from all the crying, but I manage to say, "That's epically mature."

"Fuck yeah, it is." He sighs. He's kind of relaxed and maybe a little relieved that he's got it off his chest. He squeezes my hand. "I think when it comes to you and me—we probably shouldn't have sex again."

I laugh, because it stings but that's my ego talking. I completely agree. I feel like I don't want to have sex with anyone, because I totally screwed it up. I don't trust myself anymore.

He leans over and kisses my forehead for a long moment and then he sniffles, and he's gone.

Dré's changed. Every time we talk, he's showing me

glimpses of a guy I've never seen before but absolutely admire. I want to show him that I'm changing, too.

For starters, I can tackle the last person on my list.

CHAPTER 33

I can't breathe. The last Friday of Feburary is upon us. It's opening night, and we're all hopped up on nerves, ten times more than yesterday. The veterans are cooler. Lennox, Kai, and Jackie are helping the rest of us with makeup and reminding us of our lines, and we feel like a family. We are one. A weird one.

Even Angelina is checking my props, and she helps me zip my costume. We're not exactly friends, but we coexist without being assholes. When you spend every day with the same people for hours on end, you form the kind of bond you don't get from just being friends.

Mrs. G is giving us a pep talk. "I've never been prouder," she says, scanning each and every one of our faces. I'm getting teary, knowing that we got a present and roses to give her after curtain call. It's a shirt that says Cat Wrangler and a poster-size picture of us—signed by everyone—just in case she needs a reminder of the feral cats she had to wrangle. We circle up, and she's crying when she says, "You know what to do."

"SMASH IT!"

We all mean it. We're going to freaking rock the house tonight.

I keep catching Eli's eye, and he's not avoiding me, but we aren't talking either. I stand in the wings, watching the galley fill up. I can see my mom and Gloria. A bunch of kids from school—tons of people are pouring in. It's noisy, in the front of the house and in the back.

A warm hand presses on my lower back, and I expect it to be Dré, but then I realize this smell is something so familiar and warm. It's Eli.

"Ready?" He leans on me and looks out at the front of the house.

"No." It comes out as a whisper and I clear my throat. I should say more, but I'm trying not to scare him off. I'm standing with someone I know, but so much time has gone by with us *not* talking that I've forgotten *how* we talk.

"Scared?"

I can't even face him. I'm a coward. "Completely."

"Then pretend you're someone else. Someone really kick-ass and awesome. It's what I do at gigs. Slowly, you'll realize you're not pretending anymore. It's just you. And then you'll know what everyone knew all along." He drops his hand, and he's going backstage.

"Eli," I say and turn to look at him. His hair is neatly combed but curling anyway, and his jaw is tight. I walk to him and fix the cape on his uniform. "Thanks."

He shakes his head. "Better finish getting ready."

My stomach starts flipping around and doing barrel rolls. Waiting until after opening night to apologize to Eli is starting to look like the dumbest idea I've ever had—well, top five at least. Running out the side door and moving to a new state still seems like a good idea. I go back to the girls' dressing room, because I need Lennox to talk me off whatever cliff I'm on.

As soon as I open the door, I see them. A big bouquet of flowers on my little piece of table. They're yellow and pink and orange, and I have no idea what kind of flowers they are, because I'm terrible at that stuff. But they smell nice, and the card reads, *Knock 'em dead, Livia—Al.*

I'm beaming. I didn't know if he'd get the ticket I left him at the store.

As I'm putting down the card, I see another small bouquet of flowers, hidden a little behind Al's vase. Red roses—those I know. Under them is a white envelope with a message on the outside:

Please, please don't open until you get home.
Until then, good luck. You don't need it though.
—EP

My eyes dart around the room, looking for Eli, but I'm only met with the frenzy of everyone getting ready. I want to tear the hell out of this envelope and read what's inside. It's kind of thick—but the intercom sounds and we've got five minutes to curtain, and Jackie's yelling for me to zip her dress. I finish helping her, put the envelope in my bag, and go help the crew with props.

I have a dance number in act two and until I hit the stage, I'm thinking about what's in that envelope.

However, when the lights hit my face, it doesn't feel like auditions, when I stared into deafening blackness. The audience is laughing and clapping at all the right parts, and every song gets huge reactions. We're all on fire, and backstage we're completely high off the energy. When my scene is up, I'm nervous again, but as soon as the music starts, I'm not me.

I'm not exactly Bianca either. I'm a real badass who is about to get her man, because in the world of *Othello*, the way women rule is by using what they have. It's the best performance Dré and I've ever had. We're getting whistles, and people are screaming when it's over.

Dré's wide-eyed, and backstage we hug and jump up and down together.

I get why they perform. I completely see why everyone grinds through the hours and Mrs. G's yelling. It's because just one moment onstage is everything.

We get a standing ovation. We're all out onstage, cast and crew, and Mrs. G gets her flowers and her T-shirt and she's giving a speech about us while crying, and we're all crying, too.

I don't want this moment to end.

It does though. Soon we're all in the front of the house, thanking everyone for coming, and the amount of applause we still get as people are leaving is incredible. When we've changed, we flood into the parking lot to meet our families and friends.

We all hug, and then I'm meeting Lennox's parents, Jackie's

grandparents, and Kai's huge family. My mom, Aunt Rachel, and Gloria are screaming. I remember hearing them when I was onstage. And Al's here with a big bag of candy. He's talking my mom's ear off about how I'm just about the most amazing person he's ever met and that watching me onstage was like seeing his daughter dance when she was in high school.

The night is extraordinary. It takes forever to tear me away from everyone, so we're all making plans to get pizza next, because we can't go home. Not yet.

I'm begging my mom to let me go even though we're supposed to go out to eat together; she waves me off with kisses.

It's a high. I never want to stop performing.

Never.

We're at the pizza place where we ate after auditions. Jackie's singing and making a scene—actually we're all making a scene, because the rest of us are coming in on the chorus and this is probably the next best thing to being onstage—being with these people.

I'm sitting next to Lennox, across from Dré, and he grabs the rest of my pepperoni and gives me the rest of his three-cheese slice.

Eli's in line getting more pizza, and I get up to go talk to him. I've got this feeling in my gut that if I don't make things right in this moment, it'll never be okay. But before I get to the line, Cleo grabs my shoulder.

"Hey, you." She's smiling at me, and even though I haven't been the nicest over the last month, she loops her arm in mine. "You were great tonight."

Out of the corner of my eye, I see Eli taking a few slices over to the table with Kai and Javier. My stomach drops.

"You, too," I say. I don't give Cleo enough credit for what she does. The crew ran the entire operation like invisible elves. Cleo was on lights, and without her, the magic wouldn't have been on that stage.

I stand with her as she fills up her plate with more pizza, and I listen to her go over all the show's highlights and all the near screwups backstage.

I never put Cleo on my list of people to apologize to, but standing here, listening to her go on and on about the thing she loves—the stage and the inner workings—I realize I do owe her an apology. She wanted to share all this with me from the beginning, and I let my insecurities cloud that.

"Cleo." I pull her back before we go to our separate tables. "I'm sorry I was an ass."

She winks. "You don't have to apologize to me. We're family. Plus..." she lets out a short breath as she smiles again "...I was kind of a dick. I should have stood up for you instead of getting on you about Angelina's messy ass."

I'm shaking my head, because it still doesn't excuse me being mean and assuming the worst of her.

"We're good, cuz." She pinches my arm and goes to her table.

I think I, too, often forget that, no matter what, Cleo and I are family. We're the only ones who know what it's like growing up in the trenches with our moms.

But I won't forget it again.

CHAPTER 34

It's past midnight when I get home. I rode with Dré. Eli is still using his mom's car, even though he and Dré are on speaking terms. I don't know how they made up—I never really do—but there's still this wall between them now. I spent our whole friendship mediating their battles of will to keep them from building the wall, and now I have become the wall. It wasn't only my doing, but things will never be the same again.

I'm getting out of the car when Eli pulls up. Dré looks at me and then Eli's car before he gives me a small nod. "Night."

"Night," I say.

As Dré pulls away, Eli gets out of his car and comes over to my driveway.

His hands are in his pockets, and he's rubbing his feet over the cracks in the pavement. "You get my letter?"

"Thanks." We speak at the same time as I wave the roses. "Yeah. I haven't read it yet."

He nods.

"I noticed your mom was at the show." I want to ask him about her. I want to know what's going on, but we aren't there yet.

"Yeah, she's been back a little while now." He scratches the back of his head. His curls are a mess. He's still got eyeliner under his eyes, and I don't think I'll ever stop finding him completely and utterly attractive. "Well, I'll see you tomorrow."

"Yeah."

I get this sinking feeling that whatever is in the letter isn't going to make things better. If this letter contains the end of our friendship, I have to apologize before he knows I've read it.

"Can we talk?" The flowers are getting heavy. I don't know why I didn't give them to my mom to take home with her, but I'm wishing I did because I don't want to set them on the ground, and this conversation is going to be a long one.

"Tomorrow. If you still want to."

I blink. Of course. Not now when I have this huge weight on my chest about to snuff me out of existence.

He gives me a small wave and starts walking to his house.

The pit in my stomach tightens, and I only have one thing left to do...

I'm inside and listening to my mom tell me the highlights of seeing me onstage. I'm hearing her, and I'm really glad that she's beaming and so proud of me. She's even tearing up and crying. I'm appreciative, but the envelope is burning a hole so deep into my bag I can practically smell it smoldering.

I finally get to my room, and it's in my hands. I've wanted to read it all night, and now I can't even open it.

But I'm not a coward anymore, so I tear it open and start reading.

Liv,
I don't even know where to start. You're probably thinking the beginning, but I don't know where that is.

I guess, for me, it's the day you moved in. I didn't know it—not for at least a few years after—but that's the day I always go to when I think about the past. My beginning doesn't start in kindergarten or the first time I can remember some birthday party. Those are the times without you.

Everything started for me when I let Dré talk me into spying on the girl wearing hot pink pants and a Batman shirt carrying boxes into the room across from mine. My memories are of the times we didn't have phones. Do you remember when you were grounded and we used paper and markers to write messages, and your mom threatened to nail the window shut? Or the time you ran your fingers through my hair and told me my bedhead was "way too cool" to be real?

I'm not making sense. I know I'm not making sense. I can't get shit straight in my head, and I've been trying. For weeks, I promise I've been trying, but somehow, I went from life with you to life without you again, and I'm living in this upside-down world where nothing makes sense.

You know my dad cheated. He says he didn't, that it was just emotional or whatever, but that shit is the same to my mom and me, so she left and stayed with her cousins for a while.

As you know, me and the fam aren't that cool, so my mom and I had to meet at these restaurants, and she's been a wreck because—they were it, you know, the full-on deal. I never thought this would happen to them. To us.

My mom says I'm a romantic, and maybe I am, but how do two people in love hurt each other? I guess I know now. One of them acts like a complete prick and shuts the girl he loves out of his life because he can't deal with the fact that his parents aren't soul mates and are probably getting a divorce. Simple. Ha. (Actually, that's not funny, but this is pen and I've already written too much to start over again.)

I know it's a long shot to ask for your forgiveness, but I want you to know I'm sorry. For everything. Shutting you out has been the biggest mistake of my life. You don't owe me anything, but I owe you the truth.

I love you.

I love your laugh, your smile, and the face you make when you're mad.

I love your smell, the warmth of your body next to mine, the way you say my name.

I love your eyes, the sound of your voice over the phone.

I love that you're kind, smart, and amazing, without making anyone else feel small.

I love you, Liv.

I know I've pretty much pissed you off into hating me

until the end of time, and I can live with that. I've had a lot of time to make peace with it. But you deserve the truth. You deserve the world, and if I could give you both, I would.

I'm writing this before the show tonight, but I know you're going to do great. I know you've probably stopped drinking water because you're scared you're going to pee onstage, but I hope tonight is everything you've ever wanted.

I want you to be happy, Liv. So no matter what happens, know it's okay. You're this brave, amazing girl and I'm a better person because of you.

I love you.

—Eli

CHAPTER 35

My hands are shaking and my heart is in my throat. He thinks I'm still mad. He thinks—

He *loves* me.

I knew it before, but the way that it fell out was on a street corner and—my god, I love him so much it hurts. My body, my heart, my soul. It all aches like he's been ripped from me—but he's right here, in this letter.

I go to my window and open the blinds and he's there in his bed with the light on, looking at me.

I grab my Bio II binder and rip out some paper and a marker from my desk.

I'm sorry.

I push the paper up to the window, and he's nodding, but he looks like I've punched him in the gut. I hold up my hands and write on another paper.

For being an ASS

I underline it three times, and then I'm on to the next paper when my phone buzzes.

"We have phones now, Liv." He's breathless, and he's staring at me.

"I love you, Eli." I'm laughing and crying. My eyes hurt so much from crying today, but I don't care. "I love you."

"Liv."

"I'm so sorry." My voice is cracking. I've said so much horrible stuff that I don't even know how to turn it all around. I thought he was a monster. I told everyone he was this horrible guy, going around calling me a slut, when he was just heartbroken. I feel like an ass for being too cowardly to tell Eli how I felt.

"No. Don't cry, Liv." His hand is on the window and we are such dorks because I've got my hand on mine. "I love you, too."

We stay up all night talking. The sun is coming up, and I'm lying on my bed, watching him watch me. We're ridiculous, and I wouldn't have it any other way. My eyes are heavy from crying and not sleeping for almost twenty-four hours. But no matter how many times I yawn, I won't hang up. It's Saturday, and we're not supposed to be at the theatre until noon, but I want to spend every one of those minutes with Eli.

I want to make up for all the hours we've spent together being apart.

"My mom's gone to work," I say.

"Mine, too." His mom's back, but his dad's moved to an apartment on a month-to-month basis to see if they can work things out or if he should extend his lease. Even though his dad moved out, they're doing better. Eli's not as mad anymore, he's just trying to understand how their family went from perfect to broken—but he's finding it easier to swallow the broken pieces these days.

Sometimes people fall out of love, and sometimes they need the space to figure out what love is. Sometimes they just make stupid mistakes.

"The phone is hot and my face is on fire." I've got it plugged in to charge for the second time now.

His voice is low and quiet. "Can I come over?"

"I'm going to shower first. I still have on last night's stage makeup." I'm up, grabbing some pajamas, and I take him into the bathroom with me and start the shower.

"Oh. Okay. We're doing this."

"It's not like you can see me." I'm already in the shower and washing my face.

"That's not exactly a positive."

I'm glad he can't see me grinning like a fool.

Thirty minutes later, he's in my room instead of on my phone, and we are the two most awkward people in the world. We've always been the most honest on the phone, and even though we could see each other through the window, it's not the same as him standing in front of me.

"Hi." This is the third time I've said it.

When Eli smiles, it's always lopsided and, because his lips are full, extremely sexy. He reaches for my hand and we press our palms together. His fingers are long and the tips curl over mine slightly. We're standing so close that his chest is touching mine, and his eyes go down to my lips and I'm tilting my head to meet his.

Kissing Eli is like breathing for the first time. I feel his love. It feels more powerful than the lust cloud. It's shaking me to my core, and it leaves me gasping.

My hands are on his waist and his are on my face and with each kiss we're exchanging something. He's giving me love, and I'm giving it back.

We end up on the bed kissing. I didn't know what to expect, but soon we're both fighting sleep for one more kiss, until I'm waking up, trying to turn off my phone alarm. Eli's arms are still wrapped around me, and my legs are intertwined with his.

"Eli."

He squeezes me. "I'm awake." His eyes are still closed, but he's smiling. "Just ten more minutes."

I know exactly what he means. I'm not ready to let go either. I nuzzle back into him. I want to be with him. Not casually—for as long as this thing can last. "I'm a swan." The words are already out of my mouth before I realize it doesn't sound exactly the same as it did in my head.

Eli pats my head gently. "Yes. You can be whatever you want. You're a weird but beautiful swan."

"That's not what I meant."

He laughs. "I know. You're talking about the Al thing." I suddenly remember I told Eli about the swans over the summer, because he always wanted to know what nuggets of truth Al had to offer. "Be mine."

I've got the biggest flock or flurry or wing cluster—whatever you call a bunch of butterflies—in my stomach, fluttering so hard that I can't contain myself. "If you'll be mine."

I don't think I can get any closer to Eli, but he manages to pull me in tighter. "For as long as you'll have me. And I hope that's a really, really long time."

CHAPTER 36

The second performance is as good as opening night, and in some ways it's even better. Jackie nails her song every time, but this time I feel it in my soul, and I don't think anyone escapes the magic she's got.

The main cast has Sunday off from performing, so I'm working the ticket office with Eli. And since no one comes to buy tickets in the middle of the play, instead of going backstage, we stay in the booth and make out.

We're really trying to make up for lost time, because what started out as playful kisses turns into his hand creeping up my skirt and some soft core groping.

When we are backstage helping clean up, he's already taken off his white button-down shirt so it doesn't get dingy while he and other guys move the set pieces.

The lust cloud is definitely hovering.

Lennox lifts herself onto the stage from the ground and lies down. "I'm exhausted. I've never been this excited for a Monday." We've got two days off completely, and then the understudies perform another day. I don't get to taste the stage again until Thursday, but I am so ready.

"You're staring," Lennox says. She looks between Eli and me, and a smile creeps over her face. "And so is he."

"We might be a thing."

Eli's got a piece of paper between his teeth, and I swear it's the hottest thing I've ever seen. I am love-struck—this is what that means. He could be chasing chickens or drooling in his sleep, and I think I'd find a way to see the sexy side of it.

"And all is right in the world," Lennox shouts to the rafters. I don't even care that she's embarrassing.

It's crazy. It's amazing. Eli said his life didn't really start until I moved in next door, and when I think about it, neither did mine.

"It really is about damn time, but you guys are grossing me out—*me.*"

I finally tear my eyes away from Eli. "Don't be a Grinch."

"It's not Christmas."

"It is for me." I wiggle my eyebrows, and Lennox cackles.

"See, you're a swan. You're glowing and everything." We get up to sweep the rows in the front of the house. No matter where I am, Eli's eyes find me and mine find him. We're like magnets, and maybe this is nauseating for everyone who isn't us, but for me it's absolutely crazy amazing.

"Liv." Dré's jogging down the aisle toward me. "I need to ask you something, and I want you to be honest."

I still have this goofy smile on my face, but it drops a little.

"Did you know about my mom and Yosef?"

Oh, God. I can't lie, but this is not the kind of truth I want to tell either. I just nod. "I suspected, but I didn't know for sure until Eli told me. Apparently, nothing physical happened, but you know—it was getting heavy."

Dré doesn't look mad, but he doesn't look happy either—who would be? "Whatever," he finally says, shrugging. "There isn't anything I can do about it, and it's over, apparently—fuck." He shivers a little. "Anyway..." He nods at Eli. "Y'all a thing now?"

As much as I don't want this to feel awkward, it does. "Yeah. How'd you know?"

He rolls his eyes. "Because I'm not blind, and you two have always been painfully obvious." He rocks back on his heels. "It's cool. You don't have to look at me like that. I'm cool."

I'm trying to stop blinking and smile like a normal person, but this is fucking weird. No one tells you that life is messy—I mean, everyone *says* it, but I never thought it would apply to me. "Thanks—I'm glad you were my first. I'll always be happy about that." I say it because I don't know how the three of us are going to fit together again—I don't think we do. This is so, so weird. And I think I just made it weirder.

"Jesus, Liv." He's smiling anyway. "Me, too. We're still friends—you and me. It's okay." He looks at Eli again, but he doesn't say anything about Eli and him. "Just be normal. I don't want to look in the back of the props closet and see you dry humping him."

"Oh my god." I go back to sweeping. "I promise. Jesus Christ..." We're laughing, and I see a glimmer of the future. It's not like how it was—it's something far from it. "What about you and Eli?" They aren't like they used to be, and I know it's my fault—or maybe it was never going to last, the three of us.

Dré lifts an eyebrow and gives me a long look. "Don't worry about it, Liv. We've been looking for an excuse to call it quits since before the Battle of the Bands BS."

I shake my head. "It doesn't have to be that way." I know I sound stupid. I know what I'm saying is empty and use-less, but I say it anyway, because how the hell am I going to navigate *this*?

Dré taps my nose. "It'll be okay. Nothing changes between you and me. I promise."

Every time Dré says it's okay, I wonder if he's trying to convince me or himself, but we have the rest of the year and senior year to figure it out.

Either way, this isn't how we fall apart. Different isn't al-ways bad. It's just different.

CHAPTER 37

Love is hard…and it's easy.

Love is one word, but it means a thousand different things. Love is when I can't breathe because Jackie has me bent over laughing so hard that I'm crying. Or when Lennox braids my hair. It's my mom showing me she sees *me* in the way only she can. It's my sister's key lime pie. It's what Dré and I did.

It's what Eli and I are.

I laugh whenever Jackie says her nightly love affirmations, but honestly, who wouldn't—she's just not normal. But I'm doing them, too. With love is how I should have started the Year of Fuck It. Loving myself has been the hardest of all. Love would have stopped me from doing a lot of shitty things. But as Al says, the ability to make good decisions comes from a string of fuckups. Plus, I still have eight more months to get this Fuck It thing right.

There are still times when I meet Dré's eyes, and I know love is hard. The elastic band between us that I thought snapped is still there, and whether he knows it or not, I feel a light tug whenever I catch him staring. It's going to take a while to figure out how to be *us* again. This is the hard part, but nothing worth having is easy.

It's hours before our last performance. We're all onstage dancing like idiots—legit idiots. I'm dancing to a chipmunk song like an '80s go-go dancer. If anyone had told me months ago that I'd be whipping my head around, speed jogging like I'm wearing a leotard and neon headband to a bunch of squeaky voices, I'd have called them a liar and slapped them twice.

But here I am. We're all laughing, even Mrs. G, who says I'm disrespecting her era. Eli joins me and runs the gamut of his three really weird dance moves. I don't care that Jackie and Lennox are howling and crying. I think he's sexy.

There's nothing that can bring down the mood tonight. We're all ready to close out the show on a high note, even though it's also kind of sad. It's the last time it will be just us—this exact same group of people.

I'm looking around, panting and smiling. It took a lot for all of us to get here. We've fought, we've laughed, we've cried. This musical isn't a gazillion TV shows on Thursday night, but hot damn, it's the start of something real special. I think Shonda Rhimes would approve. I like to think so—I've even got my own dance-it-out going.

She'd definitely approve.

I sneak backstage with Eli. As soon as we hit a dark corner, we're kissing. Eli's touch leaves behind this tingling sensation. He's committing another crime against humanity with those hands.

Through all the ups and downs, we came out on top.

In this theatre, if I've learned one thing, it's that Shakespeare doesn't know a damn thing about love. All he knows are the lows—and I'm pretty sure he thinks love sucks, because people always end up dead or completely delusional. Or maybe I'm being too hard on the guy who's just trying to write an entertaining tragedy.

I thought my life was playing out like some twisted version of *Othello*. I was my own Iago—his name is eerily similar to the word *ego*, and I let mine get the best of me sometimes. I thought *I* was simultaneously the innocent and selflessly devoted Desdemona; the jilted, life-hardened Emilia; and the needy and misunderstood Bianca. But I wasn't any of them *and* I was all of them at once. I'm a girl, but I'm sure as hell not one of Shakespeare's ill-fated girls.

I've always thought love stories were about two people coming together—but my love story isn't tragic, and it's not about a boy. It's about me loving me.

It's showtime.

I get it—the play is a drama, and it is hella entertaining. Shakespeare had one job, and it wasn't an obligation to present a truthful version of a woman or a decent representation of a Moor. His job was to fill seats. And he's *still* filling them.

In the wings, I can already feel what it's like when the light hits my face, and I'm full of the high I get every time all eyes are on me.

Shakespeare wrote this play. I'm having this moment because of his work. I was able to become who I am by taking a chance and auditioning for a part he wrote centuries ago. That's some scary kind of inception shit. But some old white dude isn't writing the script of my life.

Fuck that. I am.

I step out onstage.

★ ★ ★ ★ ★

ACKNOWLEDGMENTS

To all the boys I've loved before, but most notably, Juan. You continue to teach me how to love and be loved. You're my rock, my diamond in the sky, my swan. I won't turn this into a love letter but, from thirteen to thirty, you've been helping me write this story. I love you so wholly and completely it's insane.

To the New Leaf team, I shout it all the time but now it shall be in ink: Y'ALL ARE PHENOMENAL. I am grateful to be part of the New Leaf family! All of you have worked so hard for me and provided so many opportunities for Liv and the gang!

Most especially to my agent, Devin. Metal and Magic brought me to you and *Smash It!* sealed the deal. It's rare to find someone who believes in you as undoubtedly as you believe in me. That unexplainable thing—it's totally happening. This is happening.

To Suzie, you're brilliant and you've made me a better author.

The Inkyard fam, y'all are beast and I cannot thank you enough for what you've done. I know half of the work is writing the book and the other half is finding a tribe who supports it. Toast to my tribe! Most especially to my lovely editor, Tashya. You brought out the best in me. I was blessed enough to connect with you before *Smash It!* was even in my mind and twice blessed that *Smash It!* found a place in your heart.

My girls, Mckayla and Elena. Mckayla, you read the first draft and you knew then what it was and I swear, if this world goes to hell, you're my lighthouse on a dark and stormy ocean. Elena, you're my Jackie and Lennox and honestly, I LIVE for our chisme and for your light. We gon' get that bag, girl!

Paul, I borrowed some stuff. And embellished what I took. I hope you don't mind. If I could go back and tell sixteen-year-old me how lucky she is to have you, she would already know—but because she was chickenshit she wouldn't admit it until much later. Thanks for always being my best friend.

To Jimmi for letting me dig into his private life more than any friend should. Also, for being the kind of guy who re-enacted The Matrix trilogy with me in the rain instead of working like we were supposed to—RadioShack is probably out of business because of us.

To Jodi, Amara, Sasha, and Laura. I don't know what I'd do without you guys to talk to. Writing is lonely; everyone needs friends like you.

To my beta readers, you taught me a lot about this book, what it meant, how it affected you, and what it could be.

Amanda, every girl needs that one friend who sees her and

will fight for her. Though there has been a lot of time between us and we have babies now, you are my ride or die, forever.

To my whole YouTube family and online book community. Y'all gave me the courage to use the voice that's always been inside of me. I've got so much love for our little piece of the internet and it's because of each and every one of you.

And most gratefully to you, dear reader. It's because of you that Liv can shine. Whatever you're trying to do, from me to you, you got this. So, go out and SMASH IT!